revision

a NOVEL

andrea PHILLIPS

Cover and book design by Robert S. Davis
Copyediting by Lillian Cohen-Moore
Book editing by Brian J. White

Published by Fireside Fiction Company,
P.O. Box 890091, East Weymouth, MA 02189

www.firesidefiction.com

ISBN: 978-0-9861040-1-5

Fireside Fiction Company provides content notes for its books to guide readers who may wish to seek out or avoid particular story elements. These content notes may contain spoilers. The content note for this book is displayed on page 265. A current list of all the elements covered in our content notes can be found at firesidefiction.com/contentnotes.

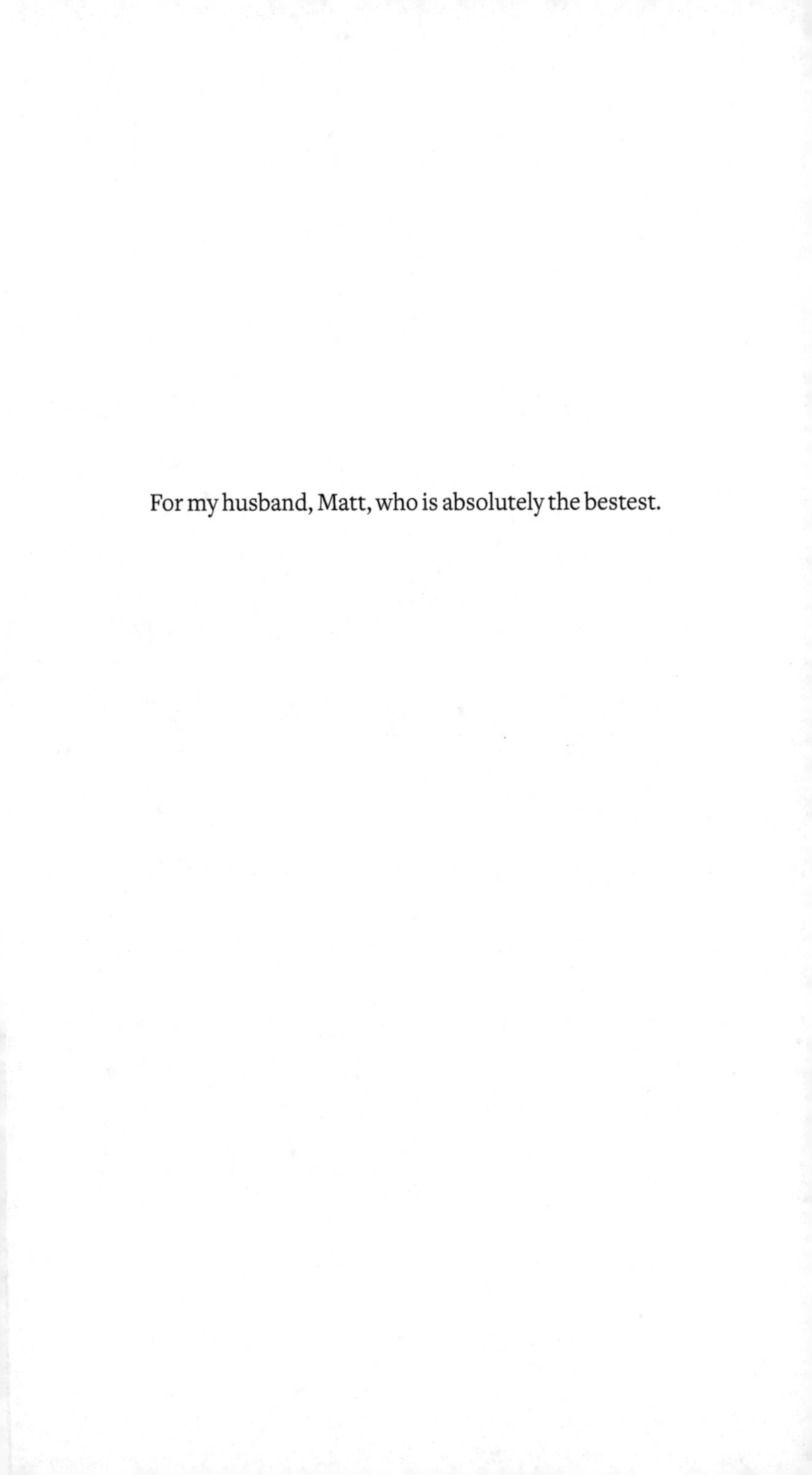

For my husband, Matt, who is absolutely the bestest.

chapter ONE

In the case of a sudden dumping, there are certain expectations about how to proceed.

Stick your spoon in a gallon of cookie dough ice cream. Bring on the chick-flicks and sob sessions with your besties. Cut up all the printed pics of the two of you together so you can burn a stack of his smirking faces in the flame of a candle. One of the candles he bought you. The ones scented like eucalyptus-mint, that he thought was so hot, and it gave you a sinus headache but you never complained because you loved him so much, and now you're sitting there with a headache and singed fingers and it isn't actually making anything better so you wonder why... why...

—Hang on, where was I?

Right, getting dumped. We'd actually been having a great night up until that part. We were cuddled up at my place watching a documentary on Tibetan architecture and eating Chinese take-out, right? I leaned in to nuzzle Benji's ear while the narrator droned on and on about murals and prayer wheels.

And then boom, like a switch had been flipped, he sat up straight as a wooden soldier and inched away from me. "This isn't working," he said.

I uncurled myself, frowning. "Oh, sorry, am I squishing you? Let me get— "

He wiped my offer away with a curt motion. "No, I mean us. We're not working."

I scrunched my nose up. "Not working? Like... "

"Like it's over, Mira. We are over."

"Wait, are you breaking up with me? Seriously?"

That's when Benji's face went all soft and compassionate, like there was any way he could be kind at this point short of taking it back. He leaned forward again and put his arm around me. "I'm getting so busy with the company lately... you know it's been bad, and it's going to get worse. I don't have time for a life. No time for you. And it's... not fair to you. You deserve better than this."

"I deserve— what? What are you talking about?" Prayer flags fluttered on TV, red and green and blue. My brain struggled to catch up with my ears. "Wait, who are you to decide what's fair for— "

"Listen, I know this is sudden, but— "

His stupid jerkface sympathy was too much to bear. "Get. Out." I said, quietly. Then, with a little more volume, "Get the HELL out of here."

He did. The door shut behind him a little louder than it needed to, leaving me with nothing to mark his passing but a table full of half-empty noodle cartons and soda bottles. I grabbed a bottle and hurled it at the closed door, imagining it smacking him right between the shoulder blades and shoving him onto his face in the hall. Instead, the cap came off mid-flight, the soda spattering in a wide arc across the room.

What a mess.

I was furious, but I didn't really know what to do with all of that righteous indignation. I turned off the documentary and stared at the blank television for a while. That didn't help much. But that's what those tried-and-true breakup rituals are for, right?

I grabbed my phone and dialed up Eli, my absolute bestest friend since grade school, but it went straight to voicemail. I shouldn't have been surprised; I could hardly reach him at all any more, much less enlist him for a little late-night shoulder sobbing. I texted him anyway, but without much hope.

Time to seek out the carbolicious comfort at the bottom of a pint of chocolate chip cookie dough swirl, then. I swung open my freezer. It held a sack of crushed ice, long melted into a single impenetrable lump; a sad scattering of kernels of corn; three nearly empty boxes of freezer-burned waffles; and, yes, a half-gallon of vanilla. When I pulled off the lid, though, there was nothing but half an inch of ice crystals at the bottom. Grrr.

I threw on a hoodie and trudged to the bodega, which as it turns out had closed eight minutes earlier. So I returned home empty-handed, muttering unflattering things about Benji and his timing, and grabbed a beer from the fridge instead. One of Benji's weird microbrew faves — not even one I liked much — but no helping it.

Next attempt: cinematic catharsis. I curled up on my sofa with a fleece blanket and tried to find something I wanted to watch. About four minutes into a classic Julia Roberts vehicle, I was seething with so much hot rage that I could've given the volcano of your choice a run for its money.

Action, then. Maybe a little symbolic destruction would help me feel better. It didn't take long to burn through all of my printed photos, all two of them, so I went to my phone and then laptop to get rid of the digitals, too, and absolutely purge every electron of the jerk from my life for good. When I was done, I just sat there, full of all this anger and no outlet for it.

That's how I wound up online reading Verity at one in the morning. Verity was Benji's company. If you asked him about it he'd start to lecture about crowdsourcing knowledge and breaking news and blah blah blah blabbity blah blah. Over time, I worked out that it was an online reference source crossed with a newspaper, something a little like Wikipedia, but bigger and deeper and scarier — breaking news as it happened, information on ordinary people, real Big Brother stuff.

So what else was I going to do? I looked up Benji's page on Verity. There was a section on what a geek-society high-profile playboy he was, updated to say that he was newly single.

Huh, I thought. That was sure fast.

But let's back up and start at the beginning. His real name was Benjamin, natch. I started calling him Benji when we first met because of his big soft puppy-dog eyes. When I said it out loud he always gave me a funny half-smile like he couldn't decide if I was making fun of him or being cute, so he couldn't decide if he should be mad or mushy over it. He was a... actually, to start with, I had no idea what he was. His daily work seemed to involve flying to a lot of conferences and getting hundreds of comments on his blog, plus he spent a lot of time meeting people over coffee.

That's how I came into the picture. I'm a barista at Joes' Buzz, the best tiki-themed coffee shop in all of Brooklyn. Before Benji and I ever hooked up, he liked to come to my shop and pretend to work on his laptop when he was really just dicking around with the latest browser game. Once in a while he'd bring people in to schmooze over lattes and snickerdoodles.

And then one day the Goth-pale woman he was with — someone at his company, I thought — spilled her double-nonfat-sugar-free-pistachio-half-caf-no-foam-no-whip all over his white button-down. "Jesus!" he said, and stood there dripping helplessly. Would you believe she just stood looking at him with her mouth open? Didn't even hand him a napkin!

"At least it didn't fry your electronics," I said. "Come on into the back, I'll help you out." I happened to have a spare shirt in my bag, so I pulled him into the break room and let him change. Not that I'm such a big altruist or anything. I'd been planning to hit the gym later, and to be honest, giving him my baggy old tee was the perfect excuse to skip it. I couldn't let an opportunity like that go to waste.

He thanked me, and I think really looked at me for the first time. When you work in the service sector, a certain kind of person tends to look right through you, like you're some kind of tree or something. Apparently he liked what he saw, because the next thing I knew he said, "Hey, when's your shift over? I'll bring your shirt back and buy you a drink."

"Coffee?" I tried not to roll my eyes. It probably didn't work.

"Nah," he said. "How do you feel about sangria?"

What can I say? He was cute, and it's not like I had anything cooking on the back burner. I smiled and flipped my hair over my shoulder as I went back to my station. "Come back at nine." The rest, as they say, is history.

It didn't last six months.

So fast-forward, and there I am, freshly dumped, staring at this stupid web page telling me Benji was single again. And I just wasn't ready for the world to know yet. I wasn't even ready to know it yet myself. I held a swallow of beer in my mouth, letting the bubbles sting my tongue. I thought about me and Benji, and I won't kid, I started feeling pretty sorry for myself. I deserved better.

Hell, he'd said it himself, not two hours gone by. Like I wasn't competent to judge that on my own. Jerk.

The tiny blue edit button glowed in the corner of the screen, tempting me to hijack his bio. Ben had left himself logged into Verity on my computer at some point, I guess one of the times he'd forgotten his bag and had a work emergency to deal with. I could tell because he'd customized his "Submit" button to say "Make It So." Dork. But I was darkly amused when I realized it would look like he'd made the change himself, if anybody ever happened to check. I jabbed the button and made a teeny-tiny little alteration: "He is deeply in love with his new fiancée, Mira Newton."

Before I hit the button, I stared at the preview for a while. I didn't know why I'd written it. It wasn't true, of course. It had never been true, and it didn't look so likely going forward, either. But for a bit, seeing it written there in black on white made it seem possible, in a way it never had been before.

Me and Benji, we never had the marrying kind of relationship. We didn't even have a tell-your-parents kind of relationship. But the words glowing there started to fill my head up with tulle and white roses and violins playing Pachelbel's Canon in D and all the other sappy wedding crap I'd always told myself I was far too cynical to care about.

I hit "Make It So."

My laptop made a satisfying click when I snapped it shut. The afterimage of the words lingered on my retinas, then they were gone, just like Benji. I took one last swig from that beer, which had grown both warm and flat, and went to bed, hoping things would look better in the morning.

When I woke up, though, it definitely wasn't morning yet. I heard a rustling from my living room. My heart stomped around in my chest like it thought it might find someplace better to go. Burglar, I thought, or maybe rats. There in the dark, for just a minute, I second-guessed my decision not to live at the place my parents kept on Fifth. Principles be damned.

I fumbled for my phone with fingers made fat by adrenaline and dialed 911, worrying the whole time about the light from the screen leaking through the door. I kept my finger hovering over the send icon and put one ginger foot in front of the other to peek out and see what I could see.

The living room was aglow with candlelight. Not so much a burglar's M.O.

The hinges on my bedroom door squealed their way open. The candles lit up a mosaic of rose petals trailing off toward the living room and ending in a puddle on my coffee table. There was a little velvet box with a diamond-and-sapphire ring, poised in the middle of this mess of floral confetti. As I stared at this tableau in muzzy incomprehension, Benji stepped out of the kitchen. He held a mismatched pair of coffee mugs and a bottle of champagne. "I'm sorry," he said. "Marry me?"

My guts were still a roiling disaster of anxiety and rejection and anger. My mind tried to formulate the biggest telling-off I had ever performed in all my life. But while my brain was blankly trying to find a few words to fit together, my mouth sprang right into action. "Yes," it said.

So that's how me and Benji the Internet Star got engaged.

chapter TWO

Joes' Buzz was one of those eclectic mom-and-pop coffee shops you keep hearing don't exist anymore (or in this case, a pop-and-pop shop). They'd hung up a shingle with that craftily placed apostrophe sometime in the early '90s and decked the place out like a tropical paradise. The walls were covered with jungle-inspired sweeps of green, blending in with clusters of potted palms and umbrella plants. Tiki masks scowled and beamed at the customers at artful intervals. The regulars were mostly brogrammers and not-so-starving artists, though there'd been a recent spike in urban moms wielding over-engineered strollers.

I shambled in the morning after my unexpected engagement very much not on time for my shift. (It would have been even later, but my mother called and woke me up about an hour after I'd turned off my alarm instead of snoozing it.) My hair was in an unwashed pony tail — the kind where your hair is so filthy you can still kind of see the strands it separated into when you pulled it back with your fingers — and I wore a Ramones T-shirt that couldn't even remember a time it hadn't been wrinkled. At least with the Ramones that's pretty much expected.

All of this could have been overlooked, and probably would have been, but my eyes were still puffy and red from all of the emoting I'd done the night before. Or a couple of hours before, to get technical. No amount of hastily applied ice had been able to fix it.

Joey was the one who caught me; Joseph liked to sleep in. The wind chimes hanging from the door jangled in Hawaiian-themed harmony, and everybody turned to get a look. Joey didn't frown at me, exactly, so much as he didn't smile. His eyebrows did that thing where they crawl up to where his hairline used to be in order to make room for all of the questions he was planning on asking.

Fortunately the morning rush was on, so I could hustle behind Joey to drop my bag in the back room and get an apron on. Then I jumped headlong into the dance of steam and caffeine.

Joey may be a gossip, but he's never in his life let anything get between him and a paying customer, aging hippie or no. So he didn't begin the inquiry into my timeliness and poor personal grooming right away. He settled for shooting me the odd meaningful glance instead. I kept my focus on the orders — well, as much as circumstances permitted — and if I prolonged one or two conversations a little more than you could have strictly called professional, well, what of it? It's not like it was the first time. And being friendly does keep 'em coming back.

But the morning rush doesn't last forever, and eventually it was me and Joey alone behind the counter. Never before in my life had I so diligently polished the espresso machine or restocked the beans, and if I say the baked goods in the display case achieved an arrangement of near-mathematical perfection, I promise I'm not just bragging.

Joey didn't buy it, though. "Late night?"

I put down the rag and slumped against the counter. "Kind of," I said. "Sorry I was so late. I just have a lot going on."

He chucked me under the chin. "You feeling OK, Mira-deara?"

"Oh, you know... it's nothing."

"... Something."

"No, I swear, it's just... "

"Is that boy of yours treating you right? Do I need to go buy a shotgun to wave at him?"

Dammit. I hadn't quite worked out for myself what had happened, and didn't know how to tell anybody else. But sometimes the best way to distill whatever's going on in your head is to talk it over. So I opened my mouth and let the words fall out, listening intently to see if any of it would explain my life to me.

"I'm getting married," I said. And then I smiled brightly, like a girl who knew exactly what she was doing would probably smile.

Joey's eyes flicked down to my belly. "Oh, honey— " he started.

"No, it's nothing like that," I said quickly. My fingers tried tying themselves into knots while I waited for something else to pop out of my mouth, but nothing came.

"Well, what is it like?" he asked.

"Benji kind of broke up with me." That... was not something I would've wanted to pop out, on second thought. Should've kept your mouth shut, Mira.

"I thought you said you were engaged." He crossed his arms and pursed his lips like a cranky old lady.

"Look, I don't even know what the hell it was about." And then the blab got the best of me. "I'm sure we're going to have some sort of stupid awkward talk about it later. He broke up with me, and then he came back a few hours later with this whole romantic candles setup, like something from a movie, and he asked me to marry him and I said yes."

"Talk about a change of heart," Joey said. He turned his back on me to rearrange the already-immaculate racks of sugar and sugar substitutes, but his rigid spine put the lie to his casual gesture. "Why on earth would you agree to marry somebody who just dumped you?"

My shoulders twisted. "I don't know," I said honestly. If there was a quaver in my voice, well look, if a night like that isn't a good enough reason for a girl to be a little emotional, what is?

There was another long silence as he turned this over for a while and tried to decide what to make of it. Levity won the day, apparently. "Did you at least get a ring? Never say yes without a ring."

I'd put Benji's great-grandma's diamonds-and-sapphires on a chain around my neck that morning, not my finger, telling myself I didn't want to scratch the thing up at work, or coat it in milk foam and syrup. I pulled it from inside my shirt and showed him. It spun around and around, sparkling like a walnut-sized disco ball.

"Mmm, boy comes from money, at least," he said, nodding with pseudo-paternal satisfaction. He pulled one of the snickerdoodles from the case and handed it to me. The scent of cinnamon-sugar made my stomach acid roil in an alarming fashion. "Congratulations, darling," he said gently. "If you need to talk about anything," his eyes jumped back down to my stomach for just the barest second, "you know Uncle Joe-Joe is always here for you."

I nibbled at the cookie in a show of gratitude, even though I couldn't bear the thought of food. Then I threw my arms around his squishy midsection and gave him a squeeze. "You're a good man, Joey," I said. "Thanks."

He let it drop with just one more searching look, like he

wanted to grill me a little more but held back because he felt sorry for me.

Did I mention how much I hate people feeling sorry for me?

The snickerdoodle did help me feel a little better, though. So did the tab of ibuprofen I popped with it. Joey's attention mostly stayed on the Times crossword after that. He always knew when to leave well enough alone.

Leaving well enough alone wasn't in the cards for me, though. I made it through the rest of the morning routine, pulling shots and slinging syrup, all the while trying to puzzle out what the hell had happened the night before. Was it all real? Had I suffered some bizarre dream?

The whole thing was too preposterous, too coincidental. Did Benji really break up with me and then propose all in a couple of hours? It wasn't because I changed his page on Verity. Couldn't be. But it was hard not to give in to completely irrational, magical thinking, that it was true because I made it true somehow.

The gem-studded nugget of a ring hung heavy on that chain around my neck, and my eyes were still so puffy and red that even my indistinct reflection in the stainless mini-fridge under the counter had clearly had a rotten night.

"Joey?" I asked abruptly.

"Hm?" He looked up from his crossword, startled.

"Do you make wishes?"

"What, like... wishing on a star?" He scratched on his beard as he thought. "I guess I used to, but not so much anymore."

"Did you ever make a wish and it came true?"

He tugged on my pony tail and grinned. "I'll say. Look around you, kiddo."

Joseph sauntered in early in the afternoon. Where Joey could have been the second coming of Jerry Garcia, Joseph looked like a Korean Ben Franklin, though I don't think anybody would have been brave enough to say it right to his face. He had an adorable round belly, a balding pate with a little ponytail holding his graying hair back, and a tiny pair of half-moon reading glasses perched at the bottom of his nose.

"Our Mira's getting married," Joey called to him, right across the whole room.

"Is she pregnant?" Joseph called back. I must have turned about five different shades of crimson. I could tell from the heat of all that blood rushing to my face at once.

The couple of regulars in the place looked at each other and then studiously focused on their phones and lattes. You could practically see their ears grow three sizes, though. Sigh.

"She says no," Joey said. "But I don't know if we believe her."

"I'm not pregnant," I said.

Joseph strolled up and carefully inspected my reddened eyes, my sallow complexion, my filthy hair. "You look terrible," he said. "I bet it's going to be a girl."

"I. Am. Not. Pregnant." My molars might as well have been mortared together.

Joseph shrugged. "Whatever you say, sweetie."

His lips twitched a little as he tried to pick just one follow-up question when he clearly had a whole collection of them. I steeled myself for a fresh inquisition. But instead he said, "I just saw your boy on the corner with some other girl."

"What?" I rushed to the window and ducked under the bamboo blinds to look. Joseph was right, of course. I even recognized the woman Benji was with. Dark hair, blue streaks, dressed all in black. She was the one who had spilled her drink on Benji the day he asked me out. I'd seen her a few times after that, either meeting Benji in the shop or at parties we'd gone to, but we'd never been properly introduced. I did know that she was involved in Verity. Today she looked pissed as hell, and was to all appearances giving him the reaming of a lifetime.

Benji held up his hands, placating, but she steamed on. She pointed one finger at the shop, right toward me, and I jumped away from the window. I went back to my post, hoping she hadn't noticed me watching.

"Trouble in paradise already?" Joey asked.

"No, he's just talking to a girl from work," I said. I wondered if their argument had anything to do with me, or if it was just about Verity. Worse — could it be both? Was it anything to do with what had happened last night?

"So," Joseph said. He tied his apron behind his back, formulating his line of attack. "This Benjamin. How long have you been seeing him, again?"

I winced. The answer was not quite five months, which didn't seem like an appropriately long time for wedding talk, now that Joseph brought it up. But the Hawaiian wind chimes on the door sparkled again and my hero — or whatever you want to call him — came in before I could possibly be required to answer.

Unlike me, Benji had enjoyed a solid several hours of sleep and a shower. But that didn't mean he looked entirely respectable. His hair was tousled, but only by artful design, and his jeans were no doubt freshly laundered, but skillfully crafted to look like somebody had dragged them behind a tractor for a few weeks. He wore a white Oxford half-tucked in, charmingly undone a button or two. I was gratified to see that he had dark circles under his eyes, at least. I tried to fluff my stringy ponytail and wished I'd gone through the bother of putting on a little lip gloss.

Joey tugged on Joseph's arm and the two of them scuttled into the break room. I couldn't decide which was the better bet: Would they loiter out of sight but still close enough to eavesdrop, or would they have a hushed catch-up chat about me and my oh-good-lord-who-knew-she-had-it-in-her personal life? Anyone's guess, really.

Benji gave me that trademark lopsided smile of his, dimpled just on the one side. He put his elbows on the counter and leaned in toward me. "Hey, M," he said. "About last night... "

My eyes started to prickle as I guessed what was coming: All a horrible mistake, forget about it, I need my space, it's not you it's me. I bit my tongue and pressed my nails into my palms; it wouldn't do to lose my composure, not here in front of the Joes and the customers. Not here in front of Benji.

But that smile lingered on his face, and the next thing he said was, "I guess we have a lot of planning to do, don't we?" He took one of my hands between his and stroked the back of mine with his thumbs.

All of the breath left me at once. "Plans," I said. Maybe this wasn't about to be Dumping Mira 2: This Time, It's For Keeps.

Benji looked into my eyes intensely as all of this tween-girl anxiety bubbled in my stomach. "Did I tell you that you look great?" And then, after a pause just a hair too short, a question rushed out of him: "Did you ever think when we first met that we'd wind up like this?"

"Like... this?"

"You know," he said, and his mouth squirmed, unable to quite make the shape of the word he needed. "Engaged."

"Not ever," I said.

"It's almost like something you'd... read, isn't it?" His eyes burned like he was waiting for me to say something in particular;

like he thought he knew what I was about to say.

My hands shook a little. Was he asking me about his bio on Verity, about that change? Was he accusing me of something?

“I’m not sure I’d call it a storybook romance, exactly,” I said carefully. “But we’re definitely great together.” I touched my free fingertips to the diamonds-and-sapphires hanging from my neck. “We should be celebrating. Right?”

His face warmed and made my insides flutter. “Yeah, we should! Come on over once you’re off shift. We’ll hit Villa Rosalita, get a bottle and some fettuccine,” he said. “And we can start thinking about what we want the rest of our lives to look like.”

“Sounds great,” I said, too fast. I never was good at playing it cool.

“Great,” he repeated, patting my hand one last time. And then he stood up straight and glanced at the specials board. “Oh hey, get me an Americano? Good girl.”

chapter THREE

By the end of my shift, I was kind of disgusted with myself, and not just because of how badly I needed a shower. Once Benji left, I could deflect the curious eyes with nothing but moxie and caffeine, but I couldn't escape from my own head. I started to second-guess myself. How could I just keep smiling and nodding and going along with whatever Benji said? Why hadn't I asked him about why he'd broken up with me, or about that argument outside with Miss Blue Streaks, or even about Verity? I wasn't That Girl, was I? The one who needed a man in her life to make everything work out OK?

On the other hand, how do you say "Honey, I was just wondering if your website changes reality," without coming off like a total loon?

To show myself I didn't need Benji — that I was a strong, independent woman who could take care of herself on her own terms and called all her own shots — I rebelled and didn't go straight to his place right after my shift. No, I went home first and finally got cleaned up and put on miles of eyeliner and in general transformed myself into a pretty, pretty princess for him. That would teach him a lesson, right? And then I went on over as fast as my kitten heels could get me back to the subway.

All the way there, I stared at the strangers on the subway and wondered how they navigated the rapids of their lives.

There was a boy bopping along to acid green earbuds with the Dominican flag blazoned on his jacket. Did he care whether his moves were the hottest? That woman with the clear vinyl kerchief on her head and the deep creases beside her mouth, the one reading the Cyrillic newspaper, was she married? The couple making out at the end of the car, were they in love? Was it going anywhere? Did they know, and did they care? If they could see the fork in the road at their feet, would they change their destination, or were they happy with where they were headed?

On the way out of the station, I brushed by an exhausted-looking Indian woman wearing a too-heavy Air Force surplus coat and a deep purple broomstick skirt. A little pin glittered from her lapel, at odds with the rest of her ensemble. It was worked from diodes and upcycled circuit boards, probably from somebody's learn-to-solder class at a hackerspace. The woman stood motionless at the top of the stairs, studying the skyline. Her hair was in a single braid that fell to her waist, but a nebula of frizz had escaped. The skin on her hands was ashy, and her eyes were bloodshot.

Homeless, I thought, and avoided any uncomfortable eye contact. There was someone who would change her life if she could. As I passed her, her chin came down, and she looked at me with hard eyes. They widened for a moment, as though she recognized me, and then quickly narrowed into a seething blend of pity and contempt. I wondered who she thought I was, but walked on, eyes straight ahead, avoiding the chance for awkward interaction.

You can't save the world, right? You can only save yourself. And that only if you're lucky.

I rapped lightly on Benji's door, then let myself in when there was no answer. His apartment was a sunny place, all honeyed parquet floors, vaulted ceilings, and windows nine feet tall, but he'd packed it to the rafters with whirring electronic things. Shame that such a gracious space had been infested with all of those nests of cables. A new thought struck: Maybe when we were married, I could clear some of it away.

Benji wasn't in evidence in the main room, but after a minute I heard his voice carrying from the office. On the phone, probably still working. Since I was stuck waiting anyhow, I tossed my purse onto his leather sofa and grabbed a garbage bag from the kitchen to start my renovation with the worst of the not-quite-empty soda cups and grease-stained take-out bags.

"Listen, I have to go, she's going to get here any minute," Benji said.

I froze, not wanting to listen in to his conversation, but unable to do anything else.

His voice was tight, defensive. "Yes, I get it, I'll figure out a way to ask her... I know it's important, you don't have to tell me. I know. You keep your eyes on your business and I'll handle mine." He wasn't talking about me. No way could he be talking about me.

He banged around in his office, from the sound of it closing drawers and stacking papers up, ready to pack it in for the day. "This might come as a shock, Marjorie, but you're not the only one with chips on the table. I'm handling it, OK? I know what I'm doing."

I bit my lip, then shoved the garbage bag under the sofa as quietly as I could. I grabbed my handbag and backed over to the door. I opened it. I slammed it shut again, the sound echoing through his apartment. "Benji, you here?" I called. My voice was steady, even casual.

"One second, phone," he called back. I heard him make his apologies and hang up. Benji emerged from his office and greeted me with a cool kiss on the forehead, but his mind seemed a million miles away. So was mine.

We weren't going to Villa Rosalita after all. "I spaced and totally forgot there's a work thing tonight," he said, hands spread out in fauxpology. "Given the investment stuff we're working on, I really have to be there. But you can come along. You'll have fun, right?"

... Right. Sure.

Benji had brought me to one of his endless work-related parties for the first time just a couple of weeks after we started dating. Its highlight was my conversation with a broad-cheekboned woman with dozens of tiny braids that set the tone for all my future interactions with his peers. It went something like this:

Her: So what do you do?

Me: Oh, I'm a barista.

Her: Hahahaha! We've all had those jobs before. So what are you trying to get into? Let me guess—you're a designer? Or are you the startup entrepreneur type?

Me: Uhhhhhhmmmmm. No? I'm OK with being a barista.

Her: Oh, um. That's great. Good for you.

Then she looked wildly around the room searching for somebody to talk to who wasn't horribly beneath her. Once was more than enough, thank you very much. The only other kind of conversation available was more or less like Benji talking about his work: a brothy soup of buzzwords all jumbled together that, upon deconstruction, amounted to a variant of "technology is awesome," or "I know about cooler stuff than you do," or sometimes "that guy thinks he's cool but really he is not."

It was as tedious, in its own way, as my parents' endless cocktail parties and fundraising dinners. The people were younger, but the conversation was always the same.

Eventually I developed a coping strategy to lubricate my way through the parties with Benji's crowd. It involved taking a couple of hits of the hardest booze on offer the second I walked in the door, and then hunching over my phone pretending to be all wrapped up in sending texts or something. If anybody tried to bother me, I'd smile and shake my head and point to my phone, apologize profusely, and say something about how the system was down and I had to take care of it.

I was so proud of myself the first time I pulled that one off. It was the perfect impenetrable armor.

Tonight's itinerary was a local tech-art meetup at a Brazilian-Korean fusion place with high slabs of a dark-polished wood as cocktail tables and a rosy filter on the lights. The air was hazy from meat-scented airborne carcinogens, and the red-aproned waiters walked among the crowd offering hunks of steak pierced on bamboo skewers. The technorati were shoulder to shoulder.

Miss Blue Streaks grabbed Benji's wrist as soon as we hit the door. "We need to talk," she said. Her eyes skipped over to me and then past, to the crowd. "It's about Prometheus."

He gave my hand an apologetic squeeze. "Verity business," he said. "Might take a while. Settle yourself in and try to have a good time. I'll make it up to you, promise."

I squeezed his hand back. "Will do." Benji and the girl weaved away in the crowd, and I lost sight of them almost immediately. No big surprise, really. It always happened sooner or later at these things. He'd come back and find me eventually.

On to coping, then. The specialty cocktail was a soju caipirinha; I grabbed one from a passing tray and squeezed into a corner next to a massive bronze jar of bamboo to claim a little breathing room. I watched the crowd for a while, monkeys trying to impress each other for status, and wished I were anywhere else.

And then, as I stood there cursing my uncomfy dress-up heels and wishing the pierced-tin ceiling didn't make the noise so much more buzzy and awful, some guy with a close-trimmed beard and these glasses with massively thick frames cornered me. His breath was hot and yeasty from the beer and he stood a normal distance away from me, but leaned forward at the waist so his face was way too close to mine to be strictly comfortable. He had good hygiene and all, just no sense of personal space. That's what I get for hiding in a corner.

I waved my phone at him, as per usual. "The system is down," I said. "Sorry, can't talk!"

"You said that last time," he said.

"Flaky system?" I looked around for Benji, hoping against hope that he was near enough to notice I'd been pinned down and come to my rescue. A little jealousy kicking in would be handy. But Benji still wasn't in evidence.

Yeast-Breath eyed me suspiciously, then leaned even further into my personal space to look at my phone screen. The soft contours of his face folded up into his frown. "You're playing Candy Crush."

I panicked. "Have to run!" I squeaked, and I pushed my way past him, out through the crowd, then further, right out the door of the restaurant.

The cool night air hit me like a bucket of water in the face, but it was a welcome change. I breathed deep. My shoulders relaxed and the pounding in my head receded.

I could see Benji through the black-shuttered window, head bent in conversation with that woman. She tilted her head; her gleaming hair swung forward. I tried to read the body language. Him hunched over, his arms crossed, while she had her chin high and her hands on her hips. A new thought struck me: Ex-girlfriend. Good luck with that, honey, he's mine now.

I walked.

I stopped at a corner a couple of blocks away, not sure exactly where I was or where to go to pass a little time. Benji had driven us here, and he was still inside talking about who even knew what. So was my handbag, for that matter. But the air was fresh and cool, the street was quiet, and out here nobody was passing judgment on my worth as a human being. Or at least not to my face. I stood there, arms crossed and sweater pulled tight across my ribs, and looked up at the sky. I wished I could see the stars, but the city lights drowned them.

"Rough night?" asked a soft voice. The asker stood about fifteen feet away from me, but she blended in with the shadows until she stepped into my puddle of lamplight. She was wearing an outsized army jacket and a broomstick skirt. A corona of frizz rose from her hair, each strand glowing. The smudges below her eyes looked like she'd had maybe four hours of sleep in the last couple of weeks. Combined.

Familiar, but I couldn't place her until I saw the pin on her lapel: She was the woman from the subway earlier. Probably about to ask me if I could spare some change.

"I... I'm sorry," I said, fumbling in my jeans pockets. "My bag is inside." I nodded at the restaurant.

She grimaced. "I don't need your money, thanks."

I thought about fate and chance and there-but-for-the-grace-of-god and I searched in my pockets a little harder. There was a credit card in my back pocket. "Hey, I was just about to get something to eat, and I'd love some company," I lied. "Come on, I'll buy you dinner."

Her face moved through a quick series of inscrutable

reactions, surprise and horror and something that might have been irritation. I couldn't be sure because it didn't last long. She studied me for another moment, the way a surgeon might study a tumor. "Sure, why not," she said.

I led her into a cheap Mexican place and ordered a mess of nachos with extra guacamole and a burrito the size of a football. I wasn't that hungry, but I figured as long as I was trying to do some good, I might as well try to go all the way and send her away with extra food.

"Big appetite, huh?" the woman said.

I nodded amiably. "I didn't eat today."

She ordered a couple of fish tacos and a veritable pail of soda, and I handed my credit card to the man at the counter. He sneered at me and pointed to a sign that read: "Cash Only."

"Oh. OH!" I twisted my credit card in my hands, thinking about my purse, probably still dumped on the floor behind that bronze jar of bamboo at the party.

The woman rolled her eyes and fished a crumpled-up twenty from an inside pocket. "I guess I'm buying tonight," she said.

"God, I'm so sorry," I said as we walked back to the table. Guilt consumed me. "Look, I swear I'll pay you back. I have cash in my purse back at the party."

She shrugged. "It's fine. Don't worry about it."

I nibbled on a chip laminated with melted cheese and tapped a fingernail on the plywood table. Silence felt awkward, but making conversation seemed awkward, too. The woman kept opening her mouth, poised on the brink of speech, and then backing away, like she'd lost her nerve.

She fiddled with punching the straw into her cup, then she caught my eye and began to talk. The words came slowly at first; it seemed like it had been a long time since she'd had the chance to really talk to anybody.

Her name was Chandra. In the course of a few minutes' conversation, I noticed a particular pomposity to the cadences of her speech as if she'd spent much, much too much time at a university. She seemed only a little older than me, though. Grad student? Unusually grubby junior professor? I worried with no small embarrassment if I had completely misread her situation.

We made pointless small talk for a while. The summer is supposed to get awful hot this year; what a shame about the latest political scandal brewing; isn't it wonderful how that fireman saved that little boy on the subway the other day.

Then she was quiet, toying with her fork like she could pick out the right words with it. "The people back at that restaurant you left," she said abruptly. "You know they're the tech scene around here."

The sudden change of subject startled me. And... had she been following me or something? "Yeah," I said, "I guess so. I'm not really one of them, though. I'm just... I'm engaged to Benjamin Adler."

"So I hear," she said. I jumped in my seat, wondering what she could possibly know about it. Before I could ask, she went on. "Are you interested in technology at all?"

I shrugged. "Not really."

"You should be," she said. "You should be afraid of it."

I wasn't quite sure what to make of this. Ever the busybody, I decided to poke at her and see what happened. "Why is that?"

"We're in a dangerous place," she said, with a furtive scan around. I wondered if she saw nonexistent fellow diners trying to eavesdrop on us, and not just the bald chef behind the counter serenading his grill in discord with the radio. "Before long, truth will be determined more by technology than by real reality. It's already happening."

I sat back, convinced I'd found the edge of her tin foil hat.

"It's like this," Chandra said. "Your bank has a computer. Let's say there's a glitch... a data-entry error, whatever... and suddenly it says you don't have any more money. That makes it real. It becomes true." She kept her eyes fixed to my face, as though looking for a particular reaction.

This was a little too much for me, a little too close to home, so I winced. "Saying something doesn't make it so."

She relaxed and sat back, shaking her head. "You're wrong. It's always been possible to change reality by saying the right thing at exactly the right moment." She waved her tiny plastic fork in the air for emphasis. "Take the Spanish American War. It was a complete fabrication. It didn't happen until a few newspaper moguls decided business was slow. They started covering a war, and both sides wound up fighting because they fell for it. They thought it was real."

"You mean writing about it as if it were already true made it true," I said. I drummed my fingers on my thighs, suddenly nervous.

"Exactly." She sat forward again, leaning onto her elbows to stare at me with burning eyes. "Words have power. But you know all about that, right? I mean... your fiancé runs Verity, right? So I'm sure he's told you everything."

"What kind of everything?" I asked slowly.

"Hasn't Ben told you what Verity really does? Verity isn't in the business of reporting reality, they're in the business of making it." She clapped her fingertips to her mouth with faux horror, and her voice became syrup-thick from bitterness. "Silly me. Not for me to spill his secrets. Forget I said anything."

I stared at her, my eyes wide, trying to think of something

to say. My upper arms were covered with goose bumps. I thought again, for about the millionth time that day, about changing Benji's Verity page. It was impossible, right? A coincidence. Saying something doesn't make it true. Everybody knows that.

I had to get out of there before I totally lost grip on reality. Real reality. I tried to think of a way to excuse myself and get back to the party. But... there was the matter of the money I owed her. I couldn't bear to stiff her on a dinner I'd asked her out to in the first place.

"Um, will you walk me back to the party?" I asked. "And then I can pay you back."

She turned her little plastic fork over and over in her hands. "I'd rather not," she said. "But I promise I'll give you a chance some other time." She set the fork down and began shredding her napkin instead. "Just do me a favor. Don't tell Ben you saw me, OK? Forget my name, forget we ever met. It's... complicated."

"Right," I said. "Whatever you say." Like I would have had any idea what to tell Benji about her anyhow.

chapter FOUR

My unsettling chat with Chandra left me even less enthusiastic about making small talk with Benji's friends and colleagues for the rest of the night. Inside again, the roar of other people having a good time combined with the heavy aromas of cumin and shredded pork nearly suffocated me. I found Benji by the bar at the back this time, wreathed in admirers and hangers-on. He was still talking to the girl with the blue streaks in her razor-sharp chin bob, though a couple of hipster dudes with matching goatees had been elevated into their conversation, too.

"Hey, Benji?" I ducked my head under his arm and put my arms around his waist, then gave the girl a half-smile by way of apology for interrupting.

She didn't return the smile, but the warm kiss Benji gave me when he saw me more than made up for it. "What up, M? Where you been?"

"I'm not feeling so hot, do you mind if we get out of here soon?" I rested my forehead against his chest to make it seem like I'd developed an awful headache. Which wasn't really so far from true, if you considered my headache to be metaphorical rather than physical.

"Already? The night is young."

"I know, I'm sorry, but I really need to get out of here. It's been a long day, you know?"

"Fine, fine, just give me a few to wrap things up." He rubbed the small of my back, only a little bit like I was his pet Labrador. I stood quietly and waited for them to finish their conversation. They had ranged deep into technical territory, and I could no more follow them than I could have followed a conversation about particle physics conducted solely in Sinhalese. I didn't have to suffer through it for long, though. After a few minutes, he stepped away from me. "I'm going to make the rounds and say my goodbyes, OK? Wait here, I'll be right back."

He wove through the crowd, dispensing a steady stream of high-fives and handshakes. I scanned the room to make sure that I hadn't popped up on Yeast-Breath's radar again. The girl with the blue highlights sat neatly on her bar stool, ankles crossed, watching me with narrowed eyes.

I tried to assemble my face into an open, friendly expression. Wide eyes, wider smile. If there's one thing my mother had taught me, it was that there's no sense in making enemies out of your future husband's long-term business associates. I leaned forward and raised my voice so she could hear me over the crowd noise. "I know I've seen you around, but I can't remember your name. Have we been introduced?"

Her lips pressed together, lengthened. "My name is Marjorie. We've met." We had met, in the sense that we'd been in the same room more than once, but I knew perfectly well we'd never been introduced. Still, sometimes you have to overlook a white lie for the sake of maintaining civility.

"You work for Benji at Verity?" Civility maintained. My mother would have been so proud.

Proud, that is, until she saw Marjorie's reaction. Her nostrils flared at the apparent insult I had offered, and one of her booted feet flexed up, like it was itching to kick me. "We work together at Verity," she corrected me. "We founded the company together."

Yowch. Not just an ex, after all; this was more along the lines of the ex-wife who shared custody of the kids. Odds were good we'd be stuck with one another for a long, long time. I definitely had to stay on her good side. Or, from the look of things, find a way to get onto her good side. "Oh wow, that's so interesting," I said.

"Where have you been all night?" She lifted her chin slightly. "I saw you leave before."

My smile flickered and went out. "I needed some air."

She snorted like she knew better, but wasn't up to calling me out on it. She stabbed at the ice in her drink with a red plastic skewer shaped like a pirate's cutlass. Sadly for me, there were no more trays of drinks in circulation, and the bartender was on a break. We were rescued from this conversational impasse by Benji's return. "Let's head out," he told me.

Marjorie stopped him, her fingers resting lightly on his bicep. It might have been an innocuous gesture, but it still boiled me in irrational jealousy. "Remember to finish your research this weekend. It won't wait." Her eyes settled on me again, heavy, like she thought I might prevent Benji from doing his job.

He shrugged. His posture said, "You're not the boss of me," but his mouth said, "I won't forget." He turned his sour gaze back to me. "Come on, M." His grip on my wrist was tighter than it needed to be, and his pace through the crowd too much quicker than mine. I had to scramble to keep from being pulled flat onto my face.

He was silent on the drive all the way back to my place. "Come up with me?" I asked him. I unbuckled my seat belt and opened the car door.

His head was turned away, watching traffic go by, so I couldn't read his expression. "Can't. Work to do tonight."

I bowed my head. "Oh. Well, good night, then. And sweet dreams."

"Yeah. Thanks."

He gave me a perfunctory peck on the lips before he drove off, but in his mind he was already gone. "Good night to you, too," I told his tail lights, a little sulky. He could've asked how I felt or wished I was better soon or offered to make me a cup of tea and tuck me in or, or... something.

My mood didn't improve any from stepping into home sweet home. The place seemed even shabbier than usual. I imagined my parents' empty apartment on Fifth Avenue with its three stories, its sweeping view of Central Park, its persistent cleanliness in the face of any amount of slobitude. My apartment smelled musty, even venturing into rancid, and the lights were too dim to keep the darkness at bay.

Benji's place was so much better. Since we were getting married, maybe I'd move in with him. Or maybe he'd break up with me again. I set my jewelry on the kitchen counter and changed into pajama pants and a tank, then stood at my bedroom window looking out at the street lights. They were bright and pure, like diamonds and promises.

Chandra had said that words have power. Chandra seemed like she knew Benji, though she hadn't said how. She couldn't possibly be telling the truth, because that would be crazy, right? But I couldn't quite find a loose corner to start pulling at her story to find where the truth ended and the lunacy began. Given the looming ambiguity of my impromptu engagement, though, I had to get to the bottom of it somehow.

I picked up my phone to message Eli so he could talk some sanity into me. I didn't tap send. Instead I hefted the phone in my hand, then tossed it down onto my bed. It bounced once and wound up under my pillow. Sometimes when the crazy is upon you, it's better to keep it to yourself. This felt like one of those times.

Maybe I could talk some sanity into myself without any outside help. If Verity had some mystical power to bend reality itself, then a little trial and error should prove it, right? Or not. I found myself at my keyboard, fingers poised, ready to remake reality in my own image. Didn't have a clue where to start, though. And I admit there was more than a little fear in my cowardly little heart. What if I proved myself a gullible idiot?

Worse, what if I didn't?

I stared at the screen, trying to come up with the perfect revision to prove that I was right or wrong, to prove whether Benji really loved me or not. My mind was blank. I clicked my laptop closed and went into the kitchen to stare at the mostly-empty half-gallon of vanilla-scented freezer burn. I went back to the window and its glittering city lights, searching for courage or peace of mind. Either one would do, but the city offered neither.

The computer drew me back. I settled cross-legged on my bed and went for a wiki walk in Verity, looking for something to change. I'd make up something that wasn't true and add it to see what happened.

I found the entry on coffee. I knew coffee. My addition was just a tiny line, but one sure to create evidence if it came true: "In 2004, a group of students at the University of Washington in Seattle created a coffee-based religion called Essence of Spirit." When I went to submit the change, there was only one button, and it was labeled "Verify." Wait, there'd been another button when I'd done this before, from Benji's account. Whatever. His vanity mods weren't relevant just now. I shook my head and clicked the button.

The change vanished into the ether. Upon refresh, the change still didn't appear on the page. I searched the web for my made-up coffee cult and found nothing. That proved it, right? I tried and I failed. Obviously the timing with my previous edit and Benji's proposal was nothing but an epic coincidence, he did really love me and want to marry me, and Chandra was somewhere on the spectrum of deranged into downright stalkerish. Simple.

Or was it? Maybe the change had been too big. Or maybe it took a little while for reality to shift to its new course. I hadn't been engaged the moment I'd clicked the button, after all; it had taken at least an hour, maybe two, before Benji came back. Maybe Essence of Spirit would be real in the morning.

I'd have to try again before reaching any conclusions. And maybe I should think of something less ambitious; something small, something that nobody else would notice. But it had to be verifiable, so I could know if it worked. I chewed on my lower lip and stared at the glowing letters on my keyboard. Maybe there was an entry on Joes' Buzz? I searched. There was.

I read the summary: location, menu, ambience, reviews, hours... hm. Hours. Maybe that was my key. I changed the article to say that the Buzz was changing its hours, effective immediately, to open half an hour later and close half an hour earlier. If it came true, maybe I could catch up on sleep.

Or maybe not. I had trouble falling asleep that night, and when I finally did, I had bad dreams.

I got to the Buzz early the next morning, but Joey was already there, Hawaiian shirt blazing. His first tiny cup of cappuccino was nearly empty. "Cranberry muffins are good this morning," he said. "Try one."

They did smell good, full of real butter and topped with a cinnamon crumble, but "It's too early for solid food," I groaned. I made myself a vat of café au lait. "Why do you have to get us up so early? Can't you open just a little later? Like half an hour. It's not like there are so many customers this time of day." I watched him closely over the steaming edge of my cup.

"And lose my quiet setup before the rush? Never!" he scoffed. "That half hour is more precious than rubies, Mira-deara."

Drat. Didn't work. But I had one more long shot to take. "Hey, I was reading about this cult in Seattle last night that made coffee into their religion. Called themselves 'Essence of Spirit.' Ever heard of 'em?" I slipped a pair of sugar cubes into my cup.

"Sounds like an urban legend to me," he said. "Don't believe everything you hear."

The jury was in, then. Chandra: wearing her crazypants. Engagement: legit and on. I took a sip of my coffee, just cool enough to drink. "You can say that again."

chapter FIVE

I had a shot at sleeping in late and paying off some of the interest on my sleep debt the next morning; I had a couple of days off. When I finally woke up at a quarter to noon, it was only because my phone was ringing. Or to be more accurate, buzzing loudly and irritatingly against the chipped blue paint of my night table. I stuck a hand from under the quilt and groped to answer it.

It was Eli. "Mira, you sleep like the dead. Come and let me in." He sounded amused, not angry. He'd had plenty of time to get used to me being not as, ah, reliable as one might hope; we'd been friends since the third grade, when he'd stuffed a mud pie down Jimmy Leitheifer's shorts because the little rat wouldn't stop pulling my ponytail.

"What?— Wait, let you in?"

"I've been standing outside your building trying to get you up for fifteen minutes already," Eli said. "Come on, I think your super is about to call the police and report a suspicious black dude."

I searched for some slippery memory of an obligation, an appointment, something, but couldn't catch one. "Were we supposed to do something today?"

"Open up and find out, pipsqueak," he said.

"Look, I'm not dressed, so it's going to be a minute. Try

not to get arrested, OK?"

"Or you could just let me come up," he laughed.

I buzzed Eli into the building, then sprinted to the bathroom to brush my teeth and throw on some clothes. He knocked with a businesslike rap-tap. I let him in with a hug and an air kiss across the cheek. He tossed his keys into the air and caught them again. "Ready to roll?"

"Wouldn't miss it for anything," I said, teetering on one foot as I pulled my other shoe on. "But where are we going?"

"Pack your bag, and hurry," he said. "I'm parked in not-a-spot, and I don't want a ticket." Bewildering, but I played along and threw a change of undies and my least-smelly shirt into a bag. And then we were in his shiny-but-perfectly-sensible black car, speeding our way to god only knew where.

"What's the hurry, are we going to be late for something?" I asked. I thumbed my phone to see if I had anything in my calendar, but either there was nothing, or I'd forgotten to put it in.

"Nah, I knew you'd still be asleep," he said. "Lucky thing we didn't need a reservation."

I faked punching him in the arm. "What, do you think I'm some kind of lazy hobo?" I protested.

"Obviously so," he nodded. "And a good thing, too, seeing as how I was right."

Here I should probably tell you a little more about Eli, my oldest and best friend in the whole world, deceptively mild but unstoppable, perpetually overprepared and overbooked. We became friends initially with the Jimmy Leitheifer mud pie incident, but we'd really bonded in the ninth grade when our dates left a school dance together to go under the bleachers, leaving me and Eli alone to commiserate.

We tried the whole inevitable boy-girl thing a couple of

months later, pushed into it by friends who insisted we would look "super cute together," but it turned out we were not, in fact, made for each other. Particularly on account of the part where I still liked kissing Danny Hanover.

So. Just friends. There are worse things in the world than being just friends with a guy like Eli Morrow.

He'd been a late bloomer, gangly with outsized teeth, and one of the most studious kids that ever walked the earth. Even now that he'd grown into his teeth and acquired a little body mass, there were days I suspected that there was nothing to him but work and responsibility. Eli: There was a man who'd never let anyone down, and least of all me.

Even so, it was a surprise to see him. Eli was just finishing his last year of law school, and it was impossible to get a piece of him. We didn't really see each other very often, anymore. Not since I dropped out of college for the vie de café and he... didn't. I missed him terribly.

But now wasn't the right time for a guilt trip about the slipping quality of his friendship. "It's great to see you," I said.

"You, too." He flashed me a smile. "That text the other night had me worried, so I thought... you know, as long as we were driving back home tonight anyway... I'd hit you a little early with a surprise to cheer you up. Something going on with you and that guy? What was his name? Benjamin?"

Ohhhhhh, right. That was it. We were supposed to go back to Westchester together. I was performing my filial obligation to visit my parents once a season, this time because the club was honoring my mother with an award for her outstanding work in... something. I'd persuaded Eli to give me a lift and spend a while with his own mom. And after the crazed series of 911 texts I'd sent Eli the other night... Duh. Of course my BFF would want to catch up.

I should've been prepared, but as usual I wasn't. "Oh. That."

Eli steamed onward. "You need me to go bust him up for you?"

My fingers went to the ring on its chain around my neck, self-conscious. "He asked me to marry him," I said.

Eli fell silent. I studied the line of his jaw, growing more anxious as the seconds slid by with no visible reaction. Finally, "And what did you say?" he asked, his fingers flexing on the steering wheel.

I shrank down into my seat. "I said yes."

He jammed into fourth gear hard and sped up as he passed a line of taxis. "Who else knows about it?"

"So far, just you," I said. I figured the Joes didn't count, especially because of the part where they couldn't tell my mother.

"And you're sure about this? Sure this is what you want to do?"

"Well," I hesitated. "It's complicated."

"Which means no, but you don't want to talk about it."

"You're the best, Eli. So understanding."

"You know I'll get it all out of you sooner or later."

We parked (legally, this time) on an unremarkable block of delis and nail salons. Then Eli dragged me by the hand another three blocks before making me put my hands over my eyes. He guided me across the street with his hands on my shoulders. "No peeking, OK?"

A bell tinkled as he pushed me through a doorway. "Open up," he said. We were in an old-fashioned ice cream parlor, complete with staff in paper hats and white collared shirts and aprons. The floor was black-and-white-checked linoleum, and vintage signs extolled the virtues of sodas I'd never heard of before. The shop was redolent with fresh waffle cones. Round swivel stools in pink vinyl and chrome ran along one wall, next to a formica counter.

"This is amazing, how did you find this place?"

He put an arm around me and squeezed. "I have ways. It sounded like you needed some cheering up, and I thought you'd like it." Then his arm dropped. "Though I guess you're celebrating today, huh?" He caught the eye of one of the scoop slingers.

We elected to share one of the shop's "world-famous" hippo-sized banana splits, just for the kitsch of it. It came in a curvy glass boat the length of my forearm. We settled onto those stools and attacked the monster dessert amicably enough.

And then, of course, Eli wanted to know more. "You haven't been seeing this guy for very long, have you?"

"It's been about six months," I said. Which was nearly true, give or take about six weeks.

"Not such a long time." He looked worried. But hey, that's what he'd signed on for with being my friend. I don't remember a time when he wasn't actively worried about some awful mistake I was making. Why ruin the streak now?

"Not such a short time, either." I fished a cherry out of the whipped cream and ate it.

"It just seems sudden."

"Yeah, I know." I'd decided to keep the whole getting-dumped-first business to myself. Not to mention the other elements of the affair that might lead him to question his already low opinion of my sanity. I'd learned a lesson from breaking the news to Joey, at least. Though that wasn't the only lesson: "And before you ask, no, I'm not pregnant."

We strip-mined our mountain of ice cream quietly for a while.

"So," Eli said tentatively, "If you're getting married, does this mean you're getting ready to... make some changes in your life?"

I tensed. "What do you mean?" I asked. But of course I knew already.

"Nothing, nothing," he said, soothing. "It's just that if you're going to get married... "

"Don't start," I warned him. "I get enough of this from my family."

He shook his head, then dropped his spoon onto the table and sat back. "I just want you to be happy," he said. "You don't have to go around feeling guilty about being who you are, Mira."

"I'm happy," I said, my voice tight. "Crazy happy. Couldn't be any happier."

"Of course you are," he said, looking down at his hands. A subject change seemed in order.

"We should go out tonight," I said. "Visit some of the old haunts. Eat the grossest thing we can find at the waffle house. It'll be a good time."

"What? No. Busy." Eli scraped his spoon through the ice cream soup.

"C'mon, you know my mom would love to see you. And I know you, you could use some R&R."

"I don't have time, Mira. I have to study, and I have my own mother to visit, too."

"You can't leave me alone with my parents all night," I said. "You might as well drive the bamboo splinters under my nails with your own hands. And anyway, we haven't hung out like this in months."

"We're hanging out right now," he protested. "I've taken too much time off today already, I'm going to take too much off tomorrow, too, and the bar exam waits for no man."

"You have to lighten up, Eli. Take a look at your priorities sometime. There's more to life than taking the next test and winning the next award."

"You'd know, wouldn't you?"

My mouth snapped shut.

"I'm sorry, Mira, I didn't mean it like that. It's just— "

I held up my hand. "Zip it, I don't want to hear it."

"Come on, you know I'd never— "

"Oh, but you did," I said. I set my spoon down and turned my head away to watch the traffic. "Look, I'll just cope by myself. Never mind."

The drive up to Westchester was quiet. And not the kind of quiet where you don't have to talk to fill up the silence because you're so comfortable together, either. This was the quiet of two people who don't have much to say to each other.

So that was it: into enemy territory with nobody to watch my back. Ugh. Eli dropped me off and drove away to visit his own loving mother.

Since it wasn't a holiday visit to the ancestral home, my sister and her kids weren't going to be there to take the focus off me and my multi-faceted failures. From the moment we crossed the bridge all the way until Eli dropped me off on the graceful gravel sweep of our driveway, I psyched myself up for defending against the assault to Make Something Of My Life.

My parents have never been too picky about what that something should be, mind. It could've been hitching my wagon to a nice man and hatching a nice basket of rosy-cheeked babies while working at the family foundation, or a high-powered career in finance hauling in buckets and buckets of cashola to help shine up the family name. They didn't care what success looked like, so long as nobody could argue that's what it was.

They just didn't want to have to face their friends at the club and admit over their dry martinis that little Mirabelle wasn't finding her way in the world. Their friends' children were investment bankers and CEOs to the last one. Or at least that's how they made it sound.

Poor little Mira working as an aproned member of the service industry and living in a building without even a concierge? It was so unimaginably brutal, such a travesty, that it reflected on mama and papa and the quality of their parenting. Not that they'd ever say it outright, of course; not like that. No, my father would inquire gruffly after my prospects and offer me a little extra financial help — "money doesn't have to be your limiting factor, darling, you know we support you in anything" — and my mother would needle me about my responsibilities toward the family.

That night was no different. I took my shoes off when I got inside so they wouldn't echo through the house. I slid on my socks into the den, noting that my mother had redone it in shades of olive and buttercream since I'd been home last. Then I collapsed onto the couch with the lights out and the TV muted, but closed captioning turned on. The only sound was the ticking of the massive golden sun clock over the sideboard. I should have been undetectable.

Eventually, as the light faded, my mother found me anyway. She perched on the arm of the suede sectional near my feet and watched me while I tried to watch a home improvement show.

"Anna says she's taking over as director of her department at the hospital, did you hear?" Ahh, the inevitable comparison to the older sister. MUCH older.

"That's great for her." I leaned to the side to get a better view of the screen. "Do you mind? You're in the way."

She stayed where she was. "It's so wonderful to see her using all of her advantages to help people, don't you think?"

"Sure, it's wonderful."

"It wouldn't hurt you to follow her example, Mira."

"I'm not a doctor, mom."

"Of course you aren't. But you aren't anything else, either."

For once, I didn't rise to the bait. I moved over by one cushion and stared at the home improvement show, where a couple with two small children were painting whimsical undersea murals for a play room. Who knew jellyfish could be so adorable?

"We just had the place on Fifth redone," my mother said, waving at the set. "You really have no good reason not to move in, Mirabelle."

My father wandered in, drawn by the sound of conversation. "She's right, sweetie," he said. "That place of yours just isn't suitable. You've been in this mopey phase of yours for long enough."

I stood up and grabbed my keys from their spot on the floor. "I'm going out," I said.

My mother stood herself, her hands fluttering. "Where are you going?"

"Out to Connelly's," I said. "I'm meeting friends." This wasn't so much the truth, of course. But in my frame of mind, anybody I ran into today that wasn't angling to inject me with some greater purpose in life could be my new bestest friend ever.

She looked at me warily and air-kissed my cheek. "Have a nice time," she said. I braced myself for what would come next from her. I could guess at all of the things floating under the surface; a thousand variations on "Are you really going to go out looking like that?" or "Don't drink too much, you'll ruin your figure," or "Don't do anything to embarrass us, sweetheart." When she said none of them, I felt a little guilty for expecting it. But I still didn't relax.

My father stepped up with his wallet and handed me a sheaf of twenties. "If you'll be drinking, take the car service," he said gruffly.

Connelly's was a faux-Irish pub, all bare brick walls and a bar of glossy blonde wood. It was packed to the gills, though I didn't recognize anybody in the dim light. The air smelled of beer and wool, just hot and humid enough to feel like a particularly mediocre sauna. I squeezed my way through the dark masses and waved at the bartender, a handsome one with dark hair and lush lips. I ordered something Belgian that was theoretically a beer but tasted more like a raspberry wine cooler, and came in a bottle with a cork.

Heavy fingers poked at my shoulder blade. "Mira," a voice shouted near my ear. "Great to see you."

I turned and beheld Mike Buchanan, former lacrosse hero and now a financier of some fortune, or so my mother led me to believe. A hulk of a man he was, topped off with unexamined confidence and a shock of sandy hair disheveled in the artless way only a $200 barber could have achieved. Arrayed behind him were a couple of his old friends, enshrouded in a communal cloud of men's body spray and machismo. I gave him a forced thumbs-up.

—Actually, now that I was looking, I recognized a lot of familiar faces dotted around the place. And to think I'd thought I was lying to my mother about meeting old friends. Though none of them were friends, exactly, were they? Anna's friends, maybe, but never mine.

"How's it going?" he said, and he gave me the same smile he'd always tried on the cute girls back in the day, the ones like me who were uncomfortably young for him.

"Oh, you know," I said, waving my hand vaguely. "Nothing much."

His eyes skimmed my body, resting too long on my hips and my breasts. "You look good," he said. "Thin." Ah, right. He'd always been like that.

"Yeah, thanks," I said, trying not to grimace. I took a deep swig from my fancy, fruity Belgian beer.

"You here with anyone?" he asked.

I shrugged with one shoulder and looked around, hoping to spot a friendlier face. "Not really," I said.

He slid his arm around my waist and tugged me closer. "Come on with us," he said. "We're having a good time." He pulled me along to the other room, where his little posse had grabbed a booth in an alcove in the back, by the restrooms. Bluh, whatever, it wasn't worth raising a fuss just to stand awkwardly by myself in the corner, right?

Mike nudged me onto the bench, and then he crammed himself in next to me, one arm draped around my shoulders as a mark of ownership. I tried to work out how to drop something about my boyfriend — my *fiancé* — but the group's eyes and conversation passed me over. I wasn't a person in this little scene, I was a prop. Mike's girl, for right now, anyway. I seemed to remember that Mike was a married man, but I glanced at his finger for a ring and saw none. Early divorce or bad memory, I couldn't say which.

Mike's fingers grazed my breast — maybe once was an accident — and then again, those meaty fingers lingering, seeking out my nipple.

I elbowed him in the ribs, hard. "Bathroom," I said, as

loudly as I could so the whole table would hear. He eased out so I could leave the booth and head toward the ladies' room. The bathroom had a line, of course, and I used the waiting time to lean against the wall with my forehead, arms crossed tight in front of me. I wouldn't go back to the table. I'd fake a phone call, and then go... where? Home to my parents? Ugh.

When my turn at the facilities finally came, I banged the door shut behind me, but it bounced back open and then I was pressed against the filthy tiles of the bathroom wall with Mike's hot breath filling my nostrils.

"Hey, babe," he said. "C'mon, let's have some fun."

His hand rested on my ass, squeezing and kneading like I was a piece of dough. I stood frozen in place, temporarily incapable of extricating myself. I tried to make a sound, but nothing came out.

Mike's other hand snaked up my shirt to cup my bra. I convulsed and found my voice. "Get away," I said. I tried to shove him back, but it was like trying to move a brick wall. Years of self-defense advice jumbled all together in my head.

Keys between the knuckles — no, that's not the one.

"Stop it," I said, but his mouth, sloppy and moist, was trailing along my neck like a slug. He ground his pelvis up against me.

Claw at his eyes? Oh god my nails were too short and my mother would never speak to me again if I blinded or disfigured him and started all that gossip.

I shoved again, shivering from adrenaline, but the strength that allegedly lets a mother lift a car in an emergency was not enough for me to lift a douchebag away from my body. "Stop," I said again.

"You know you always wanted to," he said. "Today is your lucky day." He fumbled at the button on my jeans.

Knee to the groin, right? The classic, but the angle wouldn't work. Still—

"Fuck you," I said, and I stomped on his foot hard as I could.

Mike stumbled back a step. "Fucking cocktease!" he howled, half-crouched over his injured appendage. "You're gonna regret that— " and he loomed over me, his beer-soaked reactions keeping him from acting with speed or precision. I used that tiny, precious second to duck under his arm and out of the bathroom and into the crowd in the bar where I might be safe.

Then I pushed my way out to the parking lot and stood under the street lamps, listening to my heart pound and watching clouds of my breath form and disperse like some time-lapse weather radar. I didn't cry; I was proud of that. But I still couldn't face the questions my parents would have if I came back so early. And I wouldn't go back inside for the obvious reason.

I sat on the hood of somebody else's car and thumped my head back to stare at the sky. The flood of adrenaline leached out of my blood, leaving me wilted and empty.

The cold from the metal bit through to my shoulder blades, but I had a long wait in front of me. How early could I go home, I wondered, and not have my parents ask why I was back? I closed my eyes and cupped my hands in front of my nose to keep my face warm while I tried to figure it out. Should have brought a sweater.

The car rocked and the hood flexed as another butt sat upon it. I tensed. "Fancy meeting you here," Eli said.

I opened my eyes and sat up. "I thought you were studying."

"I decided you were right and I needed a night off. I drove

up to your mom's place a while ago to see what you were up to, and she said you were here. So here I am."

"Did you just get here?" I asked, cautious.

He rubbed his hands along his thighs. "I only got here a couple of minutes ago, but I heard Mike bitching loud enough to get the general idea," he said. "It sounds like you could have used me sooner. Sorry." He studied the flickering neon in the window advertising some frat-boy brand of beer. "You know," he said, his voice slow and casual, "I heard a rumor that Mike has a federal indictment coming down the pike. Securities fraud."

"No," I said, mouth hanging slack.

He grinned, the very embodiment of mischief. "Oh, it gets better," he said. "Word on the street is his wife dumped him for his partner at the firm, and the two of them sold him down the river for immunity."

"Wow." He'd never really seemed that interesting before, you know? Who knew.

Eli shrugged, and his smile turned hard. "He's trying to make like he's still a big man, even though he's on his way down," he said. "You need me to go kick his ass for you?"

I grinned. "No, that won't be necessary."

"You sure?" Eli rubbed the knuckles of his fist. "It'd be my pleasure."

"Just sit with me for a little bit, OK?"

"If you insist." And then: "I'm sorry about before, Mira," he said, quietly. "I shouldn't have pushed you like that today. Don't be mad."

"I'm not mad."

"Look, let's go someplace a little warmer. Want to hit the waffle house and get some bad coffee?"

I slid off the car and straightened my clothes. "Sounds perfect."

Close to dawn, before staggering off to snatch a couple hours' sleep, we hugged and made easy promises to get together again soon. Real soon. That's Eli for you: Always there to pick you up when you're down.

chapter SIX

My old room at my parents' house was a perfectly preserved memento of everything my life used to be, from the cream wallpaper flecked with tiny peach roses to the lace curtains on the windows to the walnut canopy bed. Motes of dust hovered in the air, but I knew there wouldn't be a speck of it anywhere else in the room. The things in here were all carefully staged to craft the illusion of a perfection that never was: the rosebud vase with its dried spray of baby's breath and the husks of eleven roses I'd received, one at each ballet recital from the time I was four until I had decided I'd had enough. It was flanked by a porcelain-framed photograph of the family all together. Some day that had been. My dress had been too small to fit my pudgy figure but my mother wouldn't allow me to buy anything in a larger size.

The room had long been cleared of my few diffuse attempts at marking it for myself. No more posters of boy bands, the piles of unsightly paperbacks relegated to some storage area. I'd once brought back a festively loud marionette from a spring break holiday. The last time I'd been home, it had still hung from the knob of my closet's louvered doors. Not anymore. I wondered where it had gone.

Trashed, probably.

I had just barely shut my eyes after my waffle house

adventure with Eli (or it seemed like it) when mom tapped on my door twice, lightly, and then came right in, swish, over the carpet. She was carrying a tray with a delicate single-serve teapot steaming on it, a perfect little hard-boiled egg, and an unspeakably lovely fruit salad. Low-carb and low-cal. Heh.

I should explain here that from her, the tapping was more of an announcement than a request. It drove me crazy when I was fifteen, and trust me it was still like nails on a blackboard even now.

I gritted my teeth and attempted a little forgiveness, Buddha-style. She was probably here in an effort to be kind, right?

"I brought you breakfast, darling," she said. She set the tray on my dresser. "Do you have something suitable to wear at the club this evening?" Her voice was light but very cold, frost on feathers.

I... hadn't thought about it yet. And I hadn't exactly packed a full suitcase when Eli picked me up. In my defense, I'd had a lot on my plate, what with being engaged and going crazy and so on. I picked up yesterday's jeans from their heap on the floor, nearly worn through at the knees and thoroughly frayed at the cuffs. "I didn't bring anything," I said.

"Well, I'm sure it'll be fine," she said. "You have three dozen dresses still hanging in your closet, there must be something." Never mind that those three dozen dresses were still there because they were all variations on the melody of not-my-style. I'd left them behind when I moved out in hopes of never wearing any of them ever again.

"I don't know if they'll fit," I said, half-heartedly.

She sized up my hips. "You should be fine," she said. "If anything, you look like you've lost a few pounds, dear-heart. Good work."

I didn't roll my eyes, but only barely. I spent the bulk of the day back on that deliciously soft suede sectional watching cooking shows and avoiding my mother. Benji sent me a series of increasingly risqué suggestions about what I should wear to our wedding, but then he was en route to Vancouver to keynote at a conference or something and didn't have time to entertain me.

Half past six o'clock found me in the stiff leather back seat of my father's Lexus as we rolled toward the valet stand at the country club. I had decided not to fight the garment battle, so I wore a pastel green dress with Swiss dots and a white Peter Pan collar more appropriate to a toddler than a grown woman. I looked ridiculous. Or at least felt ridiculous. Probably both.

The valet was Charlie, a Jamaican gentleman who had seemed ancient when I was four and only got younger as I grew up. "Nice to see you, Miss M," he said, and he winked. Charlie had always snuck me gum and extra servings of custard when I was small, and he'd helped me to cover my tracks after an unfortunate topiary incident when I was twelve. Seeing him helped me relax just a little. Maybe this leisurely trip to the bad old days wouldn't be as bad as all that, stupid dress or no.

There was a bounce in my step and I even hummed a chipper tune as I trailed my parents toward their regular table. My mind's tongue was already savoring the club's trademark chicken cordon bleu and the piping hot French rolls they brought for the table. The club's chef was never on trend, but by god his classics were classic.

I'd only have to sit through, what, half an hour of speeches while they gave my mother whatever award she'd made up to give herself? But it was easy enough to tune all that out.

Then my mother stopped to trade air kisses with Betty Buchanan and her husband Gerald, and then with their son

Mike.

Yeah, *that* Mike.

When he saw me, his lip twitched with a nearly undetectable snarl.

I turned on my heel and went straight to the bar to get a shot of tequila, ignoring the pressure between my shoulder blades that meant my mother both noticed and disapproved of my absence. I could already tell it was going to be a long night. I wasn't going to go through it entirely sober if I could help it.

The bartender was new, so he didn't know to send me back into the dining room when the mic came on and the speeches started. I heard a polite sprinkling of applause, and then the muffled tones of some society lady pontificating on how very wonderful my mother was. Her incredible discipline and focus, right. Her dogged determination. Heh. Her bottomless empathy for the disadvantaged.

On that last one, I snorted and called for another tequila shot.

Then my mother came up to accept her award. In clipped and perfect diction, she thanked everyone for this honor, and hoped — this part was clearly written entirely for my benefit — "that the coming generation will take up our mantle of service and responsibility, and keep the way of progress moving ever forward."

The tequila didn't sit very well in my empty stomach. And I couldn't realistically stay in the bar all night. So when the speeches were finally over, I went looking for my parents. Once I saw they were seated with the Buchanans, I very nearly went back to the bar.

The wait staff were already clearing away the salad plates. My mother smiled stiffly. "So glad you decided to join us."

"Sorry mom." I settled into the empty seat. "I was

feeling a little nauseous, and I didn't want to risk ruining your big moment by running out or being sick — congratulations, though. They're very lucky to have you."

I mean it was mostly true, right?

My mother's eyes narrowed with suspicion, but Betty tsked and asked after my health.

"I had some soda crackers in the bar, so I feel a little better now," I lied. "I think it's just— you know— female troubles." With that, the table dropped the subject of how I was feeling like it was a rabid badger.

Unfortunately, my parents and Mike's had already combined forces to do that annoying thing parents do: they'd blandly arranged it so that the two single, marriageable people were sitting next to one another. I was enveloped in Mike's cloud of overpriced cologne, reminding me of the smell of urine and beer and the feeling of his hand on my breast.

I clenched my fists in my lap and practiced breathing quietly through my nose while our parents tried to sell us to each other on our suitability as marriage material.

Betty smiled at me as she poured packet after packet of artificial sweetener into her iced tea. "Are you back in town for long?" she asked. "It would be lovely to have you come to the shore to go sailing with us, don't you think, Michael?"

"Oh, of course," he said. "I'd love to have you, Mira."

"I just bet you would," I muttered, loud enough for him to hear. Out of the corner of my eye I could see the muscle by his ear twitch, and I felt a little better.

In fact, I felt better enough to feel sorry for his parents; they hadn't done anything, and there was no cause to embarrass them. Even if they had raised a massive jerk and would-be rapist. "I'm just here for a little while," I said. "Just a quick visit. I'm driving back to the city with Eli in the morning."

Betty's brow would have creased, if it weren't for the medical interventions she'd received to prevent such a potentially wrinkle-inducing tragedy. "Do you mean that boy Eli Morrow? What a nasty piece of work he is, not that he could help it, I suppose. I hear he's turned into some sort of rabble-rouser for— " she leaned forward and spoke in a hushed voice "— the wrong kind of people." Huh, progress. She hadn't said "the blacks and the Arabs" like she would have ten years ago.

"He's an amazing human being, and I am very proud of all of the civil rights work he's done," I said.

My mother kicked me under the table for being rude and contradicting an adult; and never mind that I was an adult here, too. Everyone else fixed their attention determinedly on their entrees. "The scallops are very tender this evening," my father announced. "The new chef is working out very well, don't you think?" Smooth, dad, I thought. Way to change the subject.

"We both know you'd rather have the filet!" Gerald waved his fork in the air. "It's too bad your cardiologist won't let you."

"Maybe next time I'll do it anyway. What the cardiologist doesn't know won't hurt him," my dad chortled.

I wondered what would happen if I told the charming tale of what had happened with Mike and I last night. They'll say it's your fault, whispered the little voice in the back of my head. I kept my mouth shut and checked out of the conversation, opting to stare out the window at the manicured and gazebo-adorned garden.

My deeply focused inattention persisted through the meal. I picked at my chicken, but it tasted like wet cardboard tonight. The new chef couldn't do the classics, I guess. Just like me.

The sound of my name yanked me back into the ebb and flow of the table's pointless chattering, like a summoning.

"Did you hear, Mira? Mike's giving us a progress report

on his new investment fund! They're specializing in technology firms, it's all very exciting." My mother took a small nibble of her cheesecake.

Mike grinned. "We're building the future, Mrs. Newton," he said. "Blue Ocean is getting in on some very exciting things. We're negotiating a deal right now that I expect to give us 400% ROI in the next five years. Best twenty million dollars I'll ever spend!" Our fathers guffawed and slapped the table.

"I thought you were in investment banking," I said, innocently. "Didn't that work out for you?" I looked at him through my lowered eyelashes.

His shoes scuffed the carpet. "I didn't care for it," he said. "Too much regulation."

"Say," I said, as though the idea had just struck me, "how's your wife doing, anyway?"

Mike scowled, my mother gave me yet another reproving look. Betty Buchanan looked around the club to make sure nobody was eavesdropping, and then cupped her hands to whisper to me: "D-I-V-O-R-C-E."

"Oh, that's just too bad," I said brightly. "I heard she was very popular with your business partners."

At that, Mike jerked up from the table and stalked away, knocking my goblet of mocha mousse into my lap in the process. Betty cried out and dabbed at me half-heartedly with a napkin, while my parents exchanged a private look commiserating about how completely insufferable I was.

"I think it's best if we go home now, Betty," said my mother. "I'll call you in the morning."

Gerald and my father shook hands while my mother and Betty traded air kisses again. "Lovely to see you, sweetheart," Betty told me, despite how very obvious it was that it had been anything but lovely.

"Sure," I said. Then my mother strode out of the restaurant like she was on fire, my father and I following after her like trails of smoke. The drive back to their house was silent, and took easily three times as long as the drive to the club had.

My mother brought a plate holding two exquisite almond cookies to my room while I was changing. "I thought you could use a treat since you didn't get to eat your dessert at the club." She paused for a moment, tray in her hands, like she was framing a question about my behavior toward Mike but couldn't quite focus on a way to ask that wouldn't make it all worse. Of course asking me if anything was wrong — that wouldn't occur to her.

I mustered a smile. "Thanks, mom." I leaned over and picked up one of the cookies. As I did, Benji's great-grandma's diamonds-and-sapphires, still hanging on their chain from my neck, swung forward and then back again as I straightened, a perfect pendulum.

My mother frowned. "What's that?"

I licked powdered sugar from the corner of my mouth. "What?"

Her finger prodded at the offending jewel. "This ring, where did you get it?"

My face flushed hot. "It was a gift from my boyfriend?" I didn't have the time to dissemble. Also I'm a terrible liar.

The next words from her mouth were clipped and unemotional, but ran all together in a shrill aria at the end: "You. Have. A. Boyfriend. Who. Gave. You. A. Ring. Andyoudidn'ttellmeeeeee?" A sure sign that I was in boiling-hot water. For a blinding moment, I really was fifteen again, with braces and skinned knees and a chip on my shoulder the size of a vintage 1950s automobile, and my mother had just caught me climbing in my window when I was supposed to be grounded.

I shook myself, trying to expel the adolescent version of me who had momentarily occupied my body. My mother glared at me, her eyes a portal to unfathomably deep, dark wells in the earth where rock and metal boiled.

I'd never introduced Benji to my parents. Hell, I'd never even breathed a word that he existed. I'd had a complex as broad as the ocean that he would never, ever get serious with me, and I'd done an awful lot of telling myself that it was all for fun, anyway. All just a fling, go as it may. It wasn't the kind of Facebook-it's-complicated situation you want to invite your parents into.

"I was going to tell you," I said. "It just seemed like a bad time."

Her silence wasn't stony so much as it was mountainous. Or perhaps icebergian.

"Look, can we talk about this another day? Maybe in the morning?" I gestured to my filthy dress, tossed across the bed. "I've had kind of a hard day."

Her head jerked in one short, sharp nod. "You can be certain we'll talk about this in the morning."

I sat in the wooden chair by the vanity staring at my hollow-eyed reflection for an hour and a half while the rest of the house quietly went to sleep. The bed with its nest of lace-ruffled pillows might as well have been an alligator pit.

It was well past midnight when I pulled on the T-shirt and faded jeans I'd worn that morning, stuffed the Swiss-dot dress in a trash can, and pulled out of the driveway in my dad's sports car on my way back to my own apartment. It was the responsible thing, right? The Joes had me scheduled to work the next day anyhow. Couldn't let 'em down, now could I? I was just being mature, like everyone was always telling me I should be.

Right?

chapter SEVEN

I spent the next day texting Benji-in-Vancouver terrible elephant jokes (not that there are any good ones) and deleting voicemails from my parents during quiet spells at the Buzz. I sent off apologies to Eli, too, for not keeping him company on the drive home, but I just wasn't ready to have That Conversation with my mother. I wanted to lay some groundwork first, manage some expectations. It's not the sort of thing to lay on her cold turkey.

Eli understood, of course. It was all for the best, he said. Gave him a little more time to spend with his mom, since he didn't need to shuffle me home in time for work.

I stopped and bought a bridal magazine after my shift was done. Lots of photos of improbable dresses and advice about how to gracefully deal with lost gifts and crotchety great-aunts. Nothing at all about explaining to your mother why you never mentioned to her you were seeing someone.

When my phone rang it was just about four in the morning, an hour I strongly preferred to spend sleeping. My sheets were warm and my pillow was soft, and in my slumber there were no confusing interpersonal rapids to navigate. No engagement, no Verity, certainly not my mother. I ignored the first buzz-buzz-buzz and fell asleep again, but the second time it evicted me from dreamland. I rubbed my eyes and looked at the clock and thought: This is either important, or it's a wrong number and they won't stop bothering me until I answer. I picked up my phone.

"Hello," I croaked.

"Mira?" It was my sister, Anna.

Four isn't usually her most sociable hour, either, and the shock of hearing her voice woke the rest of my brain up. I sat up in bed and hugged my quilt tight to my chest. "Is everything OK? Is dad— "

"It's Eli," she said. Her voice was somber. "I was on call at the hospital when he came in. He was on his way home, and the police say there was a drunk driver— "

A funny, empty feeling grew just behind my navel. I rocked in place. "Is he... OK?"

"I'm so sorry, Mira, but we aren't sure if he's going to make it. His family is coming to say goodbye. Just in case." Anna sounded so bleak, so cold, that I couldn't quite process the words at first.

"Goodbye," I repeated. My voice seemed small and far-away, even to myself. I could hear the static of my breath in the receiver.

"Just in case," she insisted. "There's still hope, OK?"

"OK."

"I'm sorry to wake you," she said. "Just, I thought you should know. I'm staying on shift at the hospital until we know what's going to happen for sure. I know how close you always were, so I'll... I'll keep you posted."

"Wait, should I come in, too?"

"No, they wouldn't let you in," she said. "Family only."

"Oh."

"Look, I'll call you later. OK?"

"Yeah, OK," I said.

Anna hung up. I sat there staring at the wall with the dead phone still at my ear.

Sleep was gone for good. I cried a little and thought about Eli; how hard he worked, how close he was to graduating, how terribly unfair it all was. What would become of me if I didn't have him to count on anymore? If only I'd stuck to our original plan — if I hadn't run away without him, then he'd have been home already, and then he wouldn't be —

No no no can't think like that, stop it stop. Deep breaths.

I wondered if I should be racing back to Westchester to see him, family-only or not. We were as good as family, weren't we?

Could I get there in time? Was I even safe to drive?

I watched the rising sun through the slats of my blinds, the misty gray dissolving into the uncompromising yellow of morning. I went to take a shower.

The drops did little to wash away the tension in my shoulders, but I stood there for a while anyhow, eyes closed and face tilted into the sharp spray. I thought about the possibility of losing Eli forever. My mind skittered off the idea like droplets of water off a hot frying pan. I didn't want it to be true. It just wasn't possible.

The phone rang again while I was still in there. It had to be Anna calling back, so I flung a towel around my body and scrambled to answer, dripping a river behind me. "Hello?" I said, breathless.

"Hey, Mira," Anna said. I could hear the steady beep-beep-beep of medical gadgetry through the phone. "I just wanted to check in since I'm sure you're worried. Eli's family has been here for a while. He's been hanging on so far, but he's not conscious and we're not sure if he will be. I've been making sure he's at least comfortable, but it could still go either way."

It all made sense; Anna, being both in charge of trauma and a lifelong control freak, would want to be on top of everything personally.

"Yeah. Thanks, Anna. And thanks for calling."

"So look, I know they won't let you in to visit, but is there anything you want me to say to him for you? I don't know if it would get through, but... "

I thought about it, chewing on my thumbnail. Only one thing? There was no way to condense everything I would need to tell him into a few meager phrases spoken through a middleman. "I guess give him my love," I said. "It's stupid, but I can't think of anything better."

"You have a little longer to think it over," she said.

The beeping in the background changed. It stuttered and lengthened out, and then it made that sound that you hear on television, that long, high whine that means that somebody is dead.

There was a clattering sound in my ear as the phone on the other end hit the floor. From a hundred miles away, I heard a muddle of barked commands, shouting, the sounds of a commotion I couldn't see but could easily picture. They had lost Eli, and my sister had leapt into action. The noises I heard were CPR in progress, Anna in her element wielding mysterious tubes and devices in a last-ditch effort to extend his life, even if only for a few minutes.

Eli was dead. It couldn't be true. I didn't want it to be true. Chandra's voice came to me in a flood of desperation: change reality by saying the right thing at the right moment.

I would make it false.

I ran to my laptop in my room and huddled on my bed with it, shivering and still mostly wet. Eli wasn't notable enough to have his very own page in Verity, but there was a news report about the drunk driving accident. There at the end was the part where Eli was in critical condition, and not expected to survive. I changed it: "He had been listed in very serious condition, and at one point needed to be resuscitated, but the procedure was successful." I submitted.

I listened on the phone again, where Anna's dropped cell phone served as my forgotten link to the hospital room. The noise had changed; there was still a commotion of footsteps and activity, but the shouting had gone. The faint beep-beep-beep had resumed.

It had worked. Had it worked? My lungs felt tight as I tried to work out what to think and what to do next. Was the change instantaneous? Not so far, not in my experience. So how would I know if I had changed anything at all? The screen stared back at me, unblinking; absolutely unhelpful. I listened for clues on the other end of the phone, but couldn't make words out of the distant muddle.

I went back to Verity and changed the entry again. "He had been in critical condition, and at one point needed resuscitation, but was quickly upgraded to serious but stable condition. He is expected to survive."

On the phone, I heard a murmuring sound, like a crowd sharing a gasp, and then a hoarse voice speaking — was it Eli? Had he woken up? I held my breath, hoping Anna would pick up the phone again. She didn't.

I hung up and called Joey, already at the Buzz, where I was due to come on shift in about half an hour. "Can't make it today, I'm so sorry," I told him. "A friend of mine was in a really bad accident and I'm driving up to see him in the hospital."

"Sorry to hear it." Joey sounded like he meant it, too. "I'll make Joseph get up early for once to cover for you."

“Thank you,” I said. “You’re the best.”

I pulled some clothes on over my damp skin and was in my dad’s car and on the road in less than five minutes. The drive would only take about half an hour this time of day and at my speed; plenty of time for thinking about what had just happened and all of its implications. I was already halfway there when Anna called me back. I picked up my cell phone, ignoring Eli’s voice in my head telling me what a terribly dangerous thing it was to talk and drive.

“Sorry to drop your call like that before, Mira,” Anna said. “But you’ll never guess what happened.”

“I bet I can.”

The hospital smelled cold. Its hush made even the softest noises seem painfully loud and out of place. I was self-conscious about the slapping sound my flips made against the pink-flecked linoleum as I made my way toward Eli’s room.

He was awake. I hung around the periphery for a little bit as his family and assorted medical professionals tended to him, worker bees devoted to their queen. All the while I studied his face, swollen and covered with scrapes. Both of his legs and one arm were in casts, an oxygen tube was taped into his nose, and enough wires and sensors hung from his bed to supply a biotech startup or two with all the raw materials they could need to hit IPO.

Anna touched my elbow when I arrived and steered me out the door again, into the hall. “He’s going to be all right,” she murmured, in the hushed tone people reserve for hospitals, churches, and libraries. “But we almost lost him this morning. Thank god I was in the room already.”

“Yeah,” I said, and thought about my Verity revision. “We’re all lucky you were there.”

She nudged me in the shoulder. "You're lucky I could get you in," she said. "You're not really allowed, you know."

I ducked my head so a tangle of still-wet hair fell in front of my face. "I needed to be here. I needed to see that he was really OK," I swallowed. "You're sure he's going to be OK?"

"Yep, he sure is." Anna's pearly whites gleamed under the hospital's institutional-grade fluorescents. "I guess Eli is a fighter. He's been improving all morning."

"Yeah," I said, a bit distant.

"You staying out here with mom and dad tonight?" she asked.

"I hadn't thought about it yet," I said, a little startled by the abrupt subject change. "I guess I should head back this afternoon."

"Mom is pissed," she said. "Something about you not talking to her about a boyfriend. And dad's pretty steamed you took his favorite car and snuck out without saying goodbye?"

I looked at my feet and noticed that the polish on my toenails had begun to chip away. My mother would be sure to comment on that, too. "You know what," I lied, "I really have to get back to work right away. Do you think I'll get a chance to talk to Eli myself?"

She glanced at her cell phone. "They're all going to want something to eat soon. Early for breakfast, but it's already been a long day. You could sit with him while we grab some grub. Just... not for long. He needs to rest."

"Sure," I said. And then Anna took control of the situation and somehow I found myself sitting in at Eli's side while his family members all shuffled toward the cafeteria, deep in the bowels of the medical complex.

From somewhere deep inside, I scrounged up an encouraging smile to give him.

I felt like he should be — I don't know, grateful to me, or something. Grateful for changing Verity to say he would live. I couldn't have changed reality, the very idea was ridiculous on the face of it. But I'd done it. Or I'd done something. And he was alive to tell the tale, or at least alive.

It seemed like I should say something. "It's great to see you," I managed.

Eli smiled gamely, then winced as the action creased the bruised flesh of his face. "You too," he said. His voice was jagged.

"Are you... are you all right?"

"Have to say I've been better."

My throat was tight with late-onset terror. My eyes stung but didn't spill. Anna had asked me if there was anything I needed to tell him, and here was my chance to tell him myself. "So, um, I know we've always been friends, but I wanted to make sure you knew how much I need you around... " I trailed off. Jeez, I sounded like a junior high school kid confessing a crush. Maybe the moment had passed.

He reached over, trailing an IV line, and touched my hands where they were folded together on the rail of his bed. "Me too, Mira," he said. We sat quietly together for a while. "I'm glad you're here. There was something I wanted to tell you. I had a dream while I was... I don't know. While I was gone," he said. "Maybe a vision, or a near-death experience."

"Oh?"

"I saw you, Mira. It was the weirdest thing. It was like I saw that golden light, and I was just about to step toward it, and then you were there, too, and you pulled me back."

I shivered. "I didn't do anything."

"Maybe it was just because your sister was here? Who can tell." He pressed my hand. "I know, I know, just the bizarre hallucinations of an oxygen-deprived brain. But I'm still glad you're here. And I'm happy to be alive."

"Yeah," I said. Eli's vision and my revision churned together with Benji's pop proposal, trying to make a pattern I could read. I felt like there was something there, something I might be able to understand, if only I looked hard enough. If only I could put the pieces together. Maybe Chandra wasn't wrong.

Later, on my way out of the hospital, I walked by the entrance to the psychiatric wing. I stared at those heavy doors as I passed, wondering if I belonged in there. Was this what it felt like to slip into a delusional state? I couldn't disbelieve my own experience, because what else did I have to go on? But thinking that I'd saved Eli's life — thinking I'd make Benji propose to me — just because I'd written it down in a computer? That was pretty far over the border into crazytown.

How long before I became the mayor? At this rate, I thought, it could be any day now.

chapter EIGHT

I drove back to my apartment in my daddy's sports car feeling like a popped balloon. Once I arrived, though, there wasn't anything to keep me from falling into my own head and getting lost there. So I went to the Buzz for my shift after all.

Joseph sized me up over his half-moon glasses. "Thought you weren't coming in, Mira."

"I'm super worried about my friend," I told him. "But the hospital wouldn't let me stay. Just... let me keep busy here, all right? I need something to take my mind off it. It would be a huge favor."

His stern facade crinkled up into something like sympathy. "All right, get your apron on."

It wasn't even 8 o'clock yet.

To my surprise, Benji stopped in not long after me. He was never even out of bed this time of day. Had he taken a red-eye from Vancouver? He looked terrible, like he'd been rousted from a sound sleep by an unkindly drill sergeant. His hair was mussed, but not fashionably so; it stuck in strange diagonal spikes only on the left side. His eyes were bright, if unfocused. "Hey, M," he said. "Missed you while I was gone."

Then he ordered a coffee and settled into one of the armchairs. He sat there, eyes fixed on a spot just below the cash register, the cardboard cup pressed just to his mouth so he could breath in the steam.

He didn't have his laptop bag with him. Probably the first time I'd ever seen him without it during working hours. A yawning, unsettled feeling opened inside me as I wondered why he'd come here right now, if not to work.

This was it. I steeled myself. He'd break up with me now, and it would be all over. I'd have to give that ring back and work out a way to patch things up with my mother and — for one long, horrifying moment, I had a vision of a future in which I did exactly the things she thought that I should do, and I wound up married to Mike Buchanan. Ugh.

Or worse... maybe Benji wanted to talk about Verity.

He studied my face from time to time. When I caught his eye, he'd look away again. He was naked without his computer, and with a start I realized he wasn't pecking away at his phone or tablet, either. Even the night we broke up, he'd been poking around on his phone to grab his email.

Joey noticed, too. He nudged me in the ribs with an elbow as he walked by. "What's up with the an-may? Ouble-tray in aradise-pay?"

"I don't know why he's here," I said. At least the tension gave me something else to think about than Eli. I shoved away the image of Eli's bruised face.

Joey gave me a wink and tucked a rag into the pocket of his apron. "I think it's about time for you to go on break, don't you? Take your time, we're not busy anyway. And you've had a rough morning."

I nodded slowly. I suppose I should be enthusiastic about getting permission to go and comfort my apparently troubled boyfriend, but really it seemed worse than even bathroom cleanup duty. Still, if I was planning on making a life commitment to this dude, then it behooved me to be...

supportive, I guess? Affectionate? At least kind of friendly?

I walked over and crouched down next to Benji's armchair. "Hey, sailor," I said.

He looked at me and nodded. "Hey."

"What's a guy like you doing in a place like this?"

"Oh, nothing, really," he trailed off.

"C'mon, Benji. What's dragged you out of bed so early? Something on your mind?" I crouched down by his feet so I could look up into his eyes.

He still looked glazed-over, but his voice was strong when he asked me, "Where were you this morning, M?"

I lost my balance for a second, wobbled, steadied myself with three fingers on the frigid tile floor. "Why, did you stop by?" I asked. Had he taken a red-eye from Vancouver? Did he think I was *cheating* on him?

He didn't answer.

"I went home," I said at last.

His face was still and unreadable.

"An old friend of mine was in a car accident," I said. "We weren't sure if he would make it at first, but... as soon as I heard he'd be OK I drove up and see him in the hospital."

He nodded, oh so very slightly. "You made a change on the site about it," he said.

"You saw that?" It was my turn to nod, coolly, as though this were exactly the direction I'd expected this conversation to take. As if I'd expected him to track my actions on Verity, and in no way find that creepy or an invasion of privacy. "My sister called me from the hospital and let me know how Eli was doing," I said. "It was such a relief when I heard he would be OK, I felt like I wanted to call everyone I knew and tell them. But it was only like five in the morning, so... yeah, bad idea all around."

A little bit of focus came back to him, as if he were waking up after a bad dream. So emboldened, I put on my sweetest smile and told him, "Just writing it out like that, 'Eli Morrow is in stable condition,' it was like making sure it was real. Telling the universe it couldn't go back on its promise."

His eyes narrowed at that, just for the barest second, so quickly I couldn't even be sure that they had. But then he grinned, showing the dimple on his cheek to good effect. "Wouldn't that be great?" he asked. "If words had power like that, I mean. A binding contract with the cosmos." He pulled me up into his lap and squeezed me tight around the waist like he was afraid I might vanish. His breath tingled hot on my shoulder.

"It would be," I agreed. I rubbed his knee, then, and babbled out the next thing that popped into my head: "Listen... my mother sort of knows about you — about us — that I have a boyfriend, I mean. I'm going to have to tell her that we're engaged." I froze for a long moment, terrified that he'd call my bluff and ignore my sloppy change of subject.

But no. He took my hand and brushed his lips across my wrist. "Of course you do," he said. "She's invited to the wedding, right?"

"Will you go up to visit with my family?" I wondered if I could send just him to deal with it while I hid in my apartment.

"Sure thing, M. Tell me when and I'll show up. Oh — speaking of showing up. Listen, there's a party in a couple of days. Big thing for Verity. You can fancy up for it, right? Get a prom dress or something." And then he made a big show of looking at his watch and pantomiming how shocked he was at the hour. "Hey, I have to run, but I'll call you tonight, OK? You be good." He nudged me off his lap and stretched like a tiger before standing up and straightening his jacket.

That's when I noticed it. I must have seen it a hundred

times before and it never once caught my attention. On his breast pocket there was a tiny pin worked in an unfamiliar symbol, diode and enamel, glittering in the golden morning as he kissed me and walked out the door.

No, not unfamiliar — not anymore. I'd seen that same pin somewhere before. I'd seen it on Chandra's jacket.

The afternoon turned into a drizzly dusk. I wished I'd brought a sweatshirt and an umbrella with me. The chill crept under my shirt, through my shoes and into my socks, clinging to me like I'd grown a new skin of ice. I jogged most of the way home, stopping at the Chinese place on the corner for Singapore rice noodles and soup to warm me up.

When I got home, I stripped out of my sodden clothes and put the shower on full blast, as steamy as it would go, to wash away all the worry about Eli and Benji and lunatic conspiracy theories. In a few minutes I was feeling like a warm-blooded animal again. I was toweling off my hair when I heard the telltale click-thump-thump of somebody coming into my apartment.

"Benji?" I called. "Is that you?" There was no answer.

I went cold again, scanning the bathroom for something approaching a weapon.

I took a deep breath and made a quick reality check. Likely I'd heard Benji coming in, right? Occam's razor. Someone with an actual key. But Benji hadn't said a word about coming over later.

Couldn't call the police; my phone was still at the bottom of my bag in the living room.

Bathrooms aren't the best place to look for a self-defense tool. There was the can of scrubbing powder that I might be able to fling into an assailant's eyes if I were lucky; the towel to snap with; I guess I could pull down the shower curtain and try to hurl it over an intruder's head while I made for the door. In any event, I wouldn't want to face whatever was out there naked. I pulled on my flannel pajamas and put my hair up in the towel, then walked out into my living room to see what cards fate had dealt me.

I was right. There was somebody sitting on my couch, eating my noodles straight from the carton, and it wasn't Benji. It's easy enough to psych yourself up for some kind of terrifying home intrusion, but it's another matter entirely to actually experience it. Instinct took over: I screamed, shrill, loud, and abrupt.

"Shhhh," Chandra said, waving a brown hand at me. "Your neighbors will think you're being murdered or something."

"What are you doing here?" I'm not proud of the note of panic in my voice that hadn't crept so much as barged in and taken over. I waved the canister of scrubbing powder in as menacing a fashion as I had in me.

She looked at me, mild as milk. "What, you're going to clean me to death? I just wanted to talk to you," she said. "Deep breaths, honey. Relax and count to ten."

I followed her advice: Deep breaths, relax, count to ten. "How," I asked at last, "did you get into my apartment?"

She shrugged. "I got a copy of the key from your super," she said. "Nice place, by the way. Very high-class." Then she waved her fork at me. "Are you planning on eating or what?"

I shook my head, trying to process what she'd said into something that made sense. "Why would my super give you the key?" I asked.

Her teeth flashed brilliant white against her dark face. "Social engineering is a beautiful thing. Also a trade secret." Then I guess she finally took some pity on me. "Look, I'm not here to hurt you or steal your stuff," she said. "I'm here to help you out."

"You couldn't send an email?" I asked. The immediate panic had subsided, thankfully, but taking its place was the kind of petulant crankiness generally spotted in the toy section of a department store.

"Definitely not email," she said. "Too easy to trace, and I needed to get your full attention."

I rummaged in my silverware drawer to get an extra fork and a spoon. Then I sat cross-legged in my shabby armchair and grabbed the plastic container of soup. It all seemed absurdly comfortable and familiar, like having a friend over for the zillionth time. "So, OK, you have my attention," I said. "Now tell me why I shouldn't call the police."

She twirled the fork to get a bigger bite of noodles. "I heard you have a friend who was in a bad car wreck this morning."

Christ, had everybody heard about it? Had someone sent a memo? "Yeah," I said, slowly. "He's lucky to still be alive."

"Is he really lucky to be alive?" she asked. "Or did you make him lucky with Verity?"

I put my spoon down, put my soup down, put my feet flat on the floor and leaned forward. "OK, you have my attention," I said. "Tell me what the hell is going on."

"You know it already," she said. "You can use the system to rewrite reality. You've done it a few times already, haven't you?"

I nodded, uncertain. "I think I have," I said slowly. "I don't know. I thought I might just be crazy." I frowned. "I thought you were crazy, too."

Her eyes clouded. "Sometimes I wonder if I am," she said. "I... can't remember some things I wish I did. Self-editing is a bitch."

"O-kay," I said. "Gotcha."

"It's not like that," she said. "You can use Verity to change some things, but not just anything, right?"

"Right."

"Turns out people aren't as real as we like to think," she said. "They're very... pliable."

Nausea sloshed up into my belly. "So it can change... you? People?"

"Yeah," she said. "Well, kind of. It's like being drunk. You can't make somebody do something they'd never do, but the things that bubble up could surprise you. It's easier and harder than you'd imagine. But... look, never mind all of that. Here's the thing. I need to know what your boyfriend and the company are up to, and I need your help to find out."

"So what, you want me to spy on him?"

"Something like that," she said, twirling more noodles onto her fork. "Something exactly like that."

I snorted. "You break into my place while I'm in the shower to ask me to spy on my boyfriend for you? My *fiancé*? You're kidding, right?"

She sighed. "I know I dropped by at a bad time, and I'm sorry. I shouldn't have imposed on you like this. But look... you're getting into some very deep water. If you're not careful, you're going to drown."

"Get out," I said. "Get out or I swear I'm calling the police."

She bit her lip. "You know damn well something's going on. And I'd bet cash money you haven't asked Benjamin about it yet, either. What's the matter, honey? Don't quite trust him?"

I didn't answer.

"Fine." Chandra stood up and slid her shoes on. That pin of hers glittered in the lamplight. "You don't believe me yet. But listen, you're going to be over your head real soon now.

These are dangerous people. And if they think you're a threat to them... "

"Whatever," I said. "Just don't bother me again."

"I know it sounds crazy," she said softly. "But I can prove it. Just give me one chance."

"How?"

She looked at her watch. "Sit tight right here," she said. "I need to run to the store and pick something up. I'll be back later tonight. Don't go to sleep, OK?"

"... Fine," I said. "One chance."

The door swung shut behind her. It was another twenty minutes before I realized she probably still had my key.

I lay on my sofa staring at the water spot in the ceiling while Chandra's taunt echoed around in my head. "Don't quite trust him?" Trust. You were supposed to trust someone you were in a relationship with. I had to ask, had to get to the bottom of those weird coincidences and Chandra's crazy accusations. Maybe it would be a funny story for our grandkids one day. Hey, honey, remember that one time when you—

Try as I might, I just couldn't find the punchline.

As I lay there immolated in self-doubt the gray day outside deepened into the blue of twilight, and then it was dark. Finally I sat up and grabbed my phone; the blazing screen hurt my eyes in the dark. I tapped out a message to Benji: *Can we talk?*

His response buzzed in a few seconds later. *Crazy busy. Later.*

chapter NINE

Chandra showed up back at my place just a little before eleven, letting herself in again with that key from my super. The thought struck me: If people were "pliable" like she'd said, had she done something to make him trust her?

Had she done something to me? I shoved that idea away nearly as quickly as it formed.

"Ready for a little evidence?" She settled onto my sofa, her dark eyes shining.

"Yeah," I said. "I just — look, I want some proof one way or the other. I'm tired of worrying that I'm crazy."

"I can do that." She flashed a smile. "We'll use a little fifth-grade science. You remember learning about the scientific method, right?"

"Yeah, of course," I said, indignant.

She stretched her feet out onto my coffee table and drew a sticker-encrusted computer out of her messenger bag. "So we need to develop a hypothesis, devise an experiment, and gather data."

"Right, whatever. Just tell me what you're going to do."

She handed me a pale slip of paper.

"What's this?" I stared at it.

"We're going to win the lottery tonight." She bounced a little in her seat. "I love this trick, it's my favorite."

"Win the lottery." Hoo boy.

"Here's your first lesson. Whenever there's an element of chance to how something is going to turn out, you can influence the result to fall one way or the other. Anything where the odds are equally likely. How a roulette ball will land, or," she gave me the side-eye, "whether someone's heart starts beating when they get CPR."

I bit my lip.

"But you have to know what you're changing, and this is the key part, you have to know precisely *when* to change it," she said. She plugged her laptop in, leaving the cord trailing halfway across the room.

"There are a lot of things people would love to influence. Elections, trials, legislation, that kind of thing. Lucky for the world, for most big-ticket changes like that, you'd have to nudge too many people at once to change the overall result. Doesn't scale that well."

I nodded slowly. "Nudge people? So you can control somebody's mind."

"Not... not quite. The biggest thing is you can make people decide one thing and not another. But it has to be something they might have done anyway, and you have to find a susceptible moment."

"Might have done anyway?" My pulse sped up as I thought about Benji and his pop question.

"Sure. So you couldn't make the veep suddenly assassinate the president, for example. Not unless he had it in him to begin with. But if you knew when a senator was thinking about whether to vote for or against a bill, you could push him. Timing is everything."

"That sounds really hard."

"It is really hard. And some things are just plain

impossible. If you wanted to prevent a hurricane, you'd have needed to find the right butterfly at the right second and make it beat its wings this way instead of that way before the hurricane ever started. Oh, and you can't change the past."

"So... the lottery?" I waved the pastel slip at her. "What is this, anyway?"

"Pick four," Chandra said. "It's the only kind I can win. Scratch-offs are printed long before they come into your hands, and it's too hard to do a bunch of numbers in a row manually. No way to be a big-time jackpot winner." She squinched her nose up, like she'd smelled something bad. "And I couldn't claim a big prize, anyway. There would be legal issues."

"What kind of legal issues?"

"... Forget it. It's time for them to pick some winning numbers for us. Turn on your TV."

"Right."

We sat in the living room, infused with screen glow, and waited for the end of the eleven o'clock news. Pick four was the kind of lottery where ping-pong balls are drawn from some sort of air-popper-by-way-of-aquarium. The woman who drew the balls had a fixed smile coated with a smooth pink lipstick in a shade that hadn't been fashionable in thirty years, and precisely curled blonde hair that would have made her a bombshell in her youth, but now indicated she was a Woman of a Certain Age. She said a few words, beats me what they were, and then she set the balls pinging around in their little enclosure, like a high school demonstration of diffusion.

I looked at the ticket Chandra had given me. It said the first winning number of the night would be a four. I held my breath and the instant before that first ball was sucked into its tube, I heard Chandra hit a single key. The four came up.

Chandra tabbed into another browser window after each

ball, where she had her next edit lined up just waiting to be submitted. The second number on the ticket was a seven, and so was the number that was drawn. Our third number was a 0 but I couldn't see the one that was drawn; the ball was facing in the wrong direction. Then that nice, sweet Woman of a Certain Age on the television paused to shuffle to the other end of the ball-popping contraption to pick the last number: a nine, just like the ticket in my hand. All done. She smiled her glassy smile and straightened the balls so the camera could get a better look at them: A 4, a 7, then 0 and 9. Four out of four.

My heart pumped with adrenaline levels that might have been suitable if a pack of lions were chasing me.

This was proof, wasn't it? Irrefutable proof. Evidence that I was not insane.

I pried my fingers out from the sofa cushion they'd dug into and took a deep, shuddering breath. "Amazing," I said. "God, it's nice not to be crazy."

"I'll say," Chandra said. She touched my arm. "Hey, listen... don't try to change anything else on your own," she said. "It's too dangerous for you. I run my own instance, so I can do some little things like this, but if we tried to pull this stuff on Verity Prime, they'd catch it in a second."

"So what?" I asked.

Then the lights went out, accompanied by the droning wind-down of a dozen electrical devices no longer providing their background chorus. Chandra tensed and half-stood.

I groaned. "I forgot to pay my electric bill, didn't I?"

"I sure hope so," Chandra said. "Otherwise, when the men in black break through your door, I'm jumping out the window." From the edge in her voice, she wasn't entirely joking.

"Very funny," I said. "Hang on, let me take care of it." I stumbled toward my room to get my phone, banging my shin on no less than three obstacles in the dark. I used it to check my bank balance and then winced. No way would that cover electricity. Especially if it hadn't been paid in long enough that they'd cut me off.

"Oh, hell," I muttered. I flopped down on my bed and dialed up honorary Uncle Wally, the lawyer who managed grandma's estate and the keeper of the purse strings of the trust fund I'd vowed not to ever, ever use. Except in emergencies. Which this clearly was, OK?

He answered in two rings. "Hello, Mira," he said. "Haven't heard from you in a while. Are you being a good girl?"

"Of course not," I said. "Do you even need to ask?"

His chuckle lifted my mood, the way he always lifted me and swung me around when I was small. "What can I do for you tonight?"

"Listen, I forgot to pay my electric bill and it looks like I don't have enough in my checking account. Can you take care of it?" I sucked in a breath and held it, picturing Uncle Wally's face: He had turned a delicate, mottled purple, and the far tendrils of his hedge-thick eyebrows were quivering with indignation. Cue lecture: Now.

"Mira, you can't go on like this," he scolded. "Look, why don't you just stop playing this little game of yours? You know you're breaking your mother's heart."

"Mm-hmm." I waited him out, wondering if he was as bored with delivering this talk as I was with hearing it by now.

"I know you think you're proving something to somebody, but it's just selfish. You don't know how to manage everything and then when things fall down on you — like right now things fell down on you, right? — then you inconvenience everybody else to take care of it for you. I'm not telling you to move into the place on Fifth, but at least let my office handle your bills."

"Mm-hmm." He was probably contractually obligated to say this every time I called, on account of the retainer paid by my family that had kept him in sailboats and tee times for the last thirty years. I wondered if there was even a script he had to follow.

"None of your cousins are like this," he forged onward. "You know Julia is getting a ton of press for her work at the foundation with sick kids? That's where you belong. You're a hundred times smarter than Julia ever was. And you have a responsibility to use what God and your family have provided you, to put it to good use. You could change the world for the better, Mira."

"I don't want to change the world," I said. "Look, right now I just want my electricity back on. So are you going to do it or not?"

"I'll handle it, princess, as long as you promise to think about what I said." Uncle Wally's eyebrows quivering earnestly didn't make any noise, but I knew they were doing it anyway. "Shouldn't take too long. But this is the very last time."

"It always is. Thanks, Wally, you're a sweetheart. Give Charlotte a kiss for me."

When I walked back into my living room, Chandra quirked a scandalized eyebrow at me. "Sugar daddy, huh?"

"Something like that." I dropped my phone on the table. "Except really nothing like that at all."

"Like what, then?"

I squirmed. "Family money. I don't like to talk about it."

"Benjamin landed himself a rich girl, huh?" Her lips pursed like she'd tasted something sour.

"It's not like that." I wrapped my arms around myself. "Anyway he doesn't know. Yet."

"Hey, no sweat," she said. "Your secret's safe if mine is."

"Deal."

I got a weathered book of matches out of the kitchen and went around lighting up Benji's stinky eucalyptus-mint candles, and then popped some ibuprofen to pre-empt the headache they'd give me. Better than sitting in the dark, at least.

"So what do you need me for, anyway?" I asked Chandra. "I can't believe you're telling me all of this for my benefit."

"I need information," she said. "And I don't have a way to get it without your help."

"What kind of information?" I asked.

"I need to know what's going on inside of Verity," she said. "Emails, business plans, contracts, that kind of thing."

My eyes narrowed. "What for?" I asked.

"Look, I don't mean to talk smack about your sweetheart," she said, "but Verity is doing some bad, bad stuff, and I'm trying to find a way to stop it."

Suspicion simmered to life in my heart. "Bad things like what?"

"Nothing you could take to the SEC," she said. "But I'm pretty damn sure they're revising for profit and not just for fun." She sighed. "Look, I could lie to you and say that it's creating some sort of breach in the integrity of reality, and that the more nudges happen, the looser the quantum ties of the universe hold together," she said. "But that would be a bunch of bullshit, frankly. I just really hate the idea that this incredible power is being used in such a horrible, unethical fashion."

"You still haven't told me what's so 'unethical'," I said.

She frowned. "OK, it's like this. Imagine a small tech company files a lawsuit against them for... I don't know, a patent violation or something. Things like that happen in business all the time, right?"

I nodded.

"Now imagine that it's a pretty close case, the judge could go either way. But if Verity nudged them just the right way at just the right point... "

"They'd win the case?" And I'd thought winning the lottery was a neat trick.

"Right," she said. "It's buying off the judge except without going to all that expense."

"But that's just a what-if," I said. "I'm not going to spy on my boyfriend for you just for that."

"Your loyalty is poorly placed." She grabbed her grubby messenger bag and pulled out a scrapbook. It was easily four inches thick and filled with news clippings, photos, scribbled notes. "You want a smoking gun, I can't give that to you. There's no such thing for this. But buying off a judge," she leafed through her book, "isn't even the half of it. What you need to look for is a... a distinct pattern of freak accidents and serendipitous occurrences that work to benefit either Verity or its individual owners and operators."

I blinked. "A pattern of freak accidents?"

"Yeah," she said. She tapped at a page. "For starters, we have no less than fifteen court cases dismissed or found in their favor, and not a single one against." She pulled out a paper-clipped sheaf of news articles to show me. I flipped through them. Her description was distressingly accurate.

"They have good lawyers?"

"Not done yet. We also have a first round of funding for a very, very favorable term sheet in a down market... " she handed me another couple of pages. "And then we have the scary stuff. The *accidents*."

The little crease between her eyebrows deepened. "There was the brush fire that burned down an early competitor's entire office and put them out of business... the bus that hit the journalist that was investigating their business practices... and no less than four employees have died suddenly after either quitting or being fired."

The newsprint was rubbing off on my fingers. I stared at the dark blotches in disbelief.

"Oh, and they think they killed me, too." She took one final article from her binder and brushed her thumb across the page before handing it over to me. It was her obituary.

I read it, too numb to react. According to the newspaper, she had been on a cruise just outside of Cabo for a Verity team retreat about a year ago when she fell from the ship and was lost at sea; presumably she drowned. It even included a glamour shot. She looked a lot better in it. Less tired, less worried.

"How do you know this has anything to do with... with Verity?" I asked.

She gave me a grim smile. "By the time this happened, I already knew that something was rotten in Denmark," she said. "I had a watch on my entry so it sent me a text message if anybody tried to change it. But... " she shook her head again, trying to clear away cobwebs. "It wasn't me they tried to change," she said. "They don't have my name, not my real name, so it didn't work."

"What? Then how... why do they think... "

"I did the only thing I could think of to get out of there alive," she said. "I kicked off my shoes and flung myself overboard. The ship was just leaving port at the time. Not too far to swim. So I paddled along the coast until I could get out of the water without being spotted."

"That sounds... horrible," I said, eyes wide.

"It was a bitch and a half getting home again," she said. "No money, no ID, and I didn't want to get any press attention. Took me two months to do it."

"And now you want, what, revenge?"

She shook her head. "I don't want to hurt them," she said. "I just want to stop them from hurting anyone else."

"Why can't you just call the police for attempted murder?"

"And tell them what?" She slammed her scrapbook closed. "'Oh, hi officer, I just thought you should know my friend tried to kill me by typing down that I was dead in a computer.' That'd work, sure."

"Why can't you just, I don't know, edit them so they won't do anything bad?"

Her lips twisted. "You can't change who someone is deep down."

"Even if this were true. What could I possibly do?"

"Help me find out what they're planning," she said. "Maybe once I know that, I can find a way to shut them down for good."

"I have to think about this," I said. "I don't know. I— I don't know about any of this." I stopped, stood up, sat down again.

She nodded sympathetically. "It's pretty heavy to try to process it all at once."

"How do I know you're telling me the truth about any of this?" I asked. "Hell, if you need my help so bad, why don't you just nudge me?"

"I'm never doing that again." She turned her head away from the candlelight so her face fell into shadow. "Never."

I took a deep breath. "I need a little time to think," I said. "I... you're telling me my boyfriend is some kind of criminal or something. Benji's not always Mr. Nice Guy, but he's definitely not a... a murderer."

"You can double-check all of the evidence yourself," she said. Her shrug was casual, but her words held a desperate edge.

"I don't know what else I can give you."

"Time, I need time."

Chandra grabbed my phone out of my hand and fiddled with it. "This is how to reach me," she said, handing it back. She shoved her scrapbook back in her bag, then her laptop, too. "But the longer you wait, the harder it's going to be." She stood and walked to the door, pausing halfway across the threshold. "Look, I know you're engaged and everything, but Benjamin... he's really not the guy you think he is. Watch your back." And then she left.

chapter TEN

The next day dawned bright and warm and absurdly, overwhelmingly normal. Nobody had slipped into my apartment while I slept. Nobody called me in the middle of the night. Nobody flagged me down to tell me that it turns out my mom and dad were the rulers of the mole-people that live at the center of the earth. Though that would have been in line with everything *else* that had happened lately.

So I did what I do best in a crisis: I pretended like nothing had happened at all. Went to the gym. Went to the Buzz. Went to the bodega and bought five kinds of ice cream.

Anna sent me a steady stream of updates on Eli's progress, all of them basically saying he was OK. Well, as OK as you can be when you just about died and then didn't. My mom continued her own steady stream of voicemails, but I just kept on deleting. Nothing good could come of listening, and frankly I felt I had enough on my plate already.

And Benji and I finally went out to Villa Rosalita to celebrate our engagement.

Villa Rosalita was Benji's absolute favorite pricey-yet-rustic neighborhood Italian place. Everybody knows the kind. It's got tablecloths with red checks and little kerosene lanterns at every table, but it serves its Old World dishes at a price that would have given Mama Rosalita a heart attack if anybody ever told her how high they were.

Benji and I sat side-by-side on the deep leather bench at our usual table, ankles hooked and heads bowed together as we studied the daily specials. His leg pressing against mine felt warm and familiar; all of the doubt and angst of the last few days began to dissolve.

This was Benji. I KNEW him. Just because Chandra said one thing that was true didn't mean everything she said was true. I shivered.

"Cold?" Benji slid an arm around my shoulders.

"Yeah, the air conditioning in here is always too much for me," I said. "I should have brought a sweater."

He leaned in to plant a quick kiss on the side of my head. "Let's get something to warm you up." He flagged down the waiter. "Hey, get a bottle of Dom for me and my new fiancée," he called.

"Fiancée? Congratulations, signore," said the waiter, and he didn't so much smile as his lips stretched out a bit. I'd have called it a sneer on anybody else, but since I'd never seen old stoneface make a more cheerful expression, I figured he should get the benefit of the doubt. Maybe his smiling muscles suffered from a congenital defect, or he'd had cancer of the humor gland when he was a child.

Word spread fast, and before long the whole crew of the restaurant were circled around, clapping Benji on the back and telling me what a beautiful bride I would be. Benji waved them off. "Come on, guys, give us a little privacy. I want to spend some quality time with my girl."

I rested my head on his shoulder and melted into him. A warm glow tingled in the backs of my knees and triceps, and the fear and doubt trickled away like golden syrup.

It was fine. Better than fine. Everything was going to be

wonderful, Chandra be damned.

I forgot all about Benji's fancy shindig for Verity until I got his text day-of. *Be at my place at 7 for the party?*

It took me a bit to work out what he was talking about — I'd had a lot on my mind when he'd mentioned it. But yes. Party. Wear a prom dress, he'd said.

A prom dress. There was just no way. No way.

I figured that was man-talk for "dressy," but did he mean cocktail party dressy or club dressy or Oscars dressy? No use asking him about it; he had a pretty good track record for remaining oblivious to the intricacies of women's clothing. Well, except for the fastenings.

This is why Coco Chanel invented the little black dress. Lucky for me I had such a thing floating around in my closet from after I'd stopped letting my mother dress me, but before I stopped going to my parents' events. A short one, on the sparkly side, and for bonus points an updo and lips stained the color of cherries.

When I got to his place he was in a tux, and handsome as the devil himself. His lips pursed into a silent whistle when I walked in. "You clean up good," he said. He put his hands on my waist and would have ruined all of my hard work if I hadn't backed away from his kiss.

"Later," I said firmly.

"Too bad," he said, waggling an eyebrow at me.

A black car waited for us downstairs. Benji helped me in, then sat beside me. Gentlemanly. See? I knew what I was doing in marrying him, no matter what Eli said. Or Chandra.

He stretched out, cufflinks flashing from street lights. In the quiet, everything I'd devotedly not been thinking about tried to get itself thought about.

What the hell I was doing? I should ask Benji about Chandra. I should tell him what she'd shown me. We were already engaged, right? I should just open up. Trust.

I pressed my temple to the cold window instead. The city outside was full of half-seen shadows, all questions and no answers.

Our destination was a glittering hotel ballroom filled with suited-up finance types rather than the usual flannel-and-denim crowd. Highlighted and spray-tanned creatures — probably models and actresses to the last — graced the arms of their barrel-abdomened benefactors. It was like stepping into another world and another time; cigar smoke wreathed up around the chandeliers, and the gender divide was so sharp you could use it for butchering.

I could tell what century it was only by virtue of the smartphones and wearables that adorned the attendees, like so much costume jewelry. Time travel, I thought. And yet the scene held an uncomfortable familiarity; I'd endured the same bullshit at least a couple of times a month with my parents from as far back as I could be trusted not to repeat what my dad said about his business partners to their faces.

Benji rubbed a palm along my arm. "I have to say hello to a few people, but why don't you get a drink to settle in? Oh, and get me a Scotch neat. But only if they have something better than that Glenlivet crap."

"OK," I said dully, and made my way to the bar. I needed some quality distraction to get back out of my own head, anyhow. Eyes skimmed over me as I walked by, as though I were as unremarkable as a grain of sand on the beach. The bartender, though, gave me a warmer-than-it-had-to-be smile as he slid the glasses across the bar. "Here you are, love," he said. "Come back soon."

This evidence that there were still people in the universe I hadn't disappointed yet put a little pep back into my step. I went in search of Benji a little more enthused about my prospects for an enjoyable evening.

He'd mingled himself away from where I'd left him, so that was easier said than done. I ducked my way through a dozen clusters of nearly identical men in black jackets, looking for his intentionally unruly hair.

When I finally spotted him, he was embroiled in a serious conversation with a tall, broad-shouldered man. I hung back, loath to interrupt them and get pulled into a potentially tear-inducing borefest. After a moment Benji spotted me and waved me over. The man Benji was so enthralled by turned to look at me. Surprise! It was my very own douche of the month, Mike Buchanan.

I gasped and dropped both glasses. They shattered on the marble floor, fragments skittering across the ballroom, the mixed pool of whiskey and champagne probably ruining my shoes.

"Mira!" Benji barked, storm clouds forming in the furrows of his forehead.

"S-s-sorry," I stammered. "I just— "

Mike sneered at me. "I thought you liked to slum it nowadays," he said. "What are you doing here?"

Benji's face cycled rapidly from *Wait, you know each other?* to *Don't talk to my fiancée like that* and on to *What the hell is going on here?* He raised a hand as if he were going to say something, and then he didn't say something.

A group of waiters with rags and brooms converged toward my elbows, trying to steer me out of the mess of glass. "Watch yourself, miss," they murmured, and, "step this way, please?"

Benji's awkward hand finally pointed at my feet. "You're bleeding," he said. He was right: blood was seeping from tiny gashes in my toes. I stared at them, unable to quite gather my wits. Damn, and I loved those shoes, too. I could wear them all night and never blister.

One of the waiters spoke up. "We have a first aid station, miss. Will you come with me?"

I nodded numbly and followed him, leaving tiny drops of blood behind me on the polished marble. To my surprise, Benji followed.

"So I guess you're in business with Blue Ocean or something?" I asked.

"We're getting our funding from them," he said. "We're signing the term sheet first thing in the morning. Verity needs to stay on their good side, M."

"Sorry Mike found out about me, then."

"Why? What's up with him?" Benji frowned.

"He's got a thing against me," I said.

"But... you know him, then?"

"Know him?" My face spread into the caricature of a smile. "Not as well as he'd like."

"What?" Benji's alarm raised his eyebrows up the flagpole and his voice an octave or two. I told him an edited version of that night at Connelly's in hushed pieces, after the hotel staff applied antibiotic cream and band-aids to my feet. I left out the parts about Eli; it just didn't seem like the time, and anyway, I didn't want to have to think about Eli just then.

I couldn't make myself look at Benji straight on while I was talking about it, but out of the corner of my eye I saw his expression move through astonishment to horror, and on to a kind of hard resolve.

When I was done, he squeezed me tightly and breathed

into my ear. "You don't have to be afraid of him," he said. "I didn't know he was that kind of animal. Verity needs Blue Ocean... but not him. I'll handle this."

"No, it's OK," I said. "Karma's already coming to get him. Let's just go back to the party."

Later in the evening, after I'd had a couple of drinks and my foot wounds had become adequately numb, I started to feel a little guilty about Mike and Benji, and wondered if I could smooth things over. I'd probably done enough damage for one day. True, Mike was a jerk and we definitely had an unpleasant history together, but he had been through a kind of rough patch. Maybe he deserved some slack. Maybe it was possible to rehabilitate him. Maybe he was working with a therapist to get his issues sorted out. You could never tell, right?

And hey, if I gave him the chance, maybe he'd even apologize to me; I'd never properly given him an opportunity, had I? And my ruined shoes weren't exactly his fault. I was the dumbass who'd dropped those glasses and cut myself.

Guilt won the day. Me and my vodka-fueled bravery went looking for Mike. He wasn't in the ballroom anymore, though. I peeked into one of the side rooms where Benji had been pulled into yet another impromptu business meeting; Marjorie was there with him, and they were both listening rather dispiritedly to a pair of men in tuxes gesturing emphatically. Benji had his phone out, and his gaze kept straying back to it; he'd tap out a few letters and then pretend to pay attention to the businessmen again. He saw me in the doorway and gave me a devilish grin, and then shooed me away with a nod.

I wandered off again, still in search of Mike. The air inside seemed unbearably stuffy. I had a brainwave: There was a balcony just off the ballroom. What I needed was a little fresh air and a view of the glittering skyline. I swept out into the warm spring evening and stretched my arms high over my head.

And there in the corner was Mike, his hulking shoulders stooped over, as he looked over the edge. I approached him slowly, the way you'd try to make friends with a strange dog.

There were a few other shadowy shapes out there with me, but the balcony — more of a patio, I guess — was bigger than my apartment. I didn't need to worry about eavesdropping, but I was pretty sure Mike wouldn't do anything awful to me in such a public place, either.

"Mike?"

He didn't turn to look at me, but stayed as he was: elbows on the rail, staring down at the city lights. From where we were, you could see two of the bridges lit up like constellations, but the wind blew the sound of the traffic away before it could reach us. "What do you want, Mirabelle?" he growled.

Vodka or no, I stayed a dozen feet back from him. "Hey, I wanted to... I don't know, I wanted to see if we could bury the hatchet."

He chuckled, but it was an ugly, throaty sound. "Bitch like you can only use a hatchet to cut a man's balls off," he said.

I shook my head a little; I couldn't quite believe my ears. "I'm trying to make nice with you," I said, slowly. My enunciation was excessively deliberate from the alcohol in my system. "I mean, it seems like we're stuck in the same crowd, so... "

He flipped me the bird. "I don't need you," he said. "I'm bigger and badder than you. My mom talks to your mom, and she's told me what a fucking loser you are. Making espresso for other losers all day long. I'ma sit your boy down and tell him all about you sometime."

I thought about Benji and how little he knew about me

and my family. "I'd rather you didn't," I said, though I knew Mike would completely misunderstand the reasons.

"Yeah, of course not," he said. "All you dumb bitches are nothing but liars. Fuck off before I decide to teach you a lesson."

I backed away another step, but tried one more time. "Listen, I just wanted— "

He finally turned to look at me. "Nobody cares about what you want," he said. "It's all about what I want. And what I want is for you to shut the hell up and get out of here." His voice has grown loud, and it echoed off the building. An elegant lady who had been having a quiet conversation with an equally elegant man on the other end of the balcony plucked at her companion's sleeve, and they both turned to watch us, wary.

My will to reconcile shredded and scattered in the wind. I could all but see it fluttering to the street far below. "What a piece of work you are," I said. "You can't screw me, so I'm the enemy? Is that it? What a miserable excuse for a human being you are. I was trying to be the bigger person here and make things right — offering the olive branch, forgive and forget— "

And then the hatred snuffed out of him, all at once, as quickly and thoroughly as if a candle flame had been blown out. "They're all like you, aren't they?" he said again, but the heat had seeped out of him this time, replaced by a sort of unsteady mournfulness. "Forget it. It's no use, is it?"

I was thrown hopelessly off-balance by this sudden act of conversational jujitsu. My tirade skittered to a halt. "What's no use?"

He waved toward the party inside. "This whole thing. The money scene. What am I fucking doing here? This is just a... a gas tank to put alimony in Patty's bank account while she sits on her ass on some beach in Tahiti."

I backed up another step, suddenly afraid, witnesses or

no. I would have fled entirely if it weren't for a combination of curiosity and the perceived safety lent by the shadowy others on the balcony, watching. "So why are you here, Mike?" I asked. Or maybe taunted would be a better word. "Take your ball and go home."

"That would show her, wouldn't it," he mused. "Check out of the game and leave 'em hanging."

"Probably," I said. And then I made a last attempt to get back to the matter at hand. "So... look, does this mean we're OK?"

"Sure," he said, turning back to the balcony and looking down again. "You tell yourself whatever lets you sleep at night. Bitch." He leaned further forward over the rail, and before I could blink, before I could work out the terrible thing he was doing, he had tumbled over and down and down until the darkness had swallowed him up.

Far below, a car alarm went off. It would in no way be an exaggeration to say that I freaked right the hell out.

Some of those shadowy bystanders rushed to my side in the wake of my scream: "Oh my god," they said, and "Somebody call 9-1-1," and "Is she OK?" Many hands guided me back into the relentless glare of the party and to a chair at one of the cocktail tables, where a crowd of the curious gathered around me, chattering madly with rumors and speculation about what had occurred on the balcony and the nature of Mike's relationship to me.

Ben pushed through the crowd and placed his hand at the small of my back. "You OK?" he asked. "What happened?"

"Mike," I said. "He jumped off the fucking building." The words were hard to get out, though, because my teeth were chattering.

"Ah," he said, unflustered. He rubbed his fingers behind his ear and assessed the gawkers around me. "Give the lady some space." His voice was as loud as I'd ever heard it, and held the note of command I'd heard a thousand, ten thousand times from my own father; but just this once, I was grateful. I buried my head in his ribs.

But was this... Benji's fault? Could it be? *I'll handle this*, he'd said.

I couldn't think about it. I needed the warm comfort of caring hands, no matter if they were stained with blood.

Benji snapped very effectively into the role of the diligent and loving boyfriend, I'll give him that. He kept the gawkers and gossips at bay until the police got there. They asked me what had happened with Mike, and I guess my story was corroborated by other witnesses, because they didn't keep me for long. "You've had a real bad night, miss," said one officer, her hair in a braid so tight it had to give her headaches. "Why don't you go home and get some rest?"

Benji took me home and settled me quietly into bed. He curled up behind me while my breath became quieter and slower, then left once he thought I was asleep.

I waited sixty tense heartbeats after the front door clicked shut behind him. Then I flung off the covers and dug my phone out of my bag so I could text Chandra: *I need you to check something for me.*

chapter ELEVEN

It was a long, sleepless night. Chandra didn't answer me right away; and no wonder, she was probably fast asleep like a normal person. I wondered where she stayed at night, with her income from lottery winnings and her proof-of-identity problems.

When I fell asleep myself, my dreams were filled with Mike stepping over that ledge and the sound he made when he stopped falling.

I called in sick to the Buzz in the morning. Instead I remained curled under the covers clutching my cell phone in both hands like a sacred talisman, praying for a response from Chandra. Finally she sent me a text back: *I'm on my way up now.*

My quilt landed half on the carpet in my scramble to get to the door. Chandra leaned against the far wall of the hall, holding a folded tabloid up so I could see the headline. "VC Mike Buchanan Dead," she said, then she flipped the paper around and began reading out loud to me. "Financier and trust fund baby Michael Buchanan jumped 24 stories to his death last night, eyewitnesses say— " She looked up. "Stop me if you've heard this already. Or do you want me to just skip to the juicy part about 'childhood friend and heiress Mirabelle Newton— '"

"Shut up and get in here," I hissed. I slammed the door behind her.

"Right, I forgot," Chandra said. "You're *incognito.*" She tossed the paper at me and unfolded herself onto the sofa.

I stared at the headline. In that whirlwind of shock and police reports, I hadn't quite realized that the incident would make it into the papers. I hadn't thought it would have my name in it. I hadn't thought—

My phone buzzed, the screen lighting up with Uncle Wally's smiling mug. I swore as colorfully as I knew how and threw the thing against the wall. Unhappily, it didn't shatter into satisfying pieces, nor did it stop buzzing. I let it send Wally to voicemail.

Chandra watched me with keen interest. "Who was THAT?"

"Nobody." I sank down onto the sofa beside her and stared at the paper.

I was so busted. If Uncle Wally knew, that meant my family knew, or would soon, and they'd think the paper's take was the dead truth. The tabloid laid out the whole thing as some sort of lurid love triangle between me, Mike, and Benji; they'd found somebody in the wee hours of the morning to say Mike had always carried a torch for me. Like Mike had ever been the torch-carrying kind. Fuuuuuck.

And — maybe this was worse — this meant that Benji would finally find out about my family, if he hadn't already. It was inevitable, but I'd wanted to be in control of how and when it happened. Not like things ever worked out for me when I was in control, come to think of it.

"So," Chandra said at last. "You want to tell me what I'm doing here?"

I tossed the paper onto the coffee table at her feet, but I couldn't meet her eyes. "You already know somebody died last night," I said. "And... well, I think Benji might have had something to do with it."

She leaned forward, nodding. "Right. Tell me everything you know."

I pressed my forehead to my knees. "Mike was... a complete asshole, to be frank. I've known him since I was a preschooler and he was like fourteen. He hung out with my big sister. A few days ago, he put the moves on me, and I had to kick his ass before he'd take no for an answer."

"And you think Benjamin found out?"

I shook my head. "I know he did. Last night we ran into Mike at that event and— Mike said some awful things to me. So I told Benji what had happened, for background, you know? He said something about... about protecting me." *I'll handle this.*

"That's messed up." She put a hand on my shoulder. "Hey, it's going to be OK."

I stood up and shrugged my hands deep into my hoodie pockets. "I'm going to make something. Tea. You like tea? Want some?"

She studied me. "Sure, tea is good."

I clattered around with my blue enamel kettle and a smoky loose-leaf. I thought about hiding in there until the kettle blew, but that would just be childish, wouldn't it? Little Mira, always running away from her problems. I pulled my hair back from my face, let it go again, marched back to the living room.

Chandra held the newspaper again, tapping a long finger thoughtfully against her chin. "So you think this Mike guy was nudged into jumping," she said.

"Sure, but... wait. I thought you said a nudge could only make somebody do something they might do anyway." I sank onto the edge of the coffee table. Maybe Benji had no hand in this after all.

"Well, was he suicidal?"

I snorted. "Michael Buchanan suicidal? Really, really no."

"Are you sure?" She traced circles on the newspaper in her lap. "Any truth at all to this 'love triangle' business?"

"God help me, no."

"Did this guy have anything else going on?"

"Well," my words slowed as my mind sped up. "Come to think of it, he might have been in a bad way," I said finally. "The rumor mill said his wife had cheated on him and dumped him for a business partner. And he was apparently under federal investigation."

Her eyebrows crept into apogee. "And you don't think a man in that situation would think about killing himself?"

"Not him," I said. "I told you, I've known him since I was four years old. Our parents are friends. He just wasn't the suicide type, you know?"

"Suicide doesn't have a type, peaches."

"I mean it," I insisted. "He wasn't introspective, or... I guess self-aware. I don't think he really believed anything bad could ever happen to him."

"But they did," she pointed out. "And anyway, people generally change sometime after they're fourteen years old."

"I don't know." I stood up and began to pace again. "Maybe you're right."

"Of course I'm right." She sat up straighter. "If anyone knows how it works, it's me. I built the damn thing."

"Can't you just— check the logs or something to know for sure? Didn't you do that before?"

She hesitated. "Not for something like that," she said. "Not anymore. Stuff like that, it runs with a few extra layers of security tacked on, and I can't get in to see it. Wish I could, though."

Then my brain caught up with my ears. "Wait, YOU built

Verity?" I scuffed my feet against the carpet. "I think I need to know more about... about you, and Benji, and what you have to do with any of this in the first place. I'm fucking terrified and I don't know why I should trust you more than anybody else."

"You want the big picture."

"I think I do, yeah. I have a lot of questions."

Chandra looked down at her hands. "It's questions all the way down," she said.

The tea kettle whistled. She followed me into the kitchen, this time, and we each retreated into our own thoughts as the tea steeped in the awful rose-patterned teapot my mother had given me. I fetched out the awful matching teacups and the pretty glass sugar dish, that one a gift from Eli. Chandra helped me carry the tea things back out into the living room.

She sat in the armchair, facing out toward my window on Brooklyn. She stared into her empty teacup for a while. "Where to start, where to start?"

The steam curled up around my knuckles as I poured out two cups, and the warmth and the scent gave me renewed strength. The milk was just on the brink of souring, according to the date, but it didn't quite smell off yet, so I took some anyway. I held it out to Chandra, but she waved it away.

She sighed and took a sip. The steel leaked out of her spine until she was resting her head on the back of the chair and staring up at the ceiling. "You know Chandra isn't my real name," she said abruptly. "It's what I told you, but it's not my real name."

I blinked. "So what is?"

"I'm not going to tell you," she said. "Nothing personal, just... you know. My secrets keep me alive."

"So Chandra's not... not your real name." The wheels worked in my head, trying to shift the picture I'd been looking at until it started to come back into focus. "And that's why they couldn't kill you with Verity."

"There's power in true names," she said. She shook her head, then, and took another sip of tea. "I never quite know what to make of it. I think maybe my true name, the one the universe calls me, is the one my family calls me. It's the name I have when I'm dreaming. But having another name to tell the world... maybe that saved my life."

"So it's all, what, magic? I asked.

"I'm not a witch," she snorted. "I'm a scientist." She tossed her braid back over her shoulder. "I went to MIT on a full scholarship. Started post-grad work in experimental physics, and got a stipend for it, too. My dissertation was all about the specific and measurable effects of observation on a particular kind of quantum phenomenon. I'd let you read it, but," her eyebrow quirked up, Spock-like, "I doubt you'd be able to follow it."

"Probably not."

She shrugged with one shoulder and stared at Brooklyn, or at nothing at all. I wondered what she was remembering. Then she glanced back at her tea, took another sip, and went on. "It was about that time," she said, and her voice grew tired with regret, "that I met our boy Benjamin Adler."

I bit my lip. "You were... together, weren't you?"

"No," she said, surprised. She set her cup down. "Jesus, no. It was never like that. No, I had a thing for somebody else." She shook her head to clear that apparently repulsive thought from her mind. "We were friends of friends in grad school. At the time, Benjamin was in the comp-sci department working on his next-gen news service. It was a pretty good plan — he developed a spider that searched for breaking news, scraping the social web and so on. And Marjorie worked on AI that understood what it was reading well enough to write the updates."

"That's how Verity started," I said.

"Yeah."

My phone buzzed then— Uncle Wally. I turned it face down. "So how did you get involved?"

She waved a hand. "At first, I was just tracking down interference, OK?" she said. "My gear kept picking up strange results, even when I wasn't running anything. So I tried to find the source. Eventually I figured out it was their server stack, so I set up shop with them to try to work out what was going on. Figured it out by looking at the logs afterward."

Chandra uncurled from the worn-out armchair and paced around the perimeter of the room, every so often stopping short to look at the books on my shelves, my sentimental trinkets, the awful painting of daisies my mom had bought for me. "The day I set up in Verity's server room," she said, "happened to be the same day some actor was admitted to the hospital on an OD. There were conflicting reports, and somebody hand-edited the article to say he'd just passed away."

I nodded slowly. "And it turned out he was dead after all?"

"That wasn't the surprise," she said. "It could be the person the edit came from was an orderly at the hospital, or the guy's publicist. Or just a lucky guess." She pressed her fingers to her scalp, that million-mile stare back again. "But my equipment picked up the distinctive particle burst I'd kept seeing, that interference. Only... a lot bigger."

"A nudge?"

"A nudge." Her hands dropped; she went back to pacing. "I didn't tell Benjamin what I'd found at first, but I tried to work out what had happened. I told him I was doing a quantitative review of— " she caught herself, and looked at me to make sure I was still following her. "I— look, I did a statistical comparison of the accuracy of hand-edited and machine-edited articles on Verity, right?"

"I'm still with you," I said.

"What I found," she said, "was that they were about equally accurate. But I could match the timestamps and find edits for every single instance of interference I'd seen. If you made a revision in Verity at exactly the right moment, it looked like an eight-ball breaking up a racked set on my gear. Starbursts, I called them. Proof that something weird was happening."

My fingers crept toward my neck, where Benji's great-grandmother's ring still hung.

"If I'd tried to publish on it I'm sure I'd have been laughed out of academia for the whole rest of my life. Anecdotal evidence isn't the same as data, you know? But I did a lot of trial-and-error to figure out the rules. And... to see if I could more efficiently exploit the phenomenon. As time went on I was able to predict exactly why some revisions would come true — with that burst of energy I saw, the starburst — and some wouldn't. Wondered if I could make the window a little bigger, so you could control more."

"And you could," I said softly.

She bit her lip and wrung her hands, but she also looked me straight in the eye for the first time since she'd started talking. "Yeah," she said. "I could."

Chandra stopped pacing and plucked at the tail of her braid. "I need to walk, and I'm getting nervous about Benjamin showing up here," she said. "Do you mind moving this to the park?"

"Sure. Give me a minute." I grabbed the least-dirty pair of jeans from the pile on my bedroom floor and pulled them on, then collected my phone and keys from the counter. "Walking it is."

As we left the building, my phone buzzed again. Still Uncle Wally. Still ignoring him.

We walked past the few blocks of nail salons and take-out Chinese places to Prospect Park and started along one of its meandering asphalt trails. The sky was clear and the sun bright, but the day was still cool. Morning fog hovered just out of reach, and the grass was thick with dew. A jogger in a red warm-up suit ran by us.

Chandra waited until he was out of sight before she spoke. "I'm not sure exactly what Verity is planning, but given the body count... This has to stop."

I nervously plucked a leaf off a shrub as we passed by. "Yeah."

"We can't stop Verity until we find a weak spot, something we can use to shut the whole thing down."

"What kind of a weak spot?"

Chandra shook her head. "I'm not sure anymore. If I'd had the brass ovaries to do it last year, we wouldn't be here now. I had passwords, I knew addresses... but everything has changed. I'm not even sure what it is they're planning. They stopped talking to me after... before the end."

"So how would we find out?"

Chandra hesitated. "You have access to Benjamin's apartment, right?"

"... Yeah."

"I want you to take a thumb drive and copy everything he's got on his computer. His whole email archive, every document, every photo, whatever you can find."

"Seriously? That's awful! If he caught me doing it... and we're supposed to be getting married... "

Chandra stopped and turned on me, arms crossed. "Are

you seriously telling me that you think your boy had a man kill himself last night, and you're worried about damaging the trust in your relationship?"

I was going to marry Benji, at least in theory. I'd agreed to the idea, anyway, and with that, I thought there might be a few new responsibilities. Like not spying on him on behalf of an ex-employee, or jumping to conclusions re: murder, even if the evidence looked awful fishy.

On the other hand, surely Benji had a few responsibilities to me, too, and they'd have to include basics like not double-booking when he had plans with me, not keeping secrets, and, oh yeah, not killing people before my eyes through the mysterious power of quantum mechanics.

I was slowly but surely turning into a rich, meaty stew of self-doubt, self-hatred, self-flagellation, and other self-descriptors you'd never see featured in a profile in Self magazine.

"If he's so dangerous," I said, "isn't that exactly what I should be doing? Toeing the line, afraid to cross him?"

She made an incoherent noise that nonetheless conveyed the full depth of her frustration. "Don't you want to stop this?" For a second, she sounded exactly like my mother.

"Maybe I don't." It was almost reflexive.

Her hands clenched and unclenched at her sides. She kicked a pebble in the trail and it skittered across the weathered pavement and into a mud puddle a few feet away.

I shrank a little. "Look, it's not that I'm not worried about what Benji might be up to," I said. "I just don't know what you're up to. Why should I trust you over him?"

"Ah," she said, "I see." She bent down to pick a perfect cotton ball of a dandelion and twirl it between her thumb and first finger. "What do you think would happen to ME if you told

Benjamin about these little chats we've been having?"

She blew, and the dandelion exploded into a hundred fuzzy packets of reproductive hope. "My life is in your hands, Mirabelle. You make one phone call and I'm done."

"So?"

She popped the head off the dandelion stem. "Jesus Christ, if I were the bad guy here I'd be editing you to just go along with me. What's more important to you, staying out of trouble and marrying a murderer, or *not* doing that?"

I scuffed my sneakers against the ground. "I guess... " In my brain, again and again, Mike stepped into nothingness. I didn't want to be in the dark anymore. I didn't want to be at someone else's mercy, edited on a whim. I was going to take control. "I guess it can't hurt to look. But I'm going to look, not you."

I wasn't about to send the whole kit and kaboodle over to Chandra with just her word that she'd use her knowledge for only good and not evil. I knew full well that just handing over the information she was asking for could potentially ruin Benji and destroy Verity, even if they turned out to be innocent of any wrongdoing. The range of possibilities started with identity theft and embezzlement and ran the full gamut to exotic kinds of corporate espionage. Selling business plans to competitors, say, or selling leaks to unscrupulous members of the business press.

And as for me... well, from where I was sitting, she was just showing me how to prove to myself that there was nothing shady going on, so I could move forward into wedded bliss with the air clear. Nobody could fault me for anything I did under the auspices of trying to exonerate my Benji.

Right?

My phone buzzed again, and this time it wasn't Uncle Wally. I stared at Benji's picture like the phone had suddenly turned into a man-eating squid.

"It's OK," Chandra said. "You have to pick up sometime."

So I did. "Hi, Benji."

Chandra's eyebrows shot up and she mouthed "Benji?" with some degree of snark. I turned my back on her to talk.

"Hey, M," Benji said. "Just checking in after last night. That was crazy, right? You OK?"

"Yeah, I'm fine," I said. I wondered if he'd seen the headlines yet.

He must have heard something amiss in my voice. "You sure about that, M? You sound off. Need me to come over?"

"No, really I'm fine, it's just been a— a strange day. I mean, after everything that's happened. But I can't talk long. I mean, I'm... on shift right now. At the Buzz."

He lost interest in my activities again. "Right, right. Anyway, I wanted to let you know I'm canceling my trip to Amsterdam. So you should come over tonight."

"You were going to Amsterdam?"

"Yeah, yeah, business. But now everything is up in the air with Blue Ocean, we think I'd better stick around to try and get everything settled."

"Right."

"We can bring in pizza and watch a movie. It's been a while since we had a normal night in together, not since we got engaged, so... "

"Sounds great," I said, a bit cheerlessly.

"Great. See you soon. Love you. Be good, M."

"I will," I said. "Bye." But he'd already hung up.

chapter TWELVE

Chandra sent me to a camera store and told me to buy a thumb drive — as much space as you can get, but no blinky lights, she said — and went on her merry way to god-knows-where.

But being alone in my apartment with my thoughts... that didn't work out so well for me. So I hit the gym to try to sweat some of my crazy out. My brain disengaged nicely under the combined pounding of dance beats and the elliptical trainer. Every care seeped out through my pores and left my body slick and pleasantly buzzy. Half an hour in the sauna followed up by a steaming shower sealed the deal.

I was wrung out, but relaxed and newly confident that I could deal with my train wreck of a life. Optimistic, even.

In fact, I felt so much better that when Uncle Wally called yet again, I decided to pick it up. The longer I waited to deal with this mess, the worse it was going to be for me. Not that it was going to be exactly easy, no matter what.

There were no pleasantries for this call. "Your mother is on the warpath, Mira," Wally said.

"Hello to you, too, uncle." I shouldered my gym bag and waved at the trainers on my way out.

"Have you listened to my messages?"

"No, I swear was going to call back this afternoon, but— "

"Cut the shit, Mirabelle. You were never going to call me back."

I had nothing to say to that. I mean, he was right. I let a dog walker with three frenetic bichons pass me on the sidewalk while waiting him out.

He couldn't take the agonizing silence for too long. "I'm sure I don't need to tell you the family is incredibly embarrassed and upset over seeing your name in the newspaper this morning. Very. Embarrassed."

"Look, it's all a bunch of lies. It wasn't anything like that." I must have sounded sharper than I meant to; the dog walker turned around to stare at me, just for a second.

"Then you need to sit face to face with your parents and explain it yourself. You owe it to the family."

"Whatever." I ran my thumb over the rough edges of my fingernails, mapping all of the places they should have been smooth but weren't.

"What are we going to do with you?" Uncle Wally had run out of script, it seemed. And he sounded genuinely disappointed with me for a change; usually he took my shenanigans with a grain of salt and an oversized helping of good humor. If even Wally was pissed off... A stirring of guilt arose. For once, none of the suck going on was my family's fault.

I tried to shepherd the conversation past the berating and on to the action items. "So what do I have to do? Just tell me."

"We need a show of good faith from you. Your parents who *love you* need a show of good faith."

"And that looks like?"

"That Buchanan boy's funeral. They're holding it in a few days. You'd do well to show up to it."

That would mean facing Mike's parents, too. Suddenly I felt queasy. "Do I have to?"

"I'm not done yet. That boy of yours— Benjamin, is it?"

"... Yeah."

"He comes, too. Your parents want to meet him."

I sat up. "What?" The last vestiges of my gym buzz evaporated, leaving me just as tense as I'd woken up that morning.

"You heard me, miss. Make it happen or there are going to be some serious consequences for you."

"What, they'd cut me off? So what? I don't want their stinking money anyway."

"Mira, you may not want it, but you need it. How many times last month did you call me to handle something, or dip into your account for just that one little emergency?"

"I— "

"Come to the funeral. Both of you. Be sure to wear something black."

"But I— "

"We'll see you then." Wally hung up.

I was so screwed.

When I got to Benji's place that night, he was on the phone, stalking from one room to another. He waved me inside and then turned his back to focus on his unseen assailant. "Listen, I'm the one who decides what risks I want to take. You're not— " step, step. "Marjorie— no, Marjorie, let me handle it. I've got everything under control— " step, pivot. "— Shut up for a minute and let me talk. You've made yourself clear— " step, step, pause.

"— Fine. Fine. You make whatever contingency plans you need to. But you don't need them. I've got a handle on it." He looked over at me, then. "Listen, Mira's here now, so I need to go. We'll talk about it more later." He jabbed the call off and flicked the finger at his phone before he set it down.

"Bad day?" I asked. "You haven't been... looking at the news, have you?"

"Nah, there's no time for that, I can hardly even check my email." He rubbed two fingers behind his ear, tired. "And since last night, everyone at Verity is flipping out about funding. Without Buchanan, there might not be a Blue Ocean, and nobody is sure where that leaves us and our funding deal. I've been in emergency conference calls all day."

"That's too bad," I said. I shifted uncomfortably.

"It doesn't matter," he flashed a grin at me. "Verity is the new hotness, so we'll be fine. And I always get what I want in the end." Benji stepped closer to me and put his hands on my waist. "Like you, for example."

Aw! I cradled his head behind his ears to pull his face down for a kiss, warm and slow, like there was nothing weird between us at all. There was a hard ridge behind his left ear. "What's that?" I frowned and leaned to the side so I could examine the spot more closely.

"Nothing, it's nothing, leave it alone," he said, trying to shrug me away. Before he squirmed out of reach, though, I brushed the hair away from the area long enough to see precisely what he was trying to hide. There was a small but visible lump there. It wasn't much — about the size of my pinky nail, square and only as thick as a credit card. There was a thin, angry red line of scar tissue along one edge.

"What the hell is that?" I asked him, trying to see it again.

"Nothing," he barked. "I just clubbed myself with a cabinet door a few days ago."

No cabinet door would have left a lump like that: angular and hard, like bone. But I wasn't about to press the issue, not now, when I had my secret spy agenda to deal with. "OK, sorry, jeez. I was just worried for you." A quick subject change seemed in order. "Let's find a movie."

We settled onto his pleasantly cool leather sofa to watch a couple of brain-dead action adventures starring a whole lot of CGI explosions. I couldn't tell you if they were any good, though, because it took all of my focus to keep from

a. Staring at that spot behind Benji's ear,

b. Confessing everything about Chandra and my plans for the night, or

c. Grilling him on what Verity was up to and whether he'd been responsible for Mike's tragically unsuccessful flight attempt the night before.

Luckily, I did not do any of these things.

The clock ticked onward toward midnight and bedtime. I checked my phone for messages one last time and saw the handful from Wally glowing there from earlier, disapproving of me on his behalf.

I took a deep breath and plucked at Benji's sleeve. "Sweetie? Can we talk for a minute?"

"What about, M?" I trailed him into the bathroom.

"Mike Buchanan's funeral. I have to go. My parents would be mortified if I didn't show," I said. "Even if he was an asshole and everyone knew I hated his guts."

"That's weird," he said.

"No, that's my family," I said. "They're friends with Mike's parents, and appearances are everything." I rubbed my palms on the back pockets of my jeans. "So there was something else I wanted to ask you," I said.

"Hm?" He put toothpaste on his brush and handed me the tube.

"I wanted to ask you, um," I repeated, prepping my own toothbrush. "As long as I'm going home to the funeral, can you come with me?"

"What? Why? You don't need moral support, do you? Not like you're broken up about him. You're not, right?"

I twisted the cap back on the tube and set it down. "No, it's so you could meet my parents."

"Oh." He stuck his toothbrush in his mouth and scrubbed away.

I turned to the mirror and busied myself with brushing my teeth and studying the label on the toothpaste — anything to avoid looking at Benji and reading too much into his bland, unreadable visage. Heaven forbid I should look like I was asking him to do anything that might be important to me. Heaven forbid I should let my future husband know what was and wasn't important to me.

Benji spat into the sink. "Yeah, sure, I'll come," he said. "Might make it easier to keep the deal in place, too, there might be investors there."

My knees wobbled as the wave of relief broke over me. I spat and rinsed, and then turned to hug him. "Thank you," I said. "I'll try not to make it... too awful."

"It might be awful?"

"Yeah, maybe, but... maybe not?" I flashed my clean teeth at him in something approaching a smile.

One task down, one to go.

Once in bed, I lay beside him, every muscle strung so tight it hummed, willing my breathing to stay slow and calm. Benji nestled close and put his chin on my shoulder; his hand settled light on my stomach. I wanted to curl up into him and lose myself. Here was warmth, here was the feeling of safety, even if it was all wrapped up in the source of my problems.

I caught at his wrist, instead, and rolled to turn my back. "G'night," I mumbled. He rubbed at my shoulders, just for a second, and then let me be.

My ears strained to hear Benji's breath over my own, but my heart beat like a drum. At first I kept my eyes squeezed shut, but they crept open again and again of their own accord. I stared at the reflection of the city's skyline in the mirrored door to the closet. Benji's apartment was high up enough to get a view of the city, not just a view of the offices across the street. Squares of light would flick on from time to time; cleaners or corporate spies, burners of midnight oil or burners of forbidden office passion, who could say?

The pillow grew warm against my cheek, but I dared not stir and risk disturbing Benji. At last, certain he was asleep, I eased out of bed, trying to make as little sound and create as little bounce as possible.

"Unnnhhhh," Benji said.

Damn, busted. "Bathroom," I whispered. "Back in a second."

I went into the bathroom and braced myself on the sink, staring at myself in the mirror. That face was me, but at this hour, and in this high-strung state of mind, it hardly looked like me at all. Each feature seemed assembled in a subtly incorrect fashion. Those cheekbones seemed too close to the surface of the skin, the eyelids were too oily. A stray piece of hair had pasted itself to my reflection's collarbone. I fought to mash down the idea that the tired, frightened face in the mirror would crack and fall to pieces at the slightest strain, like a poorly assembled piece of flat-pack furniture. Or maybe the one in the mirror was the one that was built right, and I was the one that would fall apart.

I flushed the toilet just in case Benji was still awake enough to pay attention, then padded back to bed.

I lay there watching the clock this time, as the minutes

unfurled one by one. Benji was still and quiet. I drew myself up onto an elbow: His eyes were closed, his breath was soft.

I snuck out of bed a second time and made my way into Benji's office. His desktop was still on, as always. The screensaver lit the whole room in swirls of mesmerizing blue and green, but I dispelled it with a quick flick of the trackpad and set about following Chandra's instructions.

She'd taught me how to set up a mail forward and run all of his existing mail through a filter, then delete it so I wouldn't leave a trace of evidence. She'd also told me where to find all of Benji's documents so I could zip them up and copy them to that thumb drive.

The transfer took a million years. I clicked open a game of solitaire as the progress bar plodded through its tortoise-like race.

The floor behind me creaked. I jumped like a startled cat. Benji's hand slid along my shoulder and down my back as he leaned over me to look at the screen. "Move the eight of hearts," he said, waving a finger in front of the screen. *Please, oh please don't let him notice the thumb drive plugged in,* I thought.

"Oh. Thanks." I forced myself to make eye contact with him and hoped it looked casual. "Sorry I woke you up," I said. "Couldn't sleep."

He nodded. His eyes were still clouded over, and I wondered if he'd even woken up enough to remember this in the morning. God, I hoped not.

"Go on back to bed," I said. I'm no Jedi, but I thought maybe he was tired enough for blunt suggestion to be good enough.

He put his nose in my hair. His breath itched as it hit my scalp. My skin crawled, but I used everything I'd ever heard a yoga teacher say about relaxation to try to keep myself from tensing up in a potentially suspicious way. His hand covered mine on the trackpad, and I bit my tongue to keep from babbling out explanations. But he only directed my hand to a different icon: some kind of downloaded puzzle game.

"I played through this one a few days ago. It made me think of you, I bet you'd love it. Or at least you'll like this a lot better than solitaire," he said. "But don't stay up too long."

He patted me on the top of my head and turned to leave, but he paused in the doorway of the office and looked back toward me. "Don't you have to work in the morning? Did you set an alarm?"

Fine time for him to start remembering my work schedule. "Yeah. I'll try to take a nap after, I guess."

Benji nodded again. His gaze lingered on me, and then on the screen, and then he turned and went back to bed.

As soon as he was clear, I wilted into the office chair like a daffodil cut five days ago. After that surge of adrenaline, I was pretty sure I'd never sleep again. My mouth was dry, my palms sweaty, and my heart hadn't raced like that since a tragically misguided flirtation with tennis lessons in my late teens.

It took a few minutes to collect myself enough to check on the copy in progress. By the time I looked, it was all done. Chandra had wanted me to grab chat logs, too, and I started to root around in the file system for them, but I came up dry. Either they weren't there, or the nerves had addled my memory of where she'd said to look. I hoped that wouldn't be important. But I could always try again another night, right?

I quickly deleted all the evidence of my completely disloyal activity — files, windows, console logs all gone, and the thumb drive neatly tucked back into my purse.

Once that was done, I thought I might as well spend a few minutes playing Benji's game, the one he'd said had made him think of me. It was a lovely thing, filled with dreamy landscapes and evocative snippets of poetry, and he was right: I loved it. I played until my eyelids drooped too heavy to continue, and then I went back into Benji's room and snuggled in behind him. I fell asleep again listening to his breath, in and out, deep and quiet and reassuring.

Not that I was entitled to take that comfort from him. Not anymore.

I didn't wake up when Benji left in the morning like I'd planned, so I stumbled into the Buzz two hours too late.

I knew it was going to be bad when I walked into the shop and all conversation stopped. Worse, both of the Joes were there together.

Oh god, they know, I thought. They read the paper, and now they know about my family and their money, and they'll never look at me the same way again.

Joseph scowled at me, hands on his hips. "Nice to see you're still interested in coming in," he said. "We thought maybe you got bored of hanging around here with the hoi polloi and set sail for Ibiza." Oh. Right. I hadn't exactly been Miss Attendance Record at the Buzz lately.

"No chance of that." I smiled with all the bravado I could muster. "Ibiza gets boring."

He looked at me over the rims of his little half-moon glasses, his nose scrunched up like I smelled bad. "So you're some heiress, huh? Why are you even working here?"

It felt like a jab straight to the solar plexus, so sharp and sudden I nearly doubled over from it. "Because," I said, "I have to make my own life."

"Let her be," Joey swatted Joseph on the arm. "She can't help who she comes from."

Joseph rolled his eyes, but he dropped the subject and went to refill the cream pitchers instead.

Joey took me aside before I could get my apron on. "Mira, we're really worried about you, after what we saw in the paper," he said. "And you know you've been calling out an awful lot lately. Is everything OK?"

I shook my head, lips pressed together. "I just have a lot going on," I said. "Sorry."

He chucked me under the chin. "Don't be afraid to talk to us. But don't disappoint us, OK? You may have a trust fund backup plan, but we really count on you to be here."

I looked at my muddy sneaks and not at him. "Yeah, I know. I'll pull it together, I swear."

He studied me another long minute, but thankfully didn't press the issue.

Later, though, when I was just starting to pack it in for the day, I tugged at his sleeve. "Hey, Joey? I have a question for you."

"What is it, sweetness?" He dried his hands on a towel and pushed his glasses up his nose.

"Let's say somebody was telling you that... that Joseph was doing something bad behind your back."

"What, like cheating on me?"

"Yeah, or... I don't know, something really bad, like breaking the law. Like... I don't know, putting rat poison in with the espresso beans."

Joey studied my face. When he finally spoke, he did it very slowly. "Honey, if somebody was telling me something like that about Joseph, I'd think the only way to get to the bottom of it would be to ask him about it myself."

"But what if you were afraid to?"

He rubbed a finger along his bottom lip before going on. "If there's something you want to know about your partner and you're afraid to ask, then maybe you have no business getting married in the first place. In a good relationship, you need to be able to talk about anything."

"I guess."

"It's not just empty words, you know. It means something."

"Yeah. You're probably right." I untied the apron from behind my back.

"You want to tell me what all of this is about?" His blue eyes cut through me.

"No, not really."

"Well... whatever it is, I think you need to sit down and have a talk with your young man. Are you going to?"

"I'll think about it real hard, anyway." I hung my apron on its hook and grabbed my bag out of its cubby. "Thanks, Joey. Have a nice night."

He tossed the towel over his shoulder and crossed his arms. "I wouldn't be in my twenties again for anything," he said. "Young people always make things more complicated than they have to be."

chapter THIRTEEN

I'd spent most of my shift at the Buzz quietly trying to figure out my plan of attack for all of the files I'd borrowed — no, let's be honest, utterly stolen — from Benji's computer. Along with the feeling guilty, of course. He'd been so sweet to me the night before. And here I was repaying all of that affection with rifling through stuff that was just plain none of my beeswax.

His email had all been sent to a one-off free account, so I felt safely anonymous where that was concerned. But I'd learned enough from Hollywood to fret that all of this could somehow be traced back to me if I looked at it from home. Maybe I'd forget to log out, or maybe he'd happen upon the login info, or mysterious high-tech tracers, whatever. As long as there was a chance that my IP could be logged, or my research otherwise traced back to me, I sure as hell didn't want ME-me at the end of it.

So I went to the library and snagged one of the public computers. It was an old, clunky thing, with a dingy beige keyboard that made that satisfying clicking sound when you pressed each key. Public and anonymous sounded just about exactly like what I needed.

The other patrons seemed harmless enough; there was a pale blonde woman browsing sales at Ann Taylor while her five-year-old ran amuck, brandishing his fire truck at the other children; a scrawny seventh grader with an overbite and dreadlocks earnestly typing away at what I could only assume was a homework assignment; a young Chinese man in a dark hoodie clicking through meme sites, switching from one to the next almost as soon as they loaded on the screen. I could hear the tinny sound of some disco song from his headphones from three seats away.

I felt a little bit ridiculous, to be honest. Here I was, objectively and baselessly paranoid, worrying that my boyfriend had sent a stranger to the library to keep tabs on me. But none of them seemed like Benji's crowd anyway. I logged into the email account to pan for the few golden nuggets of information that might help me understand what the hell was going on and what I should do.

There was no smoking gun. Nothing about mind control, nothing about Mike's death. Nothing about me, either.

But as I skimmed email after email and tried to put the pieces together, it grew clear that Verity was embarking on a huge undertaking. In their deal with Blue Ocean, they had been pursuing an absolutely epic amount of venture capital for "systemic and infrastructure improvements."

There was one particular email from Marjorie laying out a timeline, starting from the minute funds from an investor hit their bank account. She said that the software was "rock-solid" and "the primary prototype is nearly there," but they couldn't build a complete deployment of "the new device" until Mike inked the contract. "They won't let us start construction until they see that money in the bank." But I couldn't penetrate the technospeak and code names to work out what the hell this "device" was supposed to do.

On reflection, I was also impressed and a little disquieted that Mike had any sway with people holding that much money.

And then came the conversations about their future business plans. There was stuff in there that would make any conspiracy theorist writhe in ecstasy: plans to hook in with C-Span to include data on how Congress was voting on the spot, an initiative to work out a way to track individual stock traders in real time... They'd know everything about everyone. Everyone with power, anyway.

I leaned back in the creaky library chair and thought about that for a little while. The winner in a situation like that was, of course, Verity. The more they knew, the more they could exert control over a company, a situation, or even an individual. Comprehensive data could help them to... I didn't know. What did they want? Where were they going with this? Overthrowing the government? World domination? Plain old fame and fortune?

I couldn't guess. But I wondered if Chandra knew. I wondered if she'd tell me even if she did.

I scanned the library again on my way out looking for anything suspicious. Somebody paying too much attention to me or photographing the scene or something.

There wasn't anything, of course. Just paranoid.

Chandra and I met in the park again, walking under the shady boughs of another asphalt jogging trail. "So what's going on with our boy Benjamin? Found anything interesting?"

I nibbled on the ends of my hair. How much to tell her? Taking the information from Benji was crossing an important boundary, but handing it over to Chandra was torching the bridge behind me. "I think maybe," I said at last.

"Oh yeah?" She gave me the side-eye. "Anything you'd care to share?"

"I just don't know what most of it means," I hedged. "It's

all so... so..."

"Technical?" she guessed.

"Sure, technical."

She let me keep my silence as we walked on another few yards, then another and another. I tried to soak in the golden twilight and the beauty of nature, as long as I was outside; it wasn't something I did very often, after all. Frankly it's amazing I didn't have rickets.

The trail was dotted with yellowed leaves fallen early. Some tree disease, probably. Along the sides of the path were patches of tall weeds that had grown exuberantly after the last rain and not yet been mowed down.

Chandra couldn't keep up the patience and sweetness act forever, though. "C'mon," she said. "It would help a lot if you would just turn everything over to me."

"Look, I didn't see anything that convinces me Benji's definitely a bad guy. I'm still not sure— "

"But what *did* you find?"

"There were a lot of emails from Marjorie," I said. "Something about their Portland guy, and working on a prototype."

"A prototype?" she asked slowly.

"Yeah... Marjorie said something like 'the software is there, but we have to get Blue Ocean signed to build out the device.' Of course now that Mike's... well. Blue Ocean might not be in the game anymore."

"You're sure that's what it said?" she asked.

"I'm not making it up, if that's what you mean."

"No, no, I wasn't saying that. Just." She gnawed on her lower lip a little. "I wish I could get my hands on that prototype and see what it does. We have to find out more."

The trees gossiped with the wind. "I don't know if that's

a good idea."

"You're already in this," Chandra said. "The die is cast, the Rubicon is crossed. I mean, you want to find out the truth for yourself, right? We find the location, engage in a little light misdemeanor B&E to take a look at it, and we can clear your boy and your conscience, or... not."

I searched for an excuse. I hadn't seen anything more specific about the lab location when I was looking through Benji's files. And the contact was *very unhelpfully* named John Adams. Not exactly a unique and distinctive personal identifier. Nor was "Portland" for that matter. So before we could do anything else, first we had to figure out which Portland, and where the hell in Portland this prototype-building facility was, exactly.

"There's not enough information," I said. "We'll never find it."

Chandra shifted her bag onto her other shoulder and strode ahead of me. "I have ways," she called back at me. "Come on."

She led me to a cafe with wifi to try to figure it out. It was a total dive, and not in the intentional hipster way — chipped formica tables and a brownish pool on the linoleum from where the air conditioner had leaked for decades. When Chandra pulled out her laptop, the waitress marched over. She was a plump Jamaican woman in her 50s, if not a little older. "You better be ordering food if you want to camp out here," she told us.

"Cheese fries," Chandra said. "And iced tea."

I smiled defensively at the waitress. "Get me a diet?"

"Nuh-uh, you're not staying here for some three-hour business meeting on cheese fries."

Chandra passed her an unfolded ten. "Don't worry, we'll

make the table worth your while."

"Fine, fine, cheese fries and drinks. But don't blame me if the chef yells at you, he sees you sitting around a bunch of empty dishes later." The waitress shoved the money into her apron pocket and left us alone.

First we plucked the low-hanging fruit; I'd swiped a copy of the digital company directory when I copied all of those documents onto the thumb drive. Reluctantly, I let her copy just that one file from the thumb drive.

The waitress dropped our drinks at the table with an annoyed grunt.

The company directory didn't turn anything up, aside from a few new swear words that Chandra used when she saw some of the names listed as senior vice presidents. "You have got to be fucking joking," she said. "Hal Meadows? That total asshat? He was one of my lab rats when I was doing my research. No head for theoretical work, no clue what he's doing. And Kelly Petersen? God. I bet it takes both of them combined to try to fill my shoes."

"I'm sure it does," I soothed.

Our cheese fries arrived. They were gross; limp potato wedges topped by cold and congealed cheese. We ate them anyway, in the interest of appeasing the waitress and keeping our spot.

The next steps in the search were a little more complicated. Time to scour the open web and see if we could turn up something relevant. Websites, investor reports, simple search engine queries, anything that might turn up an address in one Portland or another associated with Verity. That didn't surface anything of note, except that investor's report — close examination corroborated that the company was planning on making "significant capital expenditures in order to improve our service offerings in the next fiscal year." Pending investment, of course.

Chandra said that combined with the stuff about a new prototype sounded pretty ominous. "We have to crack this and fast." She stirred the ice in her glass, then waved at the waitress to try to get a refill. The waitress stared her down instead.

"I think we're out of options. Unless you want to call up Benji and ask him." I was a little relieved, to be honest.

"Um. I do have one more idea, actually." She pulled an ice cube from her glass and popped it in her mouth. "Moleskine," she mumbled.

Oh, right. Benji had a sacred Moleskine notebook that never left his back pocket. It's where he kept not just notes but phone numbers, addresses, even passwords—a way to securely record data safely away from the cloud, so he said. Given that this location seemed to be a big freaking secret, there just had to be a note in there somewhere about Portland or John Adams or a prototype.

So if I could separate Benji and his precious notebook long enough, I could skim it for a clue to the whereabouts of this "Portland facility."

"And maybe," Chandra pointed out, "there's something in there about me, or about this Mike dude, to let you see what kind of guy Benjamin really is."

That... seemed like a great idea, actually.

The problem was, since the notebook never really left his person, there wasn't a way to get my hands on it without getting caught. He even slept with it on the nightstand beside him so he could immediately capture any blazes of brilliance bestowed upon him while he roamed sleepyland. (It wasn't uncommon for him to wake me up in the middle of the night by switching on the lamp to scribble down something that had popped into his head. It filled me with more than a little nocturnal rage; I'm a girl who prefers sleeping through the night.)

As the waitress grew ever more irritated with us, we brainstormed up a few capers, some involving a high level of creepiness (I seduce Benji and then drag him into the shower with me; meanwhile Chandra sneaks into the apartment to pilfer his notebook while he is, er, otherwise occupied.) Some were comedically unlikely to work — spilling a vat of grape juice on him and offering a pair of pants to exchange.

But Benji was coming home with me to go to Mike's funeral. He'd be staying with me at my parents' place. Surely in those unfamiliar surroundings, there would be a fifteen-minute period when I could separate Benji from his pants, right?

chapter FOURTEEN

Some days later, the Joes in their infinite compassion rearranged my schedule so I could go pack up my most somber clothes and meet Benji at his place on our way to the funeral of the late and entirely unlamented Mike Buchanan.

And so it came to pass that we climbed into his car — a sleek, curvy thing the color of gunmetal — and began the drive home with a few black clothes and a whole Best Buy full of electronics tossed into knapsacks in the back seat.

Given the whole crazy game I'd been playing, I expected the trip to be on the side of tense and awkward. I expected *me* to be tense and awkward. But we melted into normality before the first stoplight. We talked about where and when we should get married (outdoors in the fall), how we'd raise our kids (benign neglect), how we wanted to spend our golden and/or decrepit retirement years (travel).

At one point Benji glanced over at me, searched my face, and then said, "I'm so glad I have you. That I have this with you."

I smiled back at him. The car window was rolled down, and the wind blew my hair wild around my face. And I thought: Is this what it will be like when we're married? Easy, straightforward, uncomplicated. Wasn't this how love was supposed to be?

Oh god, what the hell was I doing plotting against him? What if he found out? And how could he not find out, eventually.

He'd hate me, right? What would my parents say if he found out and then told them?

What if he didn't get along with my parents?

The closer we got to my ancestral home, the worse my worry became. There were so many ways my life could take a turn for the worse from here, and not many where it wound up any better. We stopped for hot dogs at a place just a few miles away and I tried to warn him what to expect. "My parents are... very reserved," I said. "Don't expect gushy or warm. And you should know that they kind of hate my guts right now."

"It'll be fine," he murmured.

"Just... they can be real assholes, and I don't want you to take it personally," I persisted.

"I'm sure I've met worse from VCs and lawyers." He flashed his grin at me, and then we were off again.

It was only a short drive from there — too short — and my anxiety mounted with every minute. We passed all of the familiar sights of my childhood, ghosts in the headlights: the white church just off the highway; the horse breeder's pastures with the Lippizaners who would come to you at the fence and beg for sugar or apples; the old Amish barn with the faded hex painted on it.

We pulled up to the avenue leading to the house, silent under the towering oaks, and stopped at the inside of the circle.

"Holy shit, the paper wasn't lying," Benji said, his tone inscrutable. "Mira, you never told me you were fucking rich."

I looked at him, blinked, looked at the house, and back at him. Guess he'd finally found time to read the news after all. "Just comfortable," I said, "not rich."

But who was I kidding? I looked at the house where I grew up: Two stories, the wings on each side folded neatly on either side of the garden behind. Floodlights lit up the pond in the front where daddy used to keep koi fish. White columns lined the porch. It was more than just comfortable.

I squirmed in my seat. "Does it matter?" I asked.

"No, of course not," he said, and pressed a quick kiss on my wrist. Not that it helped any. He'd have had to find out eventually, of course, but... just ugh. At least I could be sure he wasn't a gold digger.

"Let's go in," I said, and swung my legs out of the car. I hooked my bag from the back and marched to the front door, then knocked firmly.

My mother answered in short order. She'd more than likely been hovering nearby, waiting for us to arrive. She was dressed to impress, or maybe intimidate, with her sternest silver suit on and the highest heels and pointiest toes she could manage. Her hair was swept up in a complicated but severe chignon, and her jewelry was heavy. She'd gone into the vault to get out some of grandma's gaudiest pieces.

I wondered just how much work and time she'd put into that ensemble. The effect would be utterly lost on Benji; I wondered how irritated she'd be to discover that fact.

My father crowded behind her a second later, his eyes rimmed with red and his bifocals askew at this time of night. He looked like he'd been reading briefs from the office, and given the redness of his nose, he'd already tapped into his evening scotch. Unlike my mother, he was wearing his coziest plaid pajamas and an old silk smoking jacket with Chinese dragons on it. My lips twitched at the mixed message. They'd never been very good at presenting a unified front.

"Hello, mom," I said. "I'd like you to meet my fiancé, Benjamin Adler... " I motioned him forward.

"Pleased to meet you," Benji said, inclining his head graciously.

My mother stood there, mouth agape, an expression that I can assure you was in no way characteristic of her usual social agility. My father straightened his bifocals and peered at Benji and then said, "Yes, Benjamin Adler. Are you really THE Benjamin Adler? From Verity?"

"That's me," Benji replied. "I'm the man who's going to marry your daughter."

"You're... engaged?" My mother's voice actually cracked. "You didn't tell us?"

"We just did," I told her, willing her to just shut up and not make a scene. Just this one time.

"Come in, boy, come in! How wonderful to meet you," my father crowed, thumping him on the back. "Welcome to the family, son. What a surprise! Can I get you a drink? I have some nice Scotch waiting around for a special occasion, and what gets more special than this?"

"That won't be necessary, sir," Benji said.

"Call me Thomas!" my dad said. "And I insist." He steered Benji toward the office, leaving me alone with my mother.

"You," she said slowly, her mouth not working quite right, "you are going to marry him?"

I nodded. "That's the plan."

"Benjamin Adler. The one who runs Verity. So help me, Mira, if this is some sort of prank... "

My fuse blew, and before I'd even left the foyer. Some kind of record. "Mother, if I were planning to play a joke on you, do you think I could get Benajmin-Adler-who-runs-Verity to come and play along with me for the hell of it?"

"Well I— I mean, of course not," she said, taken aback.

"Well, what exactly do you mean, then?"

She fidgeted with her rings. "Mira, sweetheart, you know your father and I only want what's best for you, but...

you know how difficult you can be. So when you tell us out of nowhere that you're marrying someone we've never heard a word about before now, who winds up being... well, any parent would be concerned. Any good parent, at least." And somehow her Botoxed-up eyebrows were able to confer her complete condemnation of lesser parents than she, who were incapable of the invaluable moral guidance she had to offer me.

My nails cut into the flesh of my palms. "Mother, I am an adult and I am competent to make my own decisions. Just this once, I need you to be trust that I know what I'm doing. No suspicion, no judgment, no cracks about my failures as a daughter. Just this once, act like you're happy for me and you love me. You know, as if you were my mother."

"But darling, of course I love you."

"Yeah, mom," I said. "Of course you do." And then I trailed into my dad's office, where he and Benji were already laughing and sharing Scotch like they'd known each other for a million years. My mother stalked in behind me. "Benjamin—may I call you that? Let me show you to your room so you can put down your things."

Benji flashed me an encouraging smile and followed her away. I hoped she wouldn't devour him whole once they were out of sight.

My father swirled the Scotch in his glass and beamed at me. That's when I made my next horrifying discovery. "Mira, you've done me such a big favor," my father said. "You know I've been dying to be introduced to that fellow for months now? And you just bring him home with you!"

"Why is that, daddy?" I asked, perching on the arm of his recliner.

"Do you remember poor Mike saying Blue Ocean was putting a big bet on a tech company? That company is Verity.

And the family is one of Blue Ocean's primary investors. So we have a lot of money riding on your boy! Did you know?"

"No," I said, "No. I didn't know that. That's just... that's just great."

The funeral was the next morning. The day dawned clear and sunny, like Mother Nature didn't miss Mike Buchanan either, and added in a double helping of heat so we'd all regret doing right by him in our somber black hats and pantyhose.

But I'm getting a little ahead of myself — before the funeral, we had to live through breakfast. With my family.

Mom had thoughtfully placed Benji in a guest room in the opposite wing from my room; though if she'd had any idea what the score was ahead of time, she probably would have thrown us into the same bed herself and locked the door behind us. She pulled me aside the next morning while the menfolk were reading their newspapers (the good old-fashioned kind, on actual paper) and congratulated me on "finally stepping up to your place in the world."

She paused, and I took that minute to reflect on how unflattering the morning light was, coming across the side of her face like that. The pearls in her ears glowed like little moons, but all the fine wrinkles in her face were lit up, too, like a roadmap to a country I'd never visit. And then I felt guilty because she was my mother, and because I'd been fighting her for years and years in every little thing she'd wanted me to do or say or think, when really all she'd ever wanted for me was the life she wanted for herself.

It's just that I didn't want to live her life.

"Daddy and I are very proud of the choice you've made in Benjamin," she continued. "Very proud. We need to discuss when to hold the engagement party at the club."

My ears pricked up in alarm. "Engagement party?" I asked.

"Well, of course," she said mildly. "We have to have a party so everyone can meet your nice young man."

"We don't need a party." We might not even be getting married at all, I didn't say.

"You must have a party," she said. "It would send the wrong message if you didn't."

I panicked. "I don't care what kind of a message it sends, I don't want a party."

"But darling, our friends would be— " Her friends would never let her hear the end of it if she threw an engagement party, and then I wound up not engaged anymore. Which meant I'd never hear the end of it, either.

"Mother, they are your friends and not my friends, and I don't give a rat's ass what they think," I said. "Please, can I go eat my breakfast in peace before it gets cold?"

"Mira!"

"No. Party." I pushed past her and into the Florida room, where my father and Benji were practically done already with their meals. Everything looked delicious, and I'd always had a soft spot in my heart for the housekeeper's pancakes — I suspect Miss Luanne had made them solely because I was home — but the conversation with my mother had left an acid taste in my mouth, as if the day wasn't already going to be hard enough. I poured myself a glass of orange juice and nibbled at a dry piece of toast, and promised to apologize to Miss Luanne when I got a chance.

I successfully avoided being alone with my mother again for the next couple of hours of showering and primping and dressing in our funeral best. We rode to the church in my father's car, with a slippery leather back seat wide enough for four. Benji sat next to me, resting his hand on the inside of my knee. He flashed me a wink when the car rolled out of the drive.

There was no conversation on the way there.

When we arrived at the church, my eyes were drawn to Betty Buchanan and her eyes, so red they glowed like volcanoes no matter how much netting she had on her hat to try to conceal it. The impact of it all struck me hard enough to drive the breath from my body. Her little boy was dead, and she'd never see him again. She didn't deserve this — not for a second.

I think I even found it in my heart at that moment to forgive Mike for being a misogynist asshole; in a way it wasn't his own fault, it's just what the world had expected from him, right?

My parents introduced Benji and Betty. I traded air kisses with her and murmured something about the world having lost something irreplaceable.

I'm not sure, now, if I was talking about her son, or about the blissfully ignorant life I hadn't known enough to enjoy while I still had it. Oh, sure, I still didn't have anything like a smoking gun in Benji's hand pointing to him as a murderer. And in a metaphysical sense, was he really a murderer if Mike had been on the cusp of killing himself no matter what? There was no way to tell.

One thing I did know for sure. Just a few days ago, everything had been so much simpler. Now it seemed I couldn't count on anything anymore.

Except— I felt a gentle tap on my shoulder, and I turned to see Eli, bandaged and on crutches but looking a whole lot better than the last time I'd seen him. I exclaimed and folded him into a big-but-gentle hug. "So good to see you!"

"Yeah." He patted me gingerly. "It's good to see you, too."

I pulled back and inventoried his visible damage. "Are you... I mean, are you OK? On the road to recovery and all that?"

Eli fidgeted with his crutches, trying to find a more comfortable position. "I'm going to be in physical therapy for a really long time," he said, "but I'm not going to drop dead any time soon, if that's what you're asking. My mom should be driving me back to school in a few days so I can get back to the books."

"That's wonderful." I reached out and squeezed a not-bandaged spot on his arm. Not too hard, just in case.

"Sad day, huh?" Benji said, nodding at him.

"Oh, Eli, this is Benjamin, my, um. My fiancé." I said. "Benji, this is my good friend Eli. We go way back."

"Nice to meet you." Eli nodded back soberly.

"The same," Benji said, sizing Eli up. "Were you and Buchanan close?"

Eli snorted a little too loud at that, and brought a few sharp looks our way. "God, no," he said, but at least he kept his voice lower. "He was a terror and a racist asshole. The world is better off without him."

"That's what I've heard," Benji said. "Looks like he did the world a public service, then."

"Yeah, something like that." Then Eli grimaced. "Sorry, I have to go sit down. I can't stand for very long nowadays. But hey, Mira, stop by and visit before you leave town, will you? I'm at my mom's for a couple more days, until the doctors clear me." He flicked his eyes over to Benji for a second. "I think we have a lot to talk about."

"I'll see what I can do." I adjusted my sober black skirt. It wasn't so likely, given all the crazy, but Eli knew not to count on me anyway, right?

Benji watched him hobble away. "Nice guy," he said. "I can see why you like him so much."

"Yeah," I said, as nonchalantly as I could.

"Keeping him and losing Mike was something like an even trade, huh? I mean, if you had to choose how the cards would fall." His gaze darted sideways toward me and then away to look down the pews.

I started. "I suppose," I said. That. That was as good as a confession, wasn't it? He was sending me a message. And with that, something inside me turned into a seed of ice.

All during the eulogy, my eyes kept sliding back over toward Benji. That seed of ice in me grew and grew, freezing my blood, crystallizing my spine, transforming my nerves into something brittle and needle-sharp. It felt, at long last, like resolve.

Benji sat doing his best impersonation of serious attention, though he kept sliding his phone out of his pocket to check stock prices or email or whatever the hell he did on that thing all day long. My mother would have given him any number of disapproving looks, I'm sure, except that she was sitting two rows ahead of us, with Mike's parents.

Then we all trooped out to the graveside and stood with the sun beating down on us. I deeply regretted not applying sunblock that morning, but no amount of heat was enough to melt my sudden determination.

After the usual platitudes and grandiosities, we attended to the casket one by one to pay our final respects. When it was my turn, I stood there for a moment, sweat slithering into the space between my breasts and plastering hair to my neck, trying to come up with something to say. At least, I thought, the coffin was closed, so I didn't have to say it to his face.

I shifted from one foot to another, wondering how badly my feet would stink when I got home, encased as they were in nylons. ("You can't go with bare legs," my mother had said, "it would be disrespectful to the family.")

"Hey, Mike," I said at last. My planned words of hatred withered before they hit my tongue. "Look, I'm... sorry you had it so bad at the end. You were kind of a douche, but... I guess I didn't hate you to *death*. You'd been through a lot. So. Oh, and I guess I should thank you for letting me find out... I guess what kind of person my fiancé is. Or might be. So... um. Goodbye, and I hope you're reincarnated into something that can't hurt anybody. A frog or something."

I took a deep breath and stepped away. My father patted me on the back with something he probably intended to be sympathy. "Let's head home," he said. "It's hot as hell out here." We all hurried back to his car, already a sauna from the sun.

The air in the car cooled down in no time at all, but my palms still stuck to the leather of the seats, and so did my neck. I lay back looking up at the light dome in the car ceiling, wondering if Mike had really deserved to die, and whether Benji deserved the power to make it happen. If he had made it happen. Which he probably had.

I worried about marrying Benji, who might or might not be a killer and might or might not be conspiring to, I don't know, rule the world or something. I wondered how the hell you safely break up with somebody like that. I wondered how I'd break it to my mother if I decided not to marry him after all.

And then I thought about Chandra, and about Benji's little notebook. When I stepped out of the car and back into the roiling heat, inspiration struck: "Let's get in the pool to cool off before we head back. You have time, right?"

Benji didn't bring a swimsuit, but my mother furnished him with one of my brother-in-law's; a baggy thing, violent aqua with day-glow green stripes along the sides, but it did the trick. We both changed and met on the patio.

I pushed Benji over the side of the pool. Water crashed up over the edge and wet my feet. He surfaced and grabbed at my ankles to pull me in after him, but I hopped away, laughing at how well my plan was working. "One sec," I said. "Actually I have to pee. I'll be right back."

I sauntered into the house as casually as I could, but once I was out of his sight I raced to his room and found his pants, Moleskine still in the back pocket, lying in a heap on the floor of his bathroom. I quickly riffled through the pages searching for anything that said "Portland" or "prototype" or "new device" or even "John Adams." I hit paydirt about a dozen pages back from the most recent; "John Adams," it said, along with a phone number. I took a photo with my phone and sent it off to Chandra. Then I deleted the photo and replaced the notebook in Benji's pants. Mission accomplished, easy-peasy.

When I got back to poolside, I made a big show of leaping off the diving board and swimming over to dunk Benji's head under the water. He retaliated by splashing me with huge sweeps of his arms until I cried mercy, huddled by the ladder. He didn't seem to suspect me of anything.

And if Benji seemed to give his little notebook (and me) an extra thorough once-over when he was back inside and dried off, well... surely that was nothing but my imagination, right?... Right?

chapter FIFTEEN

Finding Verity's Portland address was dead simple, once we had a phone number. Chandra called up John Adams-the-office-manager, and under the guise of being a courier service, said she needed to confirm the address for a shipment.

I started to see exactly how she'd managed to get my key from my super. When she was trying, she put out powerful waves of sincerity and trustworthiness. It was almost like she could edit reality *without* Verity.

That Portland facility turned out to be on Portland... Street, in a town about an hour and a half out of the city. Not Portland, Oregon, nor any of the other dozen states boasting their own Portlands. This was definitely a lucky break for me and Chandra and our micro-conspiracy. She'd already made it clear she didn't have any valid identity cards or documentation, so flying would have been a risky business for her. And I didn't know how I could cover up a two-week road trip across the country without tipping off Benji. Plus make my rent on time.

We took a look at the place online. It seemed to be a perfectly ordinary-but-low-rent industrial park. Not exactly the kind of place where we could blend in as part of the scenery during the day, and maybe not the safest place at night, either. I'd watched enough cop shows; I knew that's exactly the kind of place that drug deals go down and go bad, and gang warfare is waged. Right?

Still, some amount of personal risk seemed acceptable, under the circumstances. I'd never given my dad his sports car back — the subject sort of got dropped with all the other stuff going on, and it's not like he ever drove it anyway — so we decided I'd drive us out there on a Sunday afternoon. Still during daylight, so less dangerous. But also a weekend, so less populated. Our cover story if we got any unwelcome attention: we were on our way to a concert and got very, very lost.

I had a little more trouble coming up with a cover story for Benji, but in the end I didn't need to. He stopped by the Buzz during lunchtime on Friday. So sorry, he said, no time for me, he would be locked in urgent meetings all weekend.

I tried not to let the relief show in my voice. "Don't worry, I'll find some way to amuse myself without you just fine."

He laughed. "Don't have too much fun, M."

So that was that.

On the way out to Portland Street, I finally asked Chandra one of the questions that had been bothering me. "So why does it work, anyway?" I didn't need to elaborate on what "it" I meant.

"I wonder that myself," she said. "God's honest truth, I haven't got the foggiest."

"Oh, c'mon, your whole life's work is unlocking the mysteries of the unknown," I said. "If anyone has an idea, it's you."

"Well," she said. She rubbed her sleeve at a smudge on the window. "I have some ideas, but nothing you'd call a good working hypothesis."

"I don't buy it," I said. "You've been thinking about this for at least a couple of years by now, right? You have to have a theory."

She shrugged. "It could be a hundred reasons. Maybe it's just somehow choosing which branch in the multiverse you're splitting off into. Maybe we're living in a simulation and it's a bug in the code. Maybe it's because nothing outside of my head exists and this is what my consciousness has decided the world should be like." She looked at me sidelong. "I have to say, if that's the case, I wish my consciousness hadn't made you eat those onion rings for lunch. Your breath is stinking up the whole car."

I laughed and swatted her in the arm. "Don't complain. Just be glad I didn't get a bean burger, too."

Before long, the wheels crunched onto gravel at our destination. It was a desolate arrangement of rusting shipping containers backed up to a few low-slung cement-block buildings. The paint had peeled off in patches as big as my two arms outstretched, and everything was covered with a rainbow of overlapping graffiti, going as high as the would-be artists could reach or climb. They'd left a rusted pile of empty spray-paint cans by one building, half-obscured by the weeds that had sprouted up between the wall and the cracks in the soft asphalt.

"We're here," I said, entirely unnecessarily.

The late-afternoon light angled high across the rooftops and left pools of shadow hanging close to the walls. There was a long row of high windows, barred and covered from the inside with black paint. A few of the panes had cracked but never been replaced; those were blocked from the inside by squares of cardboard duct-taped in place. A door with chains, its links rusted together solid, sat at one end of the building, but it looked like it hadn't been used in decades.

"This is a weird place for a research lab," Chandra said. "Usually you'd find something like that in a pretty upscale office park, not... this."

"Maybe they don't want to attract too much attention?"

The other side of the building offered a row of docks for tractor-trailers to pull up and exchange their contents, like some sort of reproductive process. Chandra and I circled the building, looking for a way inside. We were grateful, at least, that nobody else was around. It was so quiet here that we could've been the only people in the world; you couldn't even hear the highway traffic from here, not even half a mile away.

"Hey," Chandra called at last. "Over here." She showed me a gap in the cement blocks around one of the big docking doors. It looked like a truck had hit the wall and crushed away some of the cement around the entry bay. It had been covered loosely by an arrangement of chicken wire and plywood, but that was easy enough to pull free. Once we'd unwedged the jury-rigged blockade, the hole was just big enough to wiggle through. "Give me a boost," Chandra said. I gave her my shoulder to climb up on, and she squirmed up and in. Once she was on solid footing, she turned and gave me a hand so I could scramble up after her.

We emerged into a dusty, dim cavern filled with stacks of cardboard boxes. Enough light filtered through the flaking paint on the windows and the gap in the wall to make our way to a door. It led into a sterile hall with checkerboard linoleum on the floor and cement-block walls in Institutional Mint Green, that color that makes you feel queasy after a few minutes. And if the color didn't, the flickering fluorescent lights certainly would have.

"Where do we go?" I wondered aloud.

"We have their suite number," Chandra reminded me. "We just need to find it."

That was much easier said than done. The building was enormous, the halls labyrinthine. We roamed from door to door, trying to find a pattern that would lead us to the one we were looking for.

"You are in a maze of twisty passages, all alike," Chandra said under her breath. "We should start leaving things behind us so we can find our way back again." She peered at the numbers on the door nearest us. "This one," she said, surprised.

My heart pounded in my ears. "Here goes nothing." I reached for the door, expecting it to be locked, but it swung open easily.

We stepped into a room that felt like it belonged in some other building entirely. There was gray berber carpet on the floor and a potted palm as tall as me in the corner. A desk faced us, backed by a motivational poster with a photo of a sunrise. Three conference chairs lined the wall next to a water cooler. There was another door behind the desk; that one was locked.

"Damn," Chandra said. She pulled open the desk and started looking for a key, but only uncovered a bunch of paperclips and a few pads of sticky notes. Not even a pen.

"Should we bust down the door?" she asked.

"Hang on," I said. "I bet we could climb over." The walls here were mere partitions, maybe eight or nine feet tall. The ceiling, on the other hand, was fifteen feet up. The metal struts and HVAC ducts were exposed where the building management had never seen fit to complete a drop ceiling. Together we dragged the desk to the wall, and then put one of the conference chairs on top of the desk.

All the while we worried about the noise that we were making, the time we were spending. Every second increased the odds that somebody would come into the building, or at least notice my car. But we'd come this far; it wouldn't do to chicken out now, would it?

"Hold this." I handed her my keys to stuff into her bag, then I climbed up to the top of our rickety tower and peered over, looking for a safe place to land on the other side. What I saw was as much as I would have expected, if not particularly exciting: racks of computer equipment humming quietly, tangles of wires and electronic parts on a workbench beneath me, and a row of gray metal filing cabinets lining one wall. If I put my foot down just right, I figured I could come down on the workbench and not disturb anything, and then unlock the door from the inside.

Nobody was more surprised than me when this actually worked.

Chandra joined me in the back, and we wandered through room after room just like the first one, full of desks, humming servers, and scattered pieces of equipment. It was evidence that some sort of electronic device, at least, was in fact being built here. In the deepest room in the suite, we came across an array of games: Pinball machines, consoles, even an old Zaxxon arcade machine. "I guess they're serious about their break room," I said.

"It's for testing." Chandra shook her head. "In a game you know exactly when and what random behaviors to expect, so you have a controlled environment to look for particle bursts, and an easy way to know what you've changed."

We also discovered a large area with a high wall of stacked cages holding lab mice and rabbits. That room had a steel table and drawers full of surgical tools — tiny scalpels, spools of suturing thread, drills and clamps and bandages. There was a tabletop maze, built so that the walls could be rearranged at a whim. Chandra frowned when she saw it.

"Why would they need mice?" I asked.

"If they're practicing the effects of the particles on the brain," she said slowly, "if they're trying to find the sweet spot for affecting decision-making... "

My mouth formed a round, silent "Oh." I broke out in

goosebumps.

She stuck a finger in one cage to let a rabbit sniff her. "This one has electrodes implanted in its brain or something. It's had surgery, anyway."

My memory flashed to Benji and that squared-off lump behind his ear. "What— what could they be doing with that?" I asked.

"Some kind of neural interface, maybe? A faster and more direct link to Verity?" She scrunched her nose up like she was struggling to bring up a memory. "I think I know... I think I knew something about that, but it's gone. Damn."

A horrible loud sound came from my pocket. My phone vibrating. It was a text from Eli. *Listen, Mira, we really have to talk. Call me ASAP.*

Yeah, this wasn't exactly the right moment to have any sort of talk, and especially not a "we have to talk" kind of talk. I turned away from the Frankenbunnies and took a deep breath. "So how do we know when we've found what we're looking for?"

"Not really sure." She frowned. "Shouldn't be too big. I wish I knew how far along they were in testing... "

Chandra shook her head and headed back to the rack of humming servers. She somehow unfolded a hidden keyboard and screen, like a magician pulling a dove from thin air. "If I could just get a good data dump," she murmured. The login screen waited patiently for her, black and white. She held her fingers poised over the keys, motionless.

"You have a password, right?"

She flexed her hands into tight fists. "I don't know. And... they might be tracking login attempts. If I tried to get in, it might set off an alert. They might know I'm alive."

"And that would be bad."

"Yeah." Her hands hovered over the keyboard another

moment, and then she slammed the tray back into place. "Probably encrypted anyway," she said darkly.

She stalked back to the workshop area we'd first entered and pulled open one of the filing cabinets. "At least we can raid their paper trail." She flicked her way through the hanging files, muttering to herself. She tossed a manila folder on the floor, and then a few minutes later, from another drawer, a second one. When she had gone through every drawer, she sat cross-legged on the carpet and leafed through her folders, scrutinizing each page. After several minutes, she nodded slowly and handed a fat stack of pages to me. "Go make copies of all of this," she told me. "I know what I'm looking for, now."

I set to work at the photocopier, the whir of the machine painfully loud in the hushed building. Eli buzzed me again while I waited. *This is serious, OK? Don't blow me off.* But what else could I do? I put him back in my pocket.

Meanwhile Chandra had gone back into the depths of the suite in search of the actual prototype. She emerged after several more minutes with a triumphant grin, brandishing a harmless-looking construction of circuit boards and wires. "This is it," she announced. "They'll never miss it, but this should tell me everything I need to know."

"If you say so." It looked like any other piece of electronics to me.

She collected everything from the copier's hopper and stuffed the duplicates into her messenger bag. "Now let's clean up our tracks." She replaced the original folders in those filing cabinets and then we left, locking the office door behind us.

"That was a lot easier than I expected," I said, a little nonplussed. Together we lifted the desk and muscled it back to its original position.

"Me, too," she murmured. "But then again, there's not

a huge need for physical security. Basically there's nobody in the world who could suspect what's going on in there, or understand that it was worth more than scrap if they found it."

"Except for you."

Chandra lined up the row of chairs neatly against the wall. "Yeah, and in case you forgot, I'm dead."

We wound our way out through the twisty passages back to the loading bay, and then out through the hole in the wall. It had grown dark in the time since we'd been there, and visibility was low: there were a few pools of light around some street lamps, but in between them, the terrain was invisible.

I led the way to the car, stumbling a little in the dark, but whistling a happy tune all the same. Then I rounded the corner back toward the parking lot.

I froze.

Way across the parking lot, right by our car, waited a police cruiser. Its lights were flashing. There were two cops inside; one was on the radio while the other scanned the area. He spotted me, and the cruiser wheeled toward us.

"Fuck," I said. "Now what?" I looked around, but I couldn't see Chandra in the darkness. Had she found a place to hide? I looked around trying to find an escape route myself. But the police car was faster than my feet. They cut me off before I'd gone thirty feet.

The officers climbed out of the cruiser and confronted me. "Is that your car over there, miss?"

"Um... no... I mean, kind of? It's my dad's." I stammered.

"Where you been while you left the car?" one asked. The other traced where I'd come from. His flashlight shone into the hole in the wall we'd used for entry.

"Just... walking," I said lamely.

They sized me up: young, female, white, driving her

daddy's super expensive sports car. They exchanged an eye-roll that looked like they'd decided I was more trouble than I was worth, and then they started a tag-team lecture on trespassing and how dangerous it was for me to be out at night alone like this. I looked around wondering what had happened to Chandra.

Then I saw a flicker of motion at the far end of the parking lot — she'd made it to the car. She slid inside. She started up the engine and floored it to get away.

The cops heard the motor noise and ran back to the corner just in time to see the dust kicked up in the streetlight as Chandra drove off. One officer's hands dove for his radio to put out an alert on the vehicle.

"You'd better come along with us, miss," the other officer said, suddenly grim-jawed. "We're going to need to ask you a few questions."

A sour fury grew in me. I'd trusted Chandra, finally come to see things her way, taken huge risks at her bidding, and in return she'd hung me out to dry. A less laudable part of me hoped like hell they'd catch her, too, and bust her for stealing my daddy's car.

chapter SIXTEEN

Have you ever been arrested? That was my first time. Oh, sure, the police rousted a couple of teenage beer bashes when I was in high school, and I'd been pulled over for speeding two or three or eight times... a year. But that was nothing compared to this. Handcuffs, fingerprints and mugshots, and an old-school phone with curly wire dumped in front of you so you can call for help.

There's nothing that clarifies who you are and who you can genuinely count on the way that phone call does. It makes you really face up to reality. I reviewed my options: Benji? No way. I could just see it: "Honey, can you pick me up? I got arrested trying to steal your top-secret prototype from your secret research facility."

Mom and Dad? Or Uncle Wally, which was basically the same thing? I suppose I could trust them to send somebody to come and get me instead of leaving me to rot in a holding cell. But that would turn this into A Thing. My dad would call in one of his lawyer buddies, my mom would be Very Disappointed In Me, and together they'd use this as a pulley to grab me and winch me right back into the life they wanted me to have, the one I'd been trying to escape since I was 14 years old.

There was my sister Anna, but she had too much of her own life going on to get pulled into my mess. And anyway, that would shortly become the Mom and Dad Circus anyway, because she was awful at keeping secrets from them. Or at least my secrets.

There'd been a time when Eli would drop everything and come to my aid if I needed it. But... I remembered the last time I'd sent him a 911 text, and how he definitely hadn't come running.

Probably couldn't drive yet, anyway, given those crutches.

So who else? Chandra owed me for being in here. But I wasn't sure she had the resources to spring me, no matter how much she owed me for this. And she might get busted just driving up in my dad's car. She didn't even have legal ID! Pretty sure when you get bailed out they like to know who's doing the bailing.

I hefted the phone in one hand and poised my fingers over the buttons, trying to pick the least bad of all available evils. "I can get you the number for a bail bondsman," the officer told me.

"No," I said, "that won't be necessary." And then, of their own accord, my fingers dialed a number.

Ring one...

Ring two...

Ring three... oh god I hope they don't screen me out.

"Hello?" Joey asked, voice puzzled.

"Hi boss," I said. My voice was wan and little-girl. "Sorry to bother you, but... I kind of need your help. I'm kind of in jail?"

"Oh my god," he said, and then, "we'll be right there."

By the time the Joes finally got there to pick me up, it was about eleven at night. I reviewed the schedule in my head and realized they'd probably missed their bedtime to come and get me. I felt terribly guilty over it, but also an unfamiliar warm glow. They cared about me and what happened to me!

When they arrived, they blew through the necessary paperwork and bundled me into their 1987 Lincoln Town Car as quickly as humanly possible. No questions were asked and no judgments offered regarding my brief experience with incarceration. For once, they didn't want to pry, I guess.

"Should we take you home? Should we take her home?" Joey asked.

"No, she should come back to our place," Joseph said. "You shouldn't be alone right now." He peered up into the rear view mirror to get a better look at me. "Come back to our place to spend the night, Mira. We have plenty of room."

"Thank you," I said. The guilt intensified; I didn't want to impose on them, but the stronger and more selfish part of me didn't want to be home alone, and didn't want any chance at all of running into either Chandra or Benji. At just that moment I couldn't decide which one would be the worse fate.

The two of them chattered in their old-married-couple way the whole time it took to get back to their apartment. Are there clean sheets in the guest room? Did we run out of towels this morning, or not? Do we still have those cheese crackers left?

I tuned them out and pressed my cheek to the glass of the window, eyes closed. I tried to make some sense of what had happened to me these last days, but all I could do was examine the pieces, one at a time, and then put them back down again. No matter how hard I tried, I just couldn't fit them together into something I could understand.

But the lull didn't last long. Soon the Joes had me settled in their overstuffed velvet sofa with a chenille blanket wrapped around my shoulders and a steaming mug of chamomile tea clenched in my hands. Joey bustled in the guest room putting clean sheets on their spare bed and probably dusting and such, too. They had a hushed conversation in there, no doubt speculating on what had happened to me and how they should react as a result; probably the continuation of a conversation they had in the car all the way to the police station.

Finally Joseph emerged from the doorway with an armful of toddler toys and put them in a wicker bin under the coffee table. "Our niece," he explained, with an adorable little smile. Joey followed and pronounced the guest room fit for company. Then they both settled onto the matching sofa across from me and leaned forward. Joey asked, in the gentlest, most hesitant voice I had ever heard him use (and the day before would never have believed he had in him): "Mira, honey, I know I've asked you before, but is there anything you need to talk about?"

I froze up a little. "No," I said. "If you don't mind, I... I don't want to talk about it."

Joseph nodded a little, then said, "You know, we... we care about you, Mira. I mean, we care about all of our staff, and we've worked to make the shop like a little family."

"You're all our children," Joey said, and he gave me a look so warm it would have melted glaciers. "Since we never had our own."

"That's very sweet of you," I managed.

"So Mira, if you're in any kind of trouble... we're here to help you," Joey said. He pinched at the tips of his beard. "All we ask is that you let us know what's going on."

I nodded. "I wish I could talk to you about it," I said. "It's just you wouldn't believe me. And there's nobody I can trust right now."

"Try us," Joey said.

And then I think I surprised all three of us when I burst into tears. Joseph took the mug from my hands and set it on the coffee table with a ceramic click, and Joey wrapped his thick arms around me and hugged. "Poor baby, don't cry," he murmured. "It can't be as bad as all that, can it?"

I tried to answer between sobs. "You-have-no-idea," I said.

Together they squeezed me, rubbed my back, soothed and calmed until I was quiet again.

"You need a good night's sleep," Joseph said. "Come on, let's get you settled." He led me like a toddler to the guest room.

They gave me a spare pair of what I guessed were Joseph's flannel pajamas, and then tucked me into a double bed with a cozy handmade quilt and curtains that filtered the city lights outside to a dim, even glow. I heard the door click shut, and I curled up into the safe embrace of the bed, convinced that I wouldn't be able to sleep in the unfamiliar place. I needn't have worried; the next thing I knew, sunlight was streaming across my face and morning had come.

Joseph was there when I woke, but Joey was long gone to open up the Buzz. He poured me a glass of orange juice and put a cheddar scone on a clear glass plate in front of me. He pulled a chair to sit across the formica table from me and folded his hands neatly in front of him. "Mira," he said. "You've worked with us for a while now, haven't you?"

I nodded, my mouth full of crumbs. "Couple years."

"Long enough that Joey's become very attached to you. When he says he cares about everyone at the shop like children, he means it."

I nodded again and gave a thumbs-up.

Joseph's face darkened. "I'd hate to hear of anything that suggested you were abusing his faith in you, Mira. He's a very loving man."

I stopped chewing, though my mouth was still full of scone paste. I swallowed as best I could. "I would never— "

"I'm sure you'd never do anything on purpose, but you haven't exactly been reliable lately, have you? Don't break Joey's heart, Mira. I won't let anything hurt him."

I nodded slowly.

He stood up and patted my cheek. "I'm glad we had this talk. Joey said you should have the day off, but you can't spend it here. Hurry and get out of here so I can stop thinking about you."

Chandra still had my keys.

I went to a matinee for some kid's movie and ate popcorn until the roof and corners of my mouth felt like they'd been attacked by a sandblaster. I went to a bookstore and traced the spines of the shelves of romances. I visited a park and took my aggression out on the pigeons by chasing them until they were forced to take flight instead of waddling away. Stupid pigeons.

During that time, I ignored messages from: Uncle Wally, my mother, my father, Benji, Anna, Eli.

Chandra didn't call.

But I couldn't stay away from home forever. If nothing else, there was the matter of the slime on my teeth; the Joes might be gracious hosts otherwise, but they didn't keep an extra toothbrush on hand.

If Chandra could get the super to make her a copy of my key, I could get him to let me in this one time, right? HAH. You'd think it was a part of his job, but it cost me $50 and two cases of beer delivered unto him. In advance.

But eventually I made it home to my own sink and my own dental supplies. Mid-brush, there was a knock on the door. I wondered — hoped — it was the Chinese place down the street mixing up my door and my neighbor's again. I spat out my mouthful of minty suds and went to look through the peephole.

Chandra was standing there, looking nervously over her shoulder down the hall. As I watched, she reached forward and knocked again: tap, tap, tap. She must have been watching my place, waiting for me to be home. Damn, she could've flagged me down before I was out fifty bucks plus beer.

I threw the door open. "I didn't think I'd be seeing you again," I said, petulant.

"What? What are you talking about?" She shifted her bag from one shoulder to the other.

"I'm talking about leaving me to the cops," I said. "I got arrested! I spent the night in jail, Chandra. In jail!" This was of course not *strictly* accurate, but I felt inclined to take a little artistic license. "I spent a few hours in jail and the rest of the night in my bosses' cushy guest room" doesn't have the same ring to it.

"You knew the risks coming into it, just the same as I did," she said. She pushed past me into the room, dropping her messenger bag on the floor.

I slammed the door and trailed along after her like a lost puppy. "Now I have to go to court in two months and explain what I was doing there by myself, who was driving the car, and... and... where the hell is my dad's car, anyway? God, I thought better of you. I thought you would stand by my side if things went sour like that."

"Your daddy's precious car is sitting right downstairs." She tossed the keys onto my coffee table. "What, you wanted me to stay and get arrested by your side?" She was amused, which made my irritation even worse.

"Yes," I said. "We're in this together, aren't we?"

She wasn't taking it from me, though. She dumped her bag on the floor and let me have it. "In case you forgot, I'm legally dead," she said. "I have no driver's license to hand over, no passport, no social security card. As far as anyone knows, I'm some petty con artist impersonating myself. If I got arrested with you, I'd be in for more than a little trespassing on private property and suspicion of breaking and entry."

"But— "

"But what? You just don't want to get in trouble alone? Don't you act all holy and pretend like it's only you taking risks and getting lumps out of this. I've risked my whole life, Mira. I've risked it and I damn well lost it at the table."

I flopped down on the sofa and folded my arms. "I'm trying to do you a favor by helping you at all," I said. "I've betrayed my own fiancé, pissed off my employers, I— I— "

"Oh, it's all you doing me favors, now?" she said. "And here I thought you might want to know your boyfriend was a murderous asshole with the power to control your mind. Ignorance is bliss, huh? My bad."

"That's not what I mean," I wailed.

"Then what do you mean, Mira?" she demanded. "Boo hoo, poor little rich girl, for the first time trying to do something important with her life and can't take it because it's actually *hard*."

"Don't talk to me like that. You don't know anything about me."

"Don't I?" she sneered. "I think I know a hell of a lot more about you than you do about me." Then she pulled her beat-up laptop out of her messenger bag and flipped it open. "Mirabelle Newton, born in Danbury, Connecticut, on May 5, went to Bryn Mawr with a major in humanities but dropped out in the middle of her junior year— "

"What are you looking at?" I demanded.

She turned the laptop and showed me her screen. "This,

Mira. Take a look. You've got your very own listing in Verity now. They think you're important enough they need to do something about you."

My mouth opened and shut. "Have they changed me?" I asked.

"Don't know," she said, grim. "I can't see the logs, remember? But now we know someone is thinking about it." She took her computer back and stabbed at a few keys before slapping the thing shut. "Let's walk," she announced. "I don't like to stay here too long."

I grabbed my phone and locked the door behind us. We walked aimlessly past the bodegas and boutiques, stewing together in unpleasant silence. Before long, my anger dissolved into a shapeless guilt. Chandra was right—I was inconvenienced by the police, but she would have had it way worse. I wondered, not for the first time, where exactly she stayed at night.

I didn't quite have it in me to apologize, though I knew I probably should. So I did what people in awkward situations have done since the invention of language: I changed the subject. "So did it do us any good?"

"What?" She flipped her long braid over her shoulder. "You being in Verity? I wouldn't think so."

"No, the prototype," I said. "Had any time to look at it yet?"

"Yeah, sure," she said absently. She pushed me out of the path of a cyclist barreling toward the red light. "But I don't really have all the equipment I need to study the thing, and those files we grabbed weren't as complete as I thought on first glance. Lots of seriously opaque acronyms going on, and the results of model runs that don't say what the model was doing. My advisor would've shot me if I kept records like that."

"So this whole fiasco was a waste of time, then?"

She hesitated. "I wouldn't go that far. The prototype... I think I understand what it does, and it's bad news. Seriously bad. A crime against nature bad. We have to keep Verity from building these at any scale, and then bankrupt them to keep them from ever trying it again. And I need your help to do it."

"Of course you do," I said. "What else is new." I stared at a shop window. A pet groomer; a bored poodle yawned back at me. Then a few of those pieces I'd been trying to fit together finally clicked into place. "Wait. Bankrupt? My father said the family had bet big with Blue Ocean, so if we bankrupt Verity, we might bankrupt—

She shrugged. "So we need to move fast and nip it before Blue Ocean cuts a check."

I nodded uncertainly.

"But we still need more information. Logs of what they're changing, for one thing." She kicked at a lamp post. "Dammit, I used to have so much access. Time was I could've brought the whole thing down with twenty minutes and a crappy EDGE connection. But they moved ops to a new hosting facility after my fateful cruise, and I can't think of a way to smile my way into the new one. I don't suppose you have any bright ideas?"

"Sure, I'll just ask Benji."

Chandra stopped short. She looked intently into my eyes and put her hand on my sleeve, lightly, as though to keep me from escaping. "Wait— maybe that's exactly what you should do."

I twitched away. "What? No. If he knew that I know— "

"Mira, from the sound of it he knows already and you're both just dancing around it. Maybe you should clear the air with him and ask him to let you in on everything."

"Why would he do that?"

The breeze shifted. A flag on a nearby flagpole stirred

restlessly. "You represent money and legitimacy," she said. "If he thought he might lose that... "

"What do you mean?" The hairs on my arms stood on end.

"Your family money, right? That Blue Ocean deal." she said. "Verity needs it. You could take it away from them if you wanted."

"Like my parents ever listened to me before," I protested.

"Benjamin doesn't have to know that." She shook her head, and the wind rearranged the wisps of hair around her face. "Look, it's definitely a gamble, but I think we have to take it. Tell Ben the truth, and maybe he'll take you on the inside so he can keep you and your connections."

"That's stupid. There's no way this can work."

"Then find a way to make it work," she said, and honesty painted the lines on her face in shades of worry. "I don't see what other choices are left anymore. Come on, Mira. We've come this far together. Come a little further with me."

"I'll think about it," I said. "I... give me some time."

"There isn't much time to give." Benji's face lit up on my buzzing phone. "You should really get that," she said, nodding at the screen. "Let me know how it goes, all right?"

I thumbed the call off and watched Chandra walk away.

I found myself wishing for amnesia, for time travel, to somehow wash my hands of this mess and return to a simpler time when my biggest problem was getting to the Buzz on time for my shift. I needed a moment of sanity and warmth in the middle of this ridiculous storm.

For once, I knew just where to go.

chapter SEVENTEEN

Eli lived in a cheap walk-up near the university, just around the corner from a row of sketchy sandwich shops and an electronics store that had been going out of business for twenty-five years, judging by the weathering on the signs. He buzzed me right in and I tromped up those eight flights without a grumble as my penance for making such a disaster of my entire life.

I found him with a pen tucked behind one ear and another in his teeth as he dredged through a swamp of textbooks and notebooks. The broken leg was up on a pillow. His face was a little thinner than it should have been, but his eyes were bright and his hands were steady. Definitely on the road to recovery.

"They don't even give you time off from homework when you're recovering from a major automobile accident?" I shoved my guilt gift, a sixer of craft beer, into his refrigerator.

"Mira." He didn't seem surprised I'd stopped by. But... he didn't look too happy, either.

"Hey there, tiger." I sat gingerly on the arm of the couch next to him, hoping I wouldn't jostle any of his damaged parts. "I had a little free time, so I thought I'd drop by and see you. Sick visit, right?"

He could have been made out of bronze. "You thought you'd drop by."

I bit my lip. "Come on, don't be like that."

"Mira." He was barely audible over the low hum of the air conditioner.

"So when are you done with all of this homework? Do I need to set up a jailbreak or something? Bring in some pizza?"

He just looked at me, completely unreadable, completely motionless.

"What's the matter?" I reached toward him, but realized I wasn't sure what I could touch without hurting him. Maybe nothing. I shoved my hands in my back pockets.

Eli slammed his books shut and began stacking his work in a neat pile. "Look, I don't want it to be like this, but... "

"So then don't be like this! Pretend like you're happy to see me. Fake it till you make it?"

He shoved his lap desk away. "I am happy to see you," he snapped. "I've really needed to talk to you. I've been texting you, remember?"

Ohhhhh right. It is almost never good news when somebody says they really need to talk to you. And probably even less good when it slips your mind for a while. But c'mon, this was Eli, who couldn't stay mad at me for any longer than it takes to wash up a skinned knee. "I know, I know, I'm so sorry things have been... crazy... but I'm here now. So hey, what's up?"

"I've had a whole lot of time to think lately," he said. "Turns out spending time in a hospital does that for you. So I've done a lot of thinking. About... " His eyes searched for mine, pinned them. "... About you, and about me. About us." He was so earnest, so completely sincere, and so grievously sad, that it took my breath away.

And this was exactly the conversation I hadn't ever wanted to have with him. The one I always knew had to come eventually.

I looked away. "Friends. We're friends, Eli. Don't take that away from me, OK? Not right now. I need you to be here for me. It's just— "

The tension held until his roommate burst in bearing a canvas bag overflowing with chips and two-liters. I hadn't met him before. Big guy, temple fade, looked like a linebacker gone soft in the belly. His gaze flickered from me to Eli and back again. "Oh— sorry, bud, am I interrupting something?"

Eli waved at me. "Hey Noah, this is my... This is Mira."

I smiled politely.

Noah frowned at me. "Oh, so *you're* that girl."

I tried to formulate a response, but even my mother's schooling hadn't prepared me for this. What did he mean by "that girl" exactly?

Eli saved me. Like usual. "Sorry, man, but... can you give us some privacy? You mind?"

"Oh, right, sure thing, privacy is my middle name." Noah dumped the bag of foodstuffs in the corner. He stopped in the doorway before he ducked out. "I've got my phone if you need me to come back fast, OK?"

"Don't worry, I'll keep him safe," I promised, holding up three fingers in a scout pledge. Or was it supposed to be two?

A significant look passed between the two of them. "Whatever happens I've got my phone," Noah repeated.

Once he was gone, Eli seemed at a loss for where to start over in that awkward chat we didn't want to have. I thought about changing the subject and trying to short-circuit the whole thing — how's studies, how's your mom. Or I could work up to telling him the truth about just how crazy crazy had become in the last few weeks. "I needed to talk to you about Benji," I said, by way of a warmup.

He glowered. "Are you really going to marry that guy?

Some guy you barely even know?" This might have been the first time I ever saw him truly and deeply angry with me. He hadn't even been like this when he'd caught me kissing Danny Hanover.

"You don't understand— it's complicated, it's— "

"Yeah, you always find a way to make simple things complicated," he snapped. "So tell me something I don't know."

"I really can't— not you, of all people," I pleaded. "You're my best friend, Eli. And you don't understand, I really need you right now. Benji is... he's... " Very protective? A murderer, after a fashion? What could I possibly say?

Eli had closed his eyes tight, probably counting to ten. When he looked at me again, he'd regained his calm, or something like it. "Sure, you're always here when you need me," he said. "God knows how much I love you, Mira, but it was hard enough to stand back and be supportive while you throw everything away playing coffee girl. I don't think playing at being that asshole's wife is going to work out much better. No more. I can't do this."

There was a knot in my throat so tight that I don't think I could have said anything even if I'd been able to think of anything to say. So I didn't. I turned and walked out.

So much for sanity and warmth.

I walked.

What the hell did he mean, I was *playing*. This was serious, the most serious thing I'd ever done, and there Eli was only thinking about himself and his own feelings, being completely and staggeringly selfish at the worst possible moment—

Yeah I couldn't get myself to really believe that, either. That was the horrible foundation our whole relationship had always rested on: he pined for me, and I... let him do it. It had never been right. It had never been fair.

Kinda sucked for that to become an issue right then, though. If I couldn't talk it out with Eli, there wasn't really anybody else. No port in a storm.

So now what? Break up with Benji and leave Chandra to sort it all out? Try to talk my mom and dad into pulling their investment from Blue Ocean? Lean into it and help Benji do... whatever it was he was planning on doing?

Run away from home and start over in Buenos Aires? That one sounded pretty good. I checked airfares on my phone, though, and didn't have enough room on credit to do it.

It hadn't escaped my notice that I had only Chandra's word that she was the squeaky-clean innocent party in all this. God, I was so tired of worrying and wondering what to believe and who to trust. I wished I could just clear the air. Just make it all go away.

I looked up and discovered I'd walked myself clear to Verity's offices, in a glass-sided brick of a building on the East Eide. The sunset glowed off the windows, pink and orange swirled together like sherbet. It wasn't so late, really. Benji was probably still there. Maybe I—

The lobby was all creamy marble veined with gold and brass fittings. The man at the security desk ignored me, as he always did; I'd met Benji in that lobby dozens of times. Funny, though, I'd never gone up the elevator before.

The ride up was long enough for me to change my mind several times.

The door dinged open. The receptionist, an immaculate lady who looked like she would've gotten on perfectly with my mother, looked up at me and smiled expectantly. A waterfall rippled down algae-slick tiles behind her, jade and onyx. Time to decide.

I stepped out of the elevator. To my left, there was a blown-up photo of the founders of the company, all tumbled together like eager puppies on the lawn of some college building. I stopped to stare at it, collecting details that probably didn't mean anything. The sharp angle of light, the ring Marjorie was wearing on her pinky finger, the way Chandra's body was turned away from the rest of the crowd.

"Can I help you?" the receptionist called.

"Yeah, I'm here for Benjamin Adler." I looked at his photo, large as life. He looked so young there. They all did.

"Did you have an appointment?" The furrow in her brow said she knew perfectly well I didn't have an appointment.

"No, he's not expecting me," I said. "But I'm his fiancée."

Her furrow unplowed itself. "Ah! You're Mira? How nice to meet you, I'm Silvana. Go right this way— he's the last door on the left."

When I knocked, Benji flung his door open so fast he might as well have been waiting right there just in case I showed up. His hair was uncombed and his shirt was buttoned up incorrectly. A whiteboard on his wall was filled with dense symbols. Stacks of paper spread from his desk to halfway across the floor.

He pulled me inside by the wrist, gently like he thought I might break. "Mira," he said. "What are you doing here? Is everything OK? I've been trying to reach you since last night. I've been out of my mind worrying about you."

That... that was a little more like something I'd wanted to hear. I'd thought it would come from Eli. But no.

I stepped toward Benji and put my arms around his waist. His chest was warm and real beneath my cheek, and he smelled like balsam. "I'm sorry. I... things have been crazy. I've been kind of crazy. I had to get away for a while."

He stepped back and pushed me with my shoulders. "You can't just do that," he said. "You can't just disappear on me and expect me to... to just... "

"You do it all the time," I said. "Conferences."

"Yeah, but— " Benji stopped short and searched my face. "You know what? Let's not fight right now. It doesn't matter. Not like you could go back and change it."

Benji folded me up in his arms again. I closed my eyes against all of the things I knew and suspected and worried about and listened to his heart beating, tha-thump tha-thump tha-thump.

"No," I said. "I guess I can't."

I nearly chickened out entirely. What the hell was I doing? Was this going to be the worst mistake I'd ever made? The final mistake?

"You can't change the past," I said, pulling back. "But I think you need to tell me a little more about what exactly you can change."

He sprang away from me and slammed his office door shut, then locked it. A tornado of second-guessing swirled to life in my head, accusing me of choosing poorly, thereby ruining Chandra's chances, my family's finances, my whole life, and probably the whole fate of the world to boot. The longer the silence held, the worse it became.

For once, I stood my ground.

"How long have you known?" he asked, at last. He held his finger to his lips: answer quietly.

My breath caught in my throat. The near-automatic answer that came to mind — "Known what?" — was indescribably inappropriate now, one more lie to layer on top of all the lies that had gone before. I found myself craving the earthy flavor of truthful words.

I clenched my eyes shut to keep from having to see the terrible look on his face. I took another deep breath. "I started to wonder the night you... proposed," I said. "But I didn't even guess before that. It was only a, I don't know, a petty revenge for being dumped."

He nodded slowly, as though he had known as much along. "I was sure it was you," he said. "I thought maybe you'd figured it out somehow, but I couldn't tell for sure. It could've just been an accident."

What about Mike, I didn't say. Instead: "It's time you stop keeping secrets from me."

He nodded. "I— god, I should have trusted you the whole time. I should have just talked to you from the start."

This exercise in truth-telling left me drained and limp, an overcooked piece of spaghetti. "I've been going out of my mind lately wondering if I'm insane. I need to know the truth. About everything."

Benji's breath hissed in through his teeth. He double-checked the lock on his office door, then motioned for me to keep my voice down. "Listen, Marjorie can't know that you know anything. I'd be in such deep shit if she thought I'd— "

"No more secrets between us," I said. "But fine, she doesn't have to find out. I'm not engaged to *her*."

He practically liquefied from relief. "I'm so glad to get this in the open between us, M."

"So what can it do?"

"What do you want to do?" he asked. He collapsed into his chair and kicked his feet up on the desk.

Wasn't that the million-dollar question? Like I had any idea. I grinned ruefully. "Go to Las Vegas and play the slots." I picked up a stack of papers to make room for my butt on the edge of his desk.

He laughed. "Yeah, we thought that, too. We took a big company road trip to Vegas. There are slot machines everywhere there, right?"

"Right." Almost against my will, I scanned the papers in my lap. Memo about cleaning out the refrigerator. The official company holiday schedule.

Benji didn't notice my side of the conversation had turned a little lackluster, or else he didn't mind now that our secrets were out in the open. "So we thought we'd win big. Very, very big. Break some world records."

"And did you?" Draft of a press release about a new literacy initiative they were starting up. Wait, what? I struggled to fit that into Chandra's image of Verity as an engine for world domination driven by murderers and liars.

"We lost about twelve hundred bucks before we admitted it just doesn't work."

My attention snapped back to him. "Hmm? Why not?"

He flashed his epic grin at me. "Don't know if you figured this out, but Verity can only affect random stuff. Turns out there's nothing actually random about a slot machine. It's just a really long, looping pattern. Completely predetermined. It's all in the timing."

"Crazy." I dumped the pile of papers on the carpet. Maybe, I thought, I should find out about Chandra from Verity's point of view. It had definitely occurred to me before that her story might not be totally credible, and a little due diligence was in order at this point.

"Yeah, right? But don't worry, we didn't go home without our shirts. Actually we made a pretty big chunk of cash and used it for seed money."

"How?" I could just picture how that conversation would

go: "Oh, by the way, honey, your dead ex-colleague isn't dead, and she's totally been using me to spy on you. So hey, what can you tell me about her?" Yeah, there was a non-starter.

He winked at me. "Turns out you can clean up in roulette if you have a little help."

I stood up and paced across his office to stare at the whiteboard. It said PROMETHEUS across the top in big letters, and underneath was a diagram and a jumble of barely legible dates and numbers. "So seriously, where does this leave us now?"

"Together. Right?" He followed me and grabbed me in a bear hug from behind. "This is why I tried to end it with you, M. I couldn't tell you, and it was getting too complicated to keep everything under wraps. But since you know— " He rested his chin on my shoulder.

"So will you tell me about... ?" I reached my hand behind his ear and pressed my fingertips to that squared-off lump.

He pulled away. "It's nothing," he said, subdued. "It lets me do some things without a separate computer."

"Whoa, crazy." I tensed a little. Crazy how fast he sidestepped an actual answer after all that about getting everything out in the open. More secrets?

He shrugged. "It's not as exciting as you'd think, I promise. It gives you access from anywhere, which is nice, and sometimes it lets you spot the things you can change."

"Are you the only one that has something like that?"

"No, Marjorie does, too. So far it's just us, though." He hesitated. "You have to really trust someone to give them that kind of power."

"Are you saying you don't trust me?"

His jaw worked silently for a moment. "I trust you just fine, but Marjorie... is another story." He rubbed behind his ear thoughtfully. "Eventually Marjorie's going to have to find out, though. So if we could get her to trust you... "

I snorted. "Yeah, you have your work cut out for you." Even Verity mind-control couldn't help on that front. Marjorie was about as likely to start liking and trusting me as I was to sprout branches and turn into a tree, Greek mythology notwithstanding.

"Maybe if I could get you hired on, though," he said thoughtfully. "She'd get used to you. Or maybe after a while she'd believe you stumbled onto Verity's special features on your own. Basically nobody knows about it, M, not even the ones who work here."

Hired on? With badges and passwords and access to employees-only stuff? Just what Chandra was looking for. Just what I needed, too, to figure out the truth. "So what would I get? Corporate jet? Keys to the kingdom? The power of good and evil?" Maybe I could find a way to jump off this train before it wrecked.

"Stop joking around, this is very serious," he said. A reminder chimed on his phone. "Dammit, I have to run to a dinner meeting." He grabbed his laptop bag and started stuffing papers into it.

"I'm being very serious," I answered. "Now that I'm in on your secret conspiracy, I expect a few perks."

"Conspiracy? There's no secret conspiracy." He coiled a laptop cord around his elbow and then shoved that into his bag, too.

"Whatever you want to call it. Illuminati."

Benji zipped his bag shut. "It's not like that. Just what it says on the tin. We're building the best news organization the world has ever seen." He leaned across his desk and squeezed my hip. "Advocacy journalism has always tried to change the world for the better. We're just... a lot better at it than most guys. We're aiming high, M. Stopping wars, ending hunger. Righting wrongs and delivering justice. Maybe we can get Hollywood to stop making crap sequels. Sky's the limit."

"It sounds incredible."

"It is incredible." He scanned his office, then scooped up his keys.

"Are you sure you're doing the right thing, though? Aren't there some... ethical questions?"

He shook his head. "We're changing the world for the better. It's our responsibility to mankind to use that power for the good of everyone. Wouldn't you change the world if you could?"

I thought about my family foundation, my mother's precious legacy, and my overachieving cousin Julia. I didn't answer him.

Before unlocking the door, he put one finger over his lips one last time. "Call you tonight. But not a word about any of this, OK? Ultra top secret."

"Sure," I said. "I'm great at keeping secrets."

chapter EIGHTEEN

I didn't tell Benji about Chandra. I told myself I was being wise and keeping my own counsel instead of taking sides in someone else's war.

Days passed. Benji couldn't see me much — "so many meetings," he said — but he sent me two dozen roses and a pair of earrings shaped like shooting stars by way of apology. The card read: *Make a wish, M.*

My parents and Uncle Wally weren't after me. I wasn't doubting my sanity. I made it to work on time. I did laundry.

I was even happy, for a little while. And then Benji spun up his plan to get me a job.

The Verity management meeting was set to begin at an unreasonable hour, something like eight o'clock in the morning. I stuffed myself into the most professional, responsible-looking clothes I could find in lieu of my faded denim: a tweedy gray skirt and a blue cashmere sweater I had bought to wear to job interviews, in the unlikely event I ever went to any.

I didn't want to be there at all, but Benji had said if I was going to get hired on at Verity he'd need me there to back him up. Moral support or whatever? And Chandra had agreed that getting hired by Verity would be the perfect thing. I could ride any horse I liked, they were all running toward the same finish line.

At least it had some quality catering. There was a table in the corner with a silver coffee service, neat rows of dainty cups and saucers, and a few lonely, almond-studded pastries. I paid it no mind. My stomach was roiling too much to eat anything.

Benji hovered near me, his hand floating possessively near the small of my back but never quite making contact. I knew some of the faces from the circuit of parties and other social gatherings Benji had dragged me to. There was the bearded man with no sense of personal space, there was the woman with the round glasses and the My Little Pony rainbow stripes in her hair.

On the far end of the coffee service sat a small basket filled with mobile devices. Benji dropped his own phone in and motioned for me to do the same. I clenched my jaw for a moment, thinking of Chandra's number in my address book; but she'd gone over this with me, and we had her contact listed as "Chris Cooper," a boyfriend of mine from middle school who I honestly hoped to never talk to again.

I'd felt excessively paranoid for doing it at the time, but now that I was here, placing my phone in the basket with all of the others, I was grateful for her foresight.

The conference room carried an unnatural hush, like the inside of noise-canceling headphones. There was little eye contact in this group, and even less small talk, but I nonetheless drew a handful of sharp glances. I didn't belong here, and everyone knew it. Even me.

The session was finally called to order by Marjorie, tall and sharp and dressed all in black. I was surprised to learn that she was running the show; I'd always thought Benji was the one in charge. Apparently not so much.

"We have a lot of business to attend to today, but before we get started... Ben, what in the world is *this woman* doing here?"

"I need to add an item to the agenda. I'd like to bring on Mira Newton as my personal assistant," he said. This brought a quiet rustle from the assembled staff. I think in any other group of people it might have been an outburst of chatter.

Marjorie looked at me over the top of her mug of tea for a long moment, weighing and calculating. She hadn't known ahead of time? I wondered what exactly Benji was up to. "You're Mira, Ben's *girlfriend*," she said. From her lips, it sounded like a dead insult.

Benji spoke for me: "Yes."

The corners of Marjorie's mouth turned ever so slightly downward. "We'll have to discuss this," she said. "But I'm really not comfortable having that conversation with her in the room." She looked at me through heavy eyelashes. "We need you to step outside, honey," she said. "Don't go too far. This shouldn't take very long."

I nodded and practically knocked over my chair in my haste to get out of that too-quiet room. The conference room door clicked shut behind me. I found myself standing alone in a neutral hallway with jute carpeting and inoffensive glass wall sconces. There were no chairs.

The wall between the hall and the conference room was made of glass bricks, but all I could make out from them were smears of color and the odd impression of motion. No sound came through the metal door; good soundproofing, on top of the fact that these were an unnaturally quiet bunch of people. I reached for my phone in my pocket to check the time, remembering belatedly that I'd left it inside.

Nothing to do but wait. Wait and worry. And there were so very many things to worry about, starting with what they'd decide to do about me, to why Benji had dragged me along to this, all the way to whether I was going to live through the day.

Relax, relax, relax. Surely the Mike Buchanan incident was a highly unusual confluence of passion and jealousy. They looked harmless enough, didn't they? A group of mild-mannered intellectuals and idealists, nothing to be afraid of. The tiny part of my brain that had actually paid attention in my European history classes in college whispered that intellectuals and idealists grew up to be revolutionaries, but I did my best to tune it out.

Anyway, they couldn't *all* know Verity's big secret. Benji had said as much.

I paced down the hall in search of a clock, but there was none. I strayed a little further and found the ladies' room and an institutional-style water fountain. It emitted a high-pitched whine when I took a sip from it. I went back to my hall and sat on the floor across from the door. Still closed.

A man in tinted eyeglasses and a business suit walked past. "Do you have the time— " I asked, but he gestured at me vigorously. He was on the phone, listening intently.

I closed my eyes and rested the back of my head against the wall, listening to the quiet sounds a building makes even when nobody else is around. I could only wait so long, though, before a restless energy uncoiled me and launched me pacing again down the halls, back and forth. Why was this taking so long? What on earth were they saying about me?

I grew hungry and regretted not taking one of those almond croissants before. Was it approaching lunchtime yet, I wondered?

Marjorie had told me to stay close. How close did that mean? Could I pop into the reception area to check the time? Surely I could hit the facilities when nature called. Could I go across the street and grab a cardboard cup of chicken noodle? I stood up and hesitated. Through the glass blocks, a blur oozed close to the door. My heart pounded and my breath sounded ragged in my ears as I waited for the door to open.

It did not open.

I sat back down, unnerved. Since I didn't have my phone, they couldn't call me back when they needed me. The nausea of too much adrenaline was giving way to the nausea of low blood sugar, though, and my itch to know the time was nearing a psychotic intensity.

Fuck it, I thought, and I walked out to reception. There was no clock, and the receptionist had gone missing. I turned back, defeated.

When I got there, the door wasn't closed anymore. Benji was leaning against the frame of the door, frowning down the hall. "Where were you?" he asked. "We've been waiting for you forever." I glanced into the room; a mix of scowls and curious faces looked back at me, but none were welcoming. My sour stomach amped itself up a few notches.

"I was looking for a clock," I said.

He shrugged. "Anyway, you're not in." He tossed my phone to me, and I just barely caught it. "We'll talk later."

And then he went back into that conference room. He didn't slam the door; it was just a tiny, nearly imperceptible click, but damn if it didn't seem like the most final noise I'd heard in my life.

I stopped in the ladies' restroom to plan my next steps. It was small, just two stalls and a granite sink with a spray of dried flowers for decoration. The massive mirror and its ornate brass frame seemed out of place.

It must have been Marjorie who said no. She was the one I had to deal with. I either had to win her trust, or convince her that I was too important to—

Marjorie swept in while I was lost in thought, and a sudden rage sparked in me. I busied myself with washing my hands and waited for her to emerge from her stall. When she did, I smiled and left the sink to her.

But I blocked the exit. "So, about this morning... " I said.

She looked at me in the mirror, eyes sharp, as she lathered up her hands. "I don't believe that's any of your business," she said. "And you won't be doing yourself or *anybody else* any favors to pursue this ridiculous idea any further."

I took in this information and turned it over in my head. I had thought she and Benji were very close; maybe even a little closer than I should have been comfortable with. This didn't sound like they were on good terms right now, and I wondered what had happened. Was it all about me?

Whatever.

She grabbed a paper towel to dry her hands and I smiled my shiniest, least sincere smile. "I just wanted to make sure you had all the info you needed to make a good decision," I told her. "There are a few things you might want to know, and I'm not sure Benjamin has told you everything."

She looked at me down her nose. "I know enough about you to know hiring you was a stupid idea," she said. "You're a coffee girl, you're dating him, and you obviously know your way around a blow dryer and a wand of mascara. But you don't have a college degree, no skills more relevant to us than any other waiter or busboy, and frankly you don't have the personal charisma, intelligence, or ambition to ever matter to Verity. The decision is for good reason."

She should hang out with my mother, I thought. Like minds. Marjorie moved toward the door, and I shifted to keep her from leaving. "I'm not going to take any of that personally," I said. "I'm sure you wouldn't want one unwise moment to get in the way of all of your hard work."

The breezy confidence in my voice gave her pause. "What are you talking about?" she asked, guarded.

I studied my reflection in the full-length mirror and swept my hair behind one shoulder. "You've been working on getting funding from Blue Ocean for a while now, haven't you? And that next round of capital means an awful lot to the future of Verity."

She rolled her eyes. "Stop wasting my time," she said. "If you have a point, then get to it."

I put my hands on my hips and let her have it. "You know my name is Mirabelle Newton, right? Go on, look me up in Verity, I know I'm there. My daddy is Walter Newton, as in the Newton Family Charitable Trust." Yeah, she knew that much already from the coverage of Mike's death.

It was difficult to keep the smug out of my face as the color drained out of hers while I said my next few words, though. "My dad happens to be one of Blue Ocean's primary investors, and now that Mike is gone, he just might be the one whose signature would be on that big fat check you're expecting."

She steeled herself. "So what?"

Here's where I fudged it a little; what was one more risk? "It sure would be a shame if I told daddy I didn't want him to give you the money, wouldn't it? I mean, if I had some sort of ill feeling toward you. He could never bear it if he did something that would make me so very unhappy... " She didn't have to know that pops was always a business-first, personal-feelings-later kind of guy. Or that in the last few years I'd not exactly ingratiated myself to the family.

She shook her head. "You're lying. How do I know you're not lying?"

I shrugged. "You can think I'm lying if you want. If that's a risk you're willing to take." I pulled my phone out of my purse.

"If you want, though, I could show you a little evidence." I pulled up the photo album and flipped through a choice few shots for her. "Here's daddy and me skiing at Aspen last winter... and here's the whole family all suited up. Oh, and this is daddy that week we convinced him to grow a mustache, and here's mom and daddy on their anniversary. I can call him up for you *right now* if you want to ask him yourself."

She looked me up and down, visibly reconsidering every opinion she'd ever formed regarding who and what I was and what I meant to her.

"Coffee girl doesn't quite cover it, does it?" I said.

She flinched a little at the jab. "I suppose Verity could use somebody with your personal connections," she said at last. "But why didn't Ben tell me this himself?"

I shrugged. "I guess he didn't think it was any of your business."

"Unreliable to the last," she murmured. She studied me again. "If you can bring in Blue Ocean, you're in," she said. "As Benji's personal assistant, nothing else."

"As an advisor on behalf of Blue Ocean." Maybe I could position myself to stop that check from going through after all.

Steam didn't quite come out of her ears, but I imagined it anyway. Marjorie turned to the mirror and pulled a piece of hair into place. "Fine. But no money, no spot. You don't get to sit in on meetings, no office, no salary, and you don't get a vote on anything until there's money in the bank."

"Fair enough," I said, inclining my head. "It's a deal." I held out my hand for a shake, but she ignored it.

"Can I go now?" she asked pointedly.

Unflustered, I moved aside to let her leave the restroom. "Pleasure doing business with you!" I called after her. When the door closed, I grinned at myself in the mirror and did a little victory dance: I was in. I'd won.

Time to clean up one more loose end. I took out my phone and dialed up a long-neglected number. "Daddy?" I said. "Listen— I just wanted to tell you right away. I've decided to take a position with Verity!"

He squawked enthusiastic surprise through the phone.

"Listen, daddy, just a quick favor, all right? Since this is sort of a conflict of interest for the family now, I want you to double check every scrap of due diligence before Blue Ocean wires any money. I don't want to take advantage. No, no, it's totally fine if that holds the deal up for a while longer... "

He was so proud he didn't even ask me any probing questions about his car.

On my way out, I stopped to stare at that blown-up founders photo again. Silvana the receptionist was back at her post. "Good-looking crowd, isn't it?" Her friendliness was positively effervescent, but I didn't mind it.

I matched her smile watt for watt. "Sure."

"Do you know who everyone is?"

"Hm? No— no, actually. I hardly know anybody."

She pointed with her index finger, lacquered in blue with a rhinestone embedded in the tip. "You know Marjorie and Benjamin, of course," she chirped. "Kelly and Hal are managing offsite research now, you don't see them in the office so much anymore. I'm sure you'll meet them soon, though!"

"And who are they?" I asked, nodding at Chandra and the stoic stranger lolling at her feet.

"That's Chandra Singh," Silvana said. "Unfortunately, she passed away about a year ago." Her voice fell to a respectful hush, as befitting salacious gossip of all kinds. "They say she killed herself."

"Really?" I asked. "That's too bad." I pointed at the other man. "And who's that?"

"Oh, that's Raymond Pagsisihan. It's really too bad about him... " she glanced around the empty room and her voice fell to a dead whisper. "They say he's locked up somewhere. Went totally nuts right after the company was founded."

"No kidding?" I looked at his picture a little more closely. He was an inconspicuous man, short with glossy black hair and a bland expression. He was smiling, like everyone else, but he didn't seem quite as carefree as the rest of them.

"The rumor is he and Chandra were, you know, romantic together, and she killed herself because she blamed herself for his, you know, his condition." Silvana's eyes glowed with excitement at getting to pass on the story.

I frowned. "That doesn't make sense, does it? I mean, how could she have been to blame for some kind of mental breakdown?"

She shrugged. "Don't ask me. People in love are stupid."

One of the staff came out of his office just then and waved at her. "Coffee?" he called.

"Coming," Silvana replied. And then she smiled at me and clicked her way to the kitchen to make a new pot, leaving me alone in the lobby with the giant photo and some giant new questions.

chapter NINETEEN

I had a new direction. I burned with it.

I wasn't sure what I'd be able to learn by tracking down this Raymond guy, if anything. But the story had a certain Gothic allure to it, so there was the curiosity angle, if nothing else. There was a more compelling reason to find him, too. If Raymond could tell me something more about the early days of Verity, then maybe that would help me work out if Benji was the stone-cold murderer Chandra said, or the poverty-ending crusader he sold himself as.

My first step was to search online for signs of Raymond, though it took me days to find evidence of him; he'd never been in the habit of giving interviews, and there were almost no press mentions of him. He didn't appear in Verity's own public-facing history anywhere, either, despite his prominent position in that historic company photo. Chandra had been erased, too, if not as thoroughly.

I finally found an archived press release which gave me the correct spelling for Raymond's Filipino surname. From there I unraveled a string of websites and family photos that left me not much wiser than I had begun, but with one crucial new piece of information: Raymond was suffering from a form of delusional paranoia, and had been admitted to the St. Francis Home for the Mentally Unsound for the protection of himself and others just a couple of years ago, right before Verity started to really take off.

I had to talk to him. But once I knew where to find him, I found myself reluctant to actually go.

I had many excuses. Visiting hours at St. Francis were a mere couple of hours in the middle of the afternoon, so inconvenient. I couldn't raise Benji's suspicions with an unexpected absence, nor Chandra's. What if they wouldn't let me in to see him once I was there? And anyway what would I do if I found out that Chandra was right? Or that she was lying.

I was spared from too much dissembling because Benji was spending long hours working, worse than ever before. I whiled away my evenings alone watching bad TV, eating bad food, and ignoring increasingly hyperbolic texts from Chandra.

Somewhere along the way Benji found the time to set up a few things for me by way of Verity employment — an email address I never looked at, a stack of glossy business cards, an employee handbook. Nothing that would hold up in court; nothing that opened up any new doors. Things were very touchy with Marjorie all of a sudden, he said, and the timing was bad to do anything more. But he was working on it, he swore. He wanted me on board. I just had to be patient.

In all, it was a few tense weeks between the moment I first heard Raymond's name and the moment I finally called a cab to see him face to face. Eventually the agony of not knowing was too much.

The cab dropped me off on the broad sidewalk outside the clinic. There was a bus shelter and an assortment of oaks and elms with shady branches spread wide. Marigolds and mums huddled together peaceably in alternating dots, backed by box hedges that didn't entirely distract from the fact that the windows were all just a bit too high and a bit too small. The sidewalk glittered in the afternoon sun, but the air smelled faintly of diesel. I stood still to collect myself for a moment before I walked in.

The first thing that struck me about the mental institution was how very *institutional* it was. It smelled strongly of antiseptic cleansers, that kind that aren't sold in containers any smaller than fifty gallons. There was a waiting area with a braided-rag rug and free-form soft vinyl chairs. A TV hung from the ceiling showing a soap opera in Spanish. The floors were linoleum, waxed to a high shine and uncomfortably slippery beneath my shoes.

There was nobody at the desk when I came in. I sat on the edge of a chair and tried not to drum my fingers on my thighs to show the nerves I felt.

I had just begun deciphering the goings-on in the soap opera (the woman was confessing... something?... to the man, and they were both in tears) when a nurse in pink scrubs appeared and took notice of me. "You're the one here to visit Mister Ray?" she asked.

"I am."

"How nice! You're lucky, he's all there today, so you'll be having a good visit, I bet. Come right with me."

I followed her through the very serious-looking double doors and into the hospital proper. It looked more like a hotel and less like a hospital than I'd expected, though, and my Victorian-inspired ideas of strait jackets and electroshock therapy were definitely not borne out by reality.

She brought me to a sitting room not unlike the one I had just left, though this one was supervised by a large man, also in pink scrubs, listening to the Yanks on the radio as he kept a watchful eye on his charges.

The patients here, too, were not what I'd expected. They

seemed normal, if dressed for an overgrown slumber party; they were all working on watercolors, clay pots, and collages.

"Art therapy," the nurse explained. Then she pointed to a man in a corner scribbling furiously with a pencil and a stack of sheets of office paper. "There's our Mister Ray. Don't be afraid, we haven't had a serious incident in months, not since we got his meds balanced right."

He didn't look up as I walked closer. The paper he drew on was covered in words and not pictures, all in tiny, crabbed handwriting, all packed together so tightly it was illegible. "Raymond?" I said, hesitant.

"Yes?" he answered, still not looking up from his furious scribbling.

"Hi, my name is Mira." I hovered at the table for a moment and then gingerly drew out the chair opposite him so I could sit.

"You a new shrink?"

"What? No, I don't work here."

He glanced up, briefly, flicking his eyebrows toward my jeans. "Guess not."

I perched at the edge of the chair, searching for the right way to broach my topic. "So, about that reality bending business you helped to start... " just didn't seem quite the thing.

I leaned forward to get a better look at what he was doing. The table was strewn with similar sheets, each covered with handwriting from edge to edge, no spaces between lines, no margins. Ray's hands were coated with graphite from the thick, short pencil he was using. I motioned to one of the loose sheets. "Mind if I take a look?"

He shook his head absently, still writing away. I picked it up. It was covered with variations on a theme: I can fly, I can escape, I am god, I am sane, I am free, I am rich, I am dead, I am healthy...

"Are these wishes?" I asked.

He looked up at me again, for a little longer this time. "If you write something down at exactly the right time," he said, his tone conversational and matter of fact, "it comes true."

I put the paper back on the table. "Yes," I said. "I know."

A smile broke over his face like light shining across the ocean. "You believe me! Finally, somebody who can listen to sense."

"I believe you." I nodded soberly. "I've seen it happen. And I have some questions for you."

He slapped the tabletop lightly with his palm. "Fire away. Anything for you."

I gave him my most encouraging smile. "What can you tell me," I asked, "about Verity?"

He convulsed like he'd stuck his tongue into an electrical socket. "Don't say that word," he snapped. "Killers and narcissists." He went back to furiously creating new lines of his tight script.

"Sorry," I said, folding my arms tight across my ribs. "I'm sorry, I— I just had some questions I hoped you could help with."

The corners of his mouth turned down slightly. He continued writing, but this time he asked me a question: "Did they send you? I already said I'm not helping."

I weighed the possible answers. Tell him I worked for Verity, but I was suspicious? Tell him I was working to destroy the company, along with Chandra, who might or might not have had something to do with landing him in the looney bin? Neither of these was really accurate. I decided I had nothing to lose by going with frank honesty. "No, I'm here for... just for myself."

"How do you know about— them? About revision?"

"I found out by myself, on accident," I said. "I changed something. Someone. But I wasn't sure what had happened for a long time."

"I was changed," he said. He put down the pencil. "I was changed, and it broke me. I'm broken."

"How are you broken?" I asked, cautious.

He waved his hand at the room. "That's why I'm here. I'm fine right now, but sometimes I see too much. I know too much. I was changed, and I can't be changed back."

"I don't understand."

He looked at me with pity, of all things. "You should hope you never do," he said.

"How do I prevent it? I mean, is there a way to keep someone from changing me?"

"Make sure they never know who you are."

"But if it's too late. If they know about you already."

"Who really sent you?" He pushed the glasses further up his nose. "Was it Chandra?"

I jumped at the name.

"She did send you."

"No, she didn't send me," I said.

"They can't change her, you know," he told me. "They don't know her real name."

I nodded uncertainly. "Yeah."

"They think they killed her, but they didn't. She's still alive."

My eyebrows shot up. "You know that?"

"Of course I do," he said. "She comes to visit me sometimes. The only visitor I have, since my parents are ashamed of my... sickness." He sounded wistful as he said it. "It's too bad I can't trust her to make it right." His fingers twitched toward the pencil again, but he drew them back at the last second. "She's the reason I'm here. She's the one who broke me."

"Oh." My ideas about Chandra and the sort of person she was reshuffled in my head. "What did she do, exactly?"

He didn't answer at first; instead, he picked up the pencil again and went back to writing, head down, glasses fallen down his nose. "Raymond?" I prodded gently.

He sighed and put the pencil down.

"I have to ask you," I said. "Why are you here?"

He stared at the pencil. "You caught me at a good time. Sometimes I'm... not here. I'm broken. Sometimes I see too many possibilities and I don't know which one I belong to." He went back to his writing, writing, trying to change the present again. But he kept talking while he did it. "They weren't satisfied with typing and automation. It's slow and clumsy, prone to error. They wanted to find a way to hook the brain to the system directly. Chandra was working with Hal, and they... well. Chandra asked me to volunteer." His eyes were shining like he might cry.

"Are you all right?" I asked, softly.

"I was the ops guy," he said. "Ben and Marjorie handled design and biz-dev, and Chandra made the starcatchers. You know what those are?"

I shook my head no.

"Chandra found a way to make a starburst instead of just waiting for one and hoping you were fast enough. Fast as light, your brain. Better than computer control, right? A starcatcher in your brain means you can see the possibilities and manipulate them in real time. Like a reflex." He stopped writing and clutched the pencil in two hands, like it might save him from his memories.

My skin crawled, goosebumps popping out all over

my arms and back. He had to be making it up, right? Proof of insanity. Delusional paranoia, that was what Silvana had said when she first told me about him. But I made myself ask the question. "Did it work?"

"Well, to see if it worked they needed a human subject, right? Can't teach a rabbit. Proof of concept. And if it worked, they would all do it too and become like gods."

"Right. I think I see where this is going."

He nodded at me, his lips pressed together in a thin line. "Chandra asked me to be the human subject. I would have done anything for her. Anything."

"And it didn't work right?"

He smiled beatifically. "No, my Chandra does good work. It worked perfectly. It was beautiful. Look." And then he leaned forward and ruffled the hair at the back of his neck so I could see the scar underneath; it was pink and healed up, right at the base of his skull, about three inches long. Underneath it was a small, hard lump. I reached out gingerly to touch it; it felt just like Benji's, a lump of bone, or maybe a metal device implanted there right next to his brain.

"That's a neural interface?" I asked.

"No, it's a starcatcher," he said. "So I see... I see probabilities. I can see that if I say one thing you'll believe me and if I say another you won't."

"But why are you broken?" I asked.

"Can't turn it off again," he said, "and they cut me off so I can't change anything. There's no connection from me to the system."

"No connection?" I asked.

"There was one at first," he said. "It was beautiful. But then I had a... a ten-minute grand mal seizure, and it didn't stop until they cut my access. Nobody else knew why. But they don't think they can remove the starcatcher without killing me, and I'm not fit for going out in public." His face tightened into a mask of bitterness. "I can see the web of chaos and how to nudge it, but I can't... I can't do it. My brain is fast enough but my hands aren't."

"Doesn't paper work?" I asked. "I mean... it's writing, isn't it?"

"It's timing," he said. "It's easy to write something down, but to come true, the words have to come into existence at the exact perfect instant. Writing takes too long. Forming letters takes too long. There's no single instant where you commit it to reality."

I shook my head. "I'm sorry that happened."

He frowned at me. "I'm OK right now. Glad you came. I wasn't looking for you, but this is important. You needed to be here."

"What?"

"I need to tell you what happened in that ten minutes, when I was seizing."

I wiped my unsteady palms on my jeans. "Go on."

He turned the pencil over and over in his hands. "When they switched me on," he said. "I could see the whole universe in my head. All of it. And I reached out and became something bigger than myself. Chandra would've liked that." He looked down at his hands. He had snapped the pencil in two. "It was too big," he said. "I should have looked away. I shouldn't have tried to touch it, I shouldn't have tried to fix everything. Sometimes, now, I, I, I can't stop seeing it. I just can't do anything about it. It's like being Cassandra, you remember her? You ever study Greek mythology?"

"Cassandra, the prophet," I said. "She foresaw the burning of Troy. But nobody would believe her, so she couldn't save anyone. Not even herself."

He nodded. "Like that. I can see things when I look. All of now. But I can't change it, and nobody believes me." His eyes were growing cloudy. "I've been thinking about it for too long," he said. "I mean me, in my brain, I'm not going to be here much longer. We need to hurry."

I nodded, and then the next few words tumbled out all at once. "Listen, I... I'm afraid of them. The people at... that company. And Chandra, too. I'm worried they might do something awful, and I feel like I should stop them, but I don't know how. Can you help me? Is there anything you know?"

"You'd try to stop them?" His eyes lit up like a kid in a candy shop. "I didn't look for that before. You're right. Chandra would get hurt alone but *you* could do it. Together with her. You need her. I can see it."

"I think what they're doing might be dangerous. And wrong. I have to know for sure."

He began to scribble again with one of the broken halves of the pencil, but this time on a fresh, blank sheet of paper, and the writing was different this time. Less cramped, less hurried. "I'm giving you instructions," he said. "Very secret, don't tell, but... " he trailed off, concentrating on his busy hand. After a quiet few minutes he presented me the paper with a bit of a flourish. "The keys to the kingdom," he said.

I took it and read. It was a jumble of command-line instructions and passwords. "What is this?"

"Sometimes when you don't trust the people you're working with," he said, "you leave yourself a set of traps and backdoors." A smile spread across his face slowly, like a contagious disease. "These are mine."

"Wow, thanks," I said. I chewed on my bottom lip for a second. "So... what do I do with them?"

His grin took on a decidedly wicked cast. I felt a profound flash of gratitude that he seemed to be on my side. "Let me tell you," he said. He began writing again, something like a schedule of events. They didn't make any sense.

"Just one more thing," he said. "Don't want to write this down. It would fall into the wrong hands. But... " He hesitated, his mind turning over how to say what he wanted to tell me in just the right way. "It's just... "

He stopped again and tapped the pencil on the table. "Listen, I'm not going to tell you when and why you need to know. If I do, it won't happen. It's tricky. But unless I tell you, it can't all go the right way."

Raymond's face contorted into an expression of wild desperation, his pupils shrunk to nearly nothing, his hands crabbed into claws. The papers scattered and the pencil halves clattered to the floor, but he didn't notice or pick them up. He grabbed my forearms and his eyes bored into mine. "Listen, listen, you have to listen and remember," he said. "When the moment comes, remember, remember."

"Remember what?" I tried to shrink back. "I can't remember if you don't tell me."

He pushed his face next to mine and whispered into my ear, his breath hot and smelling of institutional mouthwash. "Concentrate," he said. "Concentrate in your brain hard enough, and the wires won't matter. Just make a wish."

"What wires?" I asked, thoroughly confused.

"I can't tell you," he spat, pushing me away. "I just said I can't tell you, because if I tell you then you'll know, and then you won't be there, and then you won't be able to stop them."

"But I can stop them?"

"You can," he said. "But you'll have to hurry, and you can't turn back no matter what happens. It isn't going to be easy. It will be the hardest thing you've ever done, but not the hardest thing you'll ever do. One day— One day you might— " He shook his head, and then again, his eyes focused within. "I can't tell you, I can't tell you anything or it won't happen. But it has to happen." He squeezed his eyes shut, shook his head like a wet dog. "I'll help you, I have to help you. Paper isn't perfect but it's better than nothing... paper can change if you time it right... paper can do it even if the flesh is weak." He snatched up the working half of the pencil again and began scribbling, this time on the wall, in his tiny, crabbed script.

The nurse hurried over. "We've lost him, haven't we?" she said. "He sometimes gets like this when the other girl visits, too." She shook her head wryly. "We can't stop him now or he'll get angry, and we've found it's better to just let him write. If you stop him from writing, he becomes agitated. Sometimes violent."

"Yeah?"

She nodded. "He's a sweetheart, really, but you can't make him stop writing for anything if he doesn't want to. He won't feed himself or clean himself unless you remind him, and when he gets like this... on the walls... he won't even do that. We'll sedate him if he doesn't come out of it in an hour or so. If he doesn't snap out by then, it's going to be days, otherwise."

"Oh," I said, "I'm sorry."

"Don't be, honey," she said. "He's grateful for the visitors he gets. He gets so few, you know?" She gave me a milk-mild smile. "You should be on your way, though. He's not going to be good for visiting for the rest of the day. I'll show you the way out."

She called an aide over to attend to Raymond, who had completely forgotten I was there, as far as I could tell. Then she led me back to the entrance and called me a cab.

I opted to spend the wait outside among the carefully neutral flower beds and shrubs, pacing up and down the sidewalk, listening to the birds chirping carelessly and wondering what wires I would want to concentrate on, and what I would want to do it for. And perhaps most important... when?

chapter TWENTY

I snuck into the Buzz just a little past eleven. It was late enough that the Joes wouldn't be there anymore, but not so late that I might attract attention just for being out. The wind chimes on the door tinkled as I entered, sounding somehow ominous at this time of night. I hurried to the employee break room and shut the door to keep the light from my laptop screen from seeping into the shop. Wouldn't do to be visible from the street.

The break room was full of lights to begin with, from the security system to the alarm clock on the table that Joe used to time breaks, and the most important thing for my purposes: the array of blinking gear that kept the shop's wireless internet in operation.

One of the Joes' draws, and one of the reasons that Benji always hung out here in the first place, was the quality wifi the Joes offered. That was why I was here, too. I needed a good connection and a whopping dose of privacy. Even at home I might be interrupted by Chandra, or by Benji. But not here.

Raymond had been very clear that this part was important.

I set up my laptop and flattened Ray's notes against the table. His instructions would get me into Verity's admin system, it looked like, and from there... who knew? I held my breath as I entered each jumbled string of characters, line by line, command after command. According to Raymond, they initialized a secure connection, set it up so that I'd be a ghost, leaving behind no footprints (or more specifically, telltale entries in history logs), and gave me a few specific places to look for interesting reading material.

There was a lot there, more than I thought I could get through in a night. Files full of noise I didn't know how to read, spreadsheets full of cryptic numbers, engineering documents. Thousands of images of particle bursts — or starbursts, Raymond had called them. They were beautiful swirls of red and blue and silver on blackness.

One of them was timestamped for the exact moment Mike had tumbled over the edge.

I skipped over to a document titled Prometheus Executive Summary and read it with mingled concern and confusion. "Reconstruction of Prometheus technology is complete. We have succeeded in manufacturing starburst events, even under unfavorable conditions. Advise building out the full Verity system with this technology to maximize potential."

The words were all simple to understand, but the picture they painted wouldn't come into focus for me. Was that different? Manufacturing a starburst event?

It had already been a long day of ducking obligations and trekking out to St. Francis. My eyes were growing bleary.

I stood up to go and make myself a cup of iced tea. I figured I could risk the lights for just a few minutes, right? I needed something to occupy my hands while my mind was elsewhere. Plus I could use the jolt to keep my eyes open, and free caffeine is one of the perks of the trade, you know? No pun intended.

I'd just managed to fill a plastic cup with ice when I heard a nasty sizzle and pop. An acrid streamer of smoke drifted from the break room, thickened and spread. I raced over to see what had happened.

My laptop was a blue sheet of flame. It had already spread to the cheap plywood table, and the stacks of cardboard boxes full of coffee beans was mere seconds away from catching fire, too.

I hopped from one foot to another and snatched Ray's notes from the other end of the table, then beat them against the wall to put them out.

Fire extinguisher, I thought. But the fire extinguisher was on the wall on the far side of the fire. Call 911, I thought. But my cell phone was likewise in my bag on the floor on the far side of the fire.

A string of profanity emerged from my mouth and kept up uninterrupted as my brain darted from one impossible possibility to the next, wondering what to do. Smoke clouded up the front room. I stumbled out of the store, coughing, and had my only bright idea: I flagged down a taxi. "Fire," I called into the window. "Call 911!"

And then I had nothing to do but stand there shivering in the night air and watching. The shop filled up with pillows of smoke. I could just see the tongues of flame devouring the part of the counter with the espresso machine when the fire department finally showed. The engine announced itself with blaring sirens and spinning lights. The flashing red added another layer of hellish surreality to the scene.

The firefighters set to work.

A pair of them unspooled a hose to hook it up to the fire hydrant. Around us, cars and late-night dog-walkers stopped to gawk and gossip under the flashing red lights.

One firefighter took an axe and smashed the Joes' big plate glass window — the one with the custom gilt lettering on it — to shoot the water in more effectively. A rush of smoke and heat engulfed me as soon as the glass fell apart. I doubled over coughing so hard I thought I would vomit.

The fire had devastated the service area, taking the espresso machine and moving on to devour the pastry case. It had started an inexorable march toward the front of the store, tracing its way along the charming but dry-as-dust upcycled driftwood floorboards.

A second engine arrived. A second hose was unspooled. Great gouts of water flooded into the shop, unleashing blasts of steam. Some of the water washed out again to pool on the sidewalk at my feet.

A police officer pulled me aside to take a statement. When did she get there?

She was a nice woman with a crooked smile. She threw a blanket around my shoulders. It was wool, and scratchy against my face, but a welcome protection from the night air. My jacket had been in there, and I would never get it back.

Crooked Smile asked me if it was my shop, and what was I doing there after hours?

I explained that I worked there, and my laptop had caught on fire. She frowned dubiously and made a notation in her report. The confession poured out of me: Borrowing wifi after hours, my bumbling failure to get to a fire extinguisher, how I had flagged down a cab to call them.

"Why didn't you pull the fire alarm on the wall?" she asked.

I froze. Why didn't I? "I... I guess I panicked," I said. "I didn't even think of it, I don't know." It was like my brain had been smoked out the second the laptop battery exploded.

"We could have been here sooner." Crooked Smile wasn't smiling at me anymore.

And then I realized that the Joes would be hearing about

all of this. That I had been there, that the fire had been my fault, that I hadn't put it out or called the firemen in time to save their shop. I reluctantly handed over their phone number to the authorities who had taken over handling my latest disaster.

The Joes arrived not long after. They clung to each other in the darkness nearby, crying over the hard knock that life — my life — had dealt them.

I couldn't face them. I tried to dissolve into the background. I didn't know if they'd noticed me, but before long I saw Crooked Smile going over her notes with the Joes. The notes about my conversation with her. I wanted to die of shame.

"Can I go?" I asked one of the police officers.

"Is that your full report?" he asked me.

I nodded. "I told you everything."

"We have your contact info?"

"Yeah."

"Fine then, go get some rest."

I pulled the blanket off my shoulders and handed it back to him. My empty hands worked trying to find a bag to carry, a jacket to put on, a wallet or a phone or at least a credit card. Of course there was nothing, nothing but Ray's notes crumpled up in my hand and half-coated with ashes. Damn.

I approached the Joes. "Um," I said. "I know this is probably a bad time, but... do you have subway fare I can borrow?"

They exchanged a look. "Stay here," Joseph told Joey. "I'll take her back home and we'll talk." Then he marched me to their Lincoln Town Car and drove me silently to their place.

All the way there, I spun my excuses and promises into a beautiful tapestry in my head. It won't happen again, it was an aberration, you know I'm not really like that. I'm sorry,

I'm sure my parents will help you rebuild. But even the scene that played out in my imagination never ended well.

I walked up to their brownstone several feet behind Joseph. As he unlocked the door, I stared at the rosemary bushes in their painted clay pots through the wrought-iron fence around the Joes' tiny patio. A little bee, an early riser, sniffed at the herbs and flew away again, over my head.

The door opened. "Come inside," Joseph said. His voice was like a noose, round and rough.

I stepped inside gingerly, as onto the gallows.

He directed me into the same floral chair as the last time I'd been there and sat directly across from me. He cleared his throat a few times. I'm pretty sure he didn't look me in the eye, but I couldn't be sure, since I couldn't meet his eyes, either.

He unfolded and refolded his hands on his knee, staring at a point above and to the left of me. Those hands looked unbelievably fragile, knot-knuckled, thin brown skin crossed with blue veins. He was unsure where to start our conversation.

Finally I broke, unable to bear this delay of the inevitable. "So... how bad is the damage?" I asked.

He cleared his throat again. "We're not sure yet," he said. "The insurance adjuster will probably stop by tomorrow. Later today."

"But... how bad do you think it is?"

His jaw firmed. "We're pretty sure we won't be able to save anything," he said. "The fire destroyed all our stock, the equipment and dishes, and the smoke and flooding took everything else."

I pressed my eyes shut, wishing I could unhear the news. "So we're staying closed for a while, huh?"

"We may not be able to open again," he said. There was a subtle emphasis on the word "we" as he said it, and I flinched because I could tell I wasn't included in that anymore. "Joey and I are too old to start over. We're thinking this might be the right time to take our winnings off the table and retire. Miami, maybe. Boca."

"Oh," I said, a bit lamely. I turned this information over in my head. "I wish you would stay," I said. "I mean... we're like a family, aren't we? Didn't you say that yourself?"

He stood up, achingly slow, with the deliberate speed that meant his arthritis was bothering him. He walked over to look out at the patio, the rosemary, the little bee. "Family goes two ways," Joseph said, his voice steady. "In a family, you can count on one another. We've tried to always be there when it mattered, but... we haven't been able to say that about you, Mira. Not since you got mixed up with that boy Benjamin and his crowd."

His voice grew more and more heated as he spoke, like he'd been at a simmer for a while and the cook had turned up the heat. Now he boiled over with long-repressed anger.

He turned and finally looked me in the eye. I at once regretted that he had, because there was more than just blame there; there was grave disappointment, too.

"Mira, we've tried to respect your needs. But there are only so many car accidents and funerals and urgent appointments you could possibly have, and you were already pushing the limits of our good graces. And bailing you out of jail? You don't have anyone else?"

"I know," I squeaked.

But Joseph steamed onward to his conclusion, disinterested in anything I might have to say at this point. "And now a fire." He shook his head. "You were in the shop, by yourself, in the middle of the night, doing god only knows what, when something, what, exploded?" He glowered. "The fire might have been an accident, Mira, but it was by no means an isolated incident. It was all part of a pattern of disrespecting your job, the shop, and us personally."

I stared at the glossy blonde wood between my shoes and said nothing.

"We might rebuild the Buzz, and we might not. We'll see what insurance tells us. But *you* are fired, Mira. Don't come by again. We'll mail you your final check. Consider this an advance on it." He slid a five-dollar bill across the table toward me; the subway fare I'd asked for. Then he turned his back on me again and went back to the window.

I sat there, stunned by his vehemence, wondering if it was too late to defend myself. I tried to rally an argument in my favor: "I— "

"You may go," he cut in, voice sharp.

I bowed my head, face hot. I stood up. Walked out the door. I closed it behind me and heard the lock click shut. I turned my face toward the wind and walked and walked to try to lose myself, grappling with the ugly truth.

There was no going back now.

chapter TWENTY-ONE

I fled into the night, away from flashing lights and shouting voices. Away from the apartment I wouldn't be able to afford on my own after this. The things I cherished were slipping away one by one, everything destroyed, everything ruined. I'd lost my job and my independence and my cranky-but-sweet adoptive godfathers. *They'd* lost everything they'd built together as collateral damage. And it was all my own damn fault.

Mike's death was my fault, too, come to think of it. And Eli's car accident. And the part where Eli didn't want to be my friend anymore. Everyone around me was suffering at my hands.

Maybe my mother had always been right about me.

I'd never been to Chandra's place before, but Ray had scribbled down where to find her, as if he knew that would have to be my next stop. It was a bland hotel squatting a couple of blocks away from a subway stop, the sort of building that's completely invisible unless you're looking for it. The sort that would take cash and not ask too many questions of a long-term resident. Room 503.

Despite the hour when I got there, she wasn't asleep. But she hadn't been quite awake either. She answered the door wearing a ratty yellow bathrobe. "Mira? What are you doing here? Wait, how did you even find me?— What's wrong?" she blinked muzzily in the hallway light. "You look like hell, and not even warmed over."

"You've been lying to me," I said. "And probably nudging me, too."

She clapped her hand to her nose. "Ugh, and have you been smoking? You stink."

"I paid a visit to a very interesting man today," I said. "His name is Raymond. He seems awfully *fond* of you."

She winced and pulled her bathrobe tighter around her body, as though it might protect her from my accusation.

I pushed into her hotel room. It was a sad thing assembled from water stains and burnt-orange nylon; I'd seen SUVs with more living space. The night table was crowded with half-disassembled electronics, sticky notes, stacks of empty coffee cups. A mound of crumpled fast food bags huddled around the waste basket.

A John Hughes movie played on the tiny, fuzzy television. The comforter was mounded up at the foot of the bed where she'd thrown it to answer the door, curled around a bag of pretzels big enough to hold a toddler. What a party.

"So you met Raymond?" she asked. Her voice was still full of bravado, but it sounded hollow to my ears. She was faking it. She was scared.

"Yeah, I met him," I said, "the guy you conveniently left out of all of your stories. The one who's locked up now." I waved his now-singed scraps of paper at her. "The one who gave me his 'keys to the kingdom.'"

She actually gasped. "He gave you— "

"All his traps and backdoors, he said." I flopped onto her bed and took a handful of her pretzels.

Chandra closed her eyes and clenched her fists tight by

her sides. "I don't believe this. Ray gave you his access? Why you? He helped me to keep from being found, but he never— "

"Yeah, he said he never told you much." I mumbled through a mouthful of pretzels. "Looks like he likes me better than you now. No accounting for taste, I guess."

"You don't know what you're talking about." Her voice was flat and harsh as the desert.

"Don't I? I'll be the judge."

"Just— tell me what he said, tell me why he gave you the codes. What did he see in you that's new?" Her voice shook at the last part, just a little. And I realized that underneath her tough-girl shell, she was just as lonely and scared as I was. Maybe more. And she'd been fighting this war a whole hell of a lot longer than me.

I scooted over so Chandra could sit beside me. "He was afraid for you," I said. "The dude is obviously crazy about you, and it sounds like he always has been. Reading between the lines a little, he was worried that you would get yourself into more trouble than you're in already, but me... well, he's never met me before, and he doesn't care a rat's ass what happens to some stranger."

"Even after everything I did to him." She stared at the TV, where a teen girl was getting a makeover that would change her life forever. "How did you even find him?" she asked. "It's not exactly a... widely known chapter in the company history."

"Some good came out of Benji's idea that I should be his assistant," I told her. "I hung around the office long enough for the company gossip to try to make friends."

"Silvana?" she guessed. She plucked the bag of pretzels from my hands and stared at them without eating any.

"Yep. I feel like I should send her a basket of muffins or something." I ran my fingers through my hair and stood back up, pacing the few steps from her bed to the door and back again. "Listen, I don't know where we stand anymore. If you weren't telling me about something this big—what else are you not telling me? I don't know if I should trust you."

"Welcome to my world," she shot back. "I haven't trusted anybody in a year and a half."

I circled around her a bit, and if I were a dog I probably would have been sniffing at her tail trying to decide if she was my friend or not. "So now what?"

Chandra lay back. "You can trust me or not. I thought we wanted the same things. Guess the ball's in your court now. It sure isn't in mine."

I rubbed my eyes. Trust her or not. Raymond had told me not to trust her, but he'd told me I needed her, too. Hell, at the rate I was going, if I didn't trust her, the best way to ruin her life would be to stay close. But at this point, the only way out was through.

"Look, a lot has happened today." I told her about my big day, from visiting with Ray all the way to how my laptop had caught fire and the Joes were suddenly out of business. Somehow the second repetition wasn't as bad; I'd already told the authorities, so there was a cadence to it this time. Chandra listened, her knees drawn up to her chest.

"I just can't believe what bad luck it was," I said at last. "My battery couldn't have picked a worse time to explode. At least I saved Raymond's notes, though."

"There's no such thing as luck." She pulled her own laptop from the space between her bed and the night stand, then grabbed Raymond's papers from out of my hands. She sat cross-legged and straight-spined on the bed and got to work.

The things she did weren't a part of Raymond's instructions. Before long she was skimming through screenfuls of incomprehensible lines of code. She rubbed her cheekbone with one finger, her eyes narrowed. She cross-referenced with another file, and another. After a while, she grimaced and closed the machine.

"Well, I think we're completely screwed," she said. "Not much to do now but plan our funerals. We lost."

"What? What are you talking about?" Pink lines of code danced on her face as I looked at her, the afterimage burned into my retinas from staring at her screen.

She sank back onto her pillows and looked up at the ceiling. "Marjorie set a bomb for you."

"A bomb? In my laptop?!" I wondered how this would affect the Joes and their insurance claim. I'd have to make it right with them, dip into the trust, and—

"No, not that kind of bomb. This one, it was just theoretical last I knew. I didn't think they were that far along," she said. "They were waiting for somebody to access that executive summary you read, and they had a... a process waiting for it. That thing tried to do everything you could imagine to destroy either the machine accessing that data or else the person doing it."

"How is that possible?"

"The magic of automation. The software tries eighteen million changes every twenty seconds, and the hardware shows it which possibility would make a particle starburst light up all pretty-like." She smiled at me, but there was nothing happy about it. "You got out lucky that the battery in your laptop is the one that burst, and not the one where you have an aneurysm and drop dead on the spot."

"They could do that?"

"They sure as hell tried," she said.

"And now they know who looked at the file?"

She hesitated. “Not exactly,” she said. “The bomb was set to guard against access, but since you came in Ray’s back door, they won’t know who you are. If even Marjorie or Benjamin had accessed that page without defusing the bomb first, the same hunter-killer process would have gone off.”

“So... then we’re still safe?”

She shook her had. “Nope. They’ll know from the same logs I just looked at that the process went off, and which burst took place. Probably already got a text alerting them. I’d bet cold cash. So right now they’ll know that somewhere there was a burst laptop battery, and not much else. But as soon as Benjamin hears about that fire at the Buzz, and he finds out about your laptop... well, he’s certainly bright enough to put two and two together.”

“Maybe we’ll be lucky.”

“You know what I think about luck.” She looked away, studying the radiator under her window. “And there’s—something else you should know, as long as we’re putting all our cards on the table. About that prototype,” she said. “If they scale up, they’ll be like unto gods.”

“What the hell does that mean?”

She stopped pacing and stood in front of me, arms crossed, eyes hard and flat. “When we first set Verity up, if they wanted you dead, they could make a trigger for you getting hit by a bus. And if you got close enough to a bus while it’s trying that, it’s curtains for you.”

“But if there’s no bus in your neighborhood, or you’re in the middle of the ocean or something... ”

“Right. Zero potential there, nothing that can be nudged. You’re perfectly safe.”

“OK. But now it’s different?”

“Yeah. Smarter, and a lot more powerful. Like the bomb.

The software looks for different paths to get the desired outcome, no matter how unlikely, and keeps trying all the options." She grimaced. "If they want you dead and you're near a bus, you get hit by a bus. Or maybe you fall down the stairs and break your neck. Or you drown in the bathtub. Or you contract pneumonia, or a tweaker stabs you in broad daylight. Or— "

My mouth had fallen open as I got it. "Oh. Oh. It finds a way." On TV, the John Hughes movie was over. We'd missed the happy ever after and the credits were rolling.

"It's a very intense process, it takes a lot of computing power, but if you have enough money and enough time, you can have the system wait around for the thing you want to be possible, however briefly, and then make it happen. But the prototype makes it much, much worse."

I frowned. "Worse how?"

"The new hardware they're making, Prometheus. It can also instigate possibilities were there were none before. It makes more starbursts. The window of opportunity won't be a tiny window you can climb through anymore, so much as a goddamn highway you can take to anywhere you want."

She clicked off the TV, and the room went dark. "This isn't about the ability to game the stock market and make a few extra billion to retire on. Once they build this, they'll be able to do anything at all. No matter how unlikely it seems."

My heart was thudding fast in my chest, flooded with adrenaline but with nowhere to run. "Anything at all."

"They can topple governments," she said. "Manufacture plagues, maybe create earthquakes and hurricanes."

I waved weakly. "But maybe they can, like Benji told me, feed the hungry and avert wars. Don't you think they could use it for good?"

Chandra reached her hand to mine. "In all of human

history," she said, "has there ever yet been an innovation used only for good?"

And she was right, of course. If it's possible for a human being to use a tool to get a leg up on an enemy, real or imagined, there was no way to avoid it. Explosives. Atomic power. The internet itself.

"What can we do?" I asked.

"If there's anything you'd really miss from home, pack it up now, before he finds out what happened," she said. "And then get out of there. I think you're going to have to run like hell. Just like me."

chapter TWENTY-TWO

When I got back to my apartment, I couldn't do anything for a while but stand listlessly in the center of my living room, turning in slow circles to look at everything and wondering what exactly it is you pack when you're running away from a secret cabal with its eyes set on world domination via your dead body.

You'd think that the adrenaline would force some clarity of action into you. Instead, I was in the throes of muzzy-headed fatigue and already had an adrenaline hangover. A headache pulsed just above my eyes. I had no reserves left. Spent. Wrung out. Used up. But I had to get this done and get lost before Verity came to get me.

Focus, focus, no time to waste. I obviously couldn't bring my laptop, already reduced to slag back at the Joes' Buzz. Clothes, I thought. One thing I need is clothes. And a bag, I need a bag to carry everything in.

I grabbed my gym bag and pulled the fragrant, never-laundered sports bra and sweats from it, then abandoned the whole bag as too indelibly gym-odored to save. I had a set of monogrammed luggage from when my parents had sent me off to Europe in the summer before college, but that was too heavy to even consider. I turned slowly, looking for anything else that might be suitable. My eyes fell on Benji's go pack, dumped in its usual spot next to my shabby sofa.

Benji. He was here.

I bit my lip and wondered if there was any chance he might have forgotten his bag here the last time he was over. Yeah, wishful thinking.

I prodded open the door to my bedroom. The night was already dissolving into the first breath of dawn. Benji's jaw was limned in silver as he lay, hand cradling his face, lips soft and arm splayed protectively over the spot where I should have been sleeping. I crept toward my closet and, as silently as I could manage, grabbed an armful of clean laundry off the floor. I edged out of my room again.

I sorted through it: A sweatshirt, a couple of T-shirts, a clean pair of jeans. It would have to do. I'd want some underwear, though, and some other things while I was here, since I didn't know when — if! — I'd ever make it back. My grandmother's brooch in my jewelry box, the little cut crystal perfume bottle I'd bought for myself in Paris, the shoebox full of dried rose petals and movie tickets and other memorabilia of a life that wouldn't be mine much longer. I ventured back into my bedroom, holding my breath and moving my weight gradually from one foot to the next so the floor wouldn't creak.

This time, though, Benji's eyes were open, watching me. I froze in the doorway, then fixed a rigid smile on my face. "Go back to sleep, honey," I said.

He sat up. "Cut the act, M. I know."

My pulse thudded faster and my breath quickened. I crossed my arms tight across my ribs, but I fought to keep my voice easy. "Know what?"

His lips curled down at the edges. "I know all of it. I know there was a fire at your coffee shop tonight, and I know how it happened."

My hands dropped to my sides. I walked over to the edge of the bed and dropped to sit by him. "What are you going to do?" I asked him, my voice low.

He studied me for a moment, and then his finger lifted to trace the line of my neck down to my shoulder. "I don't know," he said. "Turns out I don't know a lot of things. Who are you really, Mira? What's your game?"

"You know who I am." I started to reach toward him, but retrieved my fingers before I made contact.

"Then how did you get to that file? Don't tell me it was an accident this time. Fool me twice, shame on me." He sat up, then, and scrubbed his fingers through his hair. It stood up like a bird's nest. "You make me crazy, M," he said. "I don't know if it was something you did or if it was me all along... "

"You know I couldn't have made you do anything you didn't want to do," I said.

"I wonder about that." His eyes were lined with red from lack of sleep. Probably mine were, too.

I pressed my hands between my knees. "What are you going to do?" I asked again.

"I want to run away with you," he said.

"So let's do it," I whispered. "We can run away together and forget about all of this."

He shook his head. "She'd never let us go."

"We could find a way to make her," I pleaded. "I know we could."

He looked me in the eye, then, and I wondered how I'd ever thought his eyes were puppy-dog soft, when clearly they were made of stone. "I don't want to give it up, M."

I twisted my shoulders. "Money is easy," I said.

"Money," he scoffed. "You're right, money is easy. But what I want is the chance to make history. Mira, we could take the world and make it right."

"But you'd be robbing everybody else of their free will," I said. "Don't you think that's wrong? You always said you believe in democracy, didn't you? Freedom of speech, freedom of the press, freedom of information— "

"Stop trying to throw my words back at me," he said. "This is about trying to create the best possible world."

"For you, maybe," I said.

"For everybody."

"But who are you to decide what's best for everybody? How the hell do you know what the whole rest of the world wants? You're just a... a little boy who wants to play god with the whole planet."

His eyes had narrowed. "I love you, M, but you're not making my choice any harder, are you?"

"So you won't give it up," I breathed.

"I can't. I can't leave all of that up to someone else."

"Not even for me?"

He caressed my shoulder. "Not even for you. Some things are more important than... personal weaknesses."

After worrying about it for so long, this conversation wasn't really that bad the second time around. Maybe because so many worse things had happened in between. "So I'm a personal weakness." I touched his great-grandma's diamonds-and-sapphires hanging from my neck. "I guess we're done here."

His eyes never left me. "I'm supposed to call Marjorie right now," he said, "and tell her you're here."

"You were waiting here because she told you to."

"Maybe," he said. There was no uncertainty in his voice.

"What were you supposed to do with me if you found me?"

It took him a little while to calculate the right answer. "We weren't sure you were still alive," he said. "Marjorie thought you might have died in the fire and it hadn't hit the news yet."

"Clearly no."

"But if I found you... I was supposed to finish the job. You're an enemy of Verity now. There's no coming back from this."

"No," I said softly. "There wouldn't be, would there?"

He said nothing.

"Are you going to do it, then? Kill me?"

He squeezed my hand. "I don't want to."

"So we're at an impasse," I said. "You won't come with me, and I can't go with you."

"So it would seem."

And then I saw it, the analyzing glint in his eyes, like he was getting close to making a decision. I wondered if he weren't using that chip in his brain already to set up— something. A lump rose in my throat. "Let me go," I blurted.

"I don't think I can," he said.

"Marjorie will never know I've been here," I said. "Just... just let me grab a few things, and I'll leave. You'll tell her I never came back again, your conscience will be clear, and... and after that... "

"After that?"

"I'll stay out of your way. I'll disappear. Maybe we'll never see each other again."

He closed his eyes, but his fists stayed clenched by his sides on top of my homely quilt. The sun had crept up a little further while we talked, and color had begun to return to the room, enough that I could see the tattoo on his bicep, red and blue and silver twisted together in the shape I now knew was a starburst of probabilities requited. He was branded in the flesh, and for him there really was no going back.

"Go," he said. "You have ten minutes to get what you can and get out of here. After that all bets are off."

I bowed my head. "It's a deal." Then I scrambled. If he said ten minutes, I'd want to be gone in five. I stuffed a few clothes into the previously rejected gym bag. My spare credit cards, the shoebox of mementoes, a few granola bars, and a first aid kit. The urban survival gear Benji had given me three days after the first time he'd slept over.

He watched me pack up without comment, but I knew the minutes were ticking by like a metronome in his head.

When I was done, I paused by the side of the bed, unsure what the right protocol was for our situation. Emily Post certainly never covered how to say goodbye to your boyfriend in the few minutes he gave you to flee before he'd deliver on a promise to kill you dead.

"I guess this is it," I said.

"Yeah. Mira? It's been great. I'm going to miss you."

"Me too," I said. I nearly bent down to kiss him, but I felt like that would be overstepping the invisible wall that had sprung up between us. Instead I pressed his grandmother's diamonds-and-sapphires into his hand. "Take care of yourself."

His fingers closed around the ring. "*You* don't need to worry about *me*."

"Thanks." I paused again, awkward to the finish, then pulled the bag up on my shoulder. "Bye." I turned and walked toward the front door.

"Mira?" he called after me.

"Yes?" I spun back, flooded with sudden hope that he'd change his mind and make a stand with me.

He stood in the doorway to my bedroom, my blanket on the floor behind him. The sunlight flooding in silhouetted him so I couldn't see the expression on his face. But I didn't need to;

his voice was ice cold. "If I see you again, I won't give you another chance like this. From now on, we're going to be enemies."

"I know," I said. And then I walked out.

Chandra and I and my daddy's car all met up again to plan our next step in a brunch spot pleasantly far from anyone who could possibly know either one of us. The diner was a faux-'50s work of high kitsch, all pink neon and curvy deco embellishment. There were tiny five-song jukeboxes at every table. The place smelled of fried eggs and sour coffee. There was a single harried waitress on duty — I'd be harried too in that pink shirtdress and beehive wig — and she jerked her head toward a table by the front window when she saw us. The floor was a chessboard in black and cream linoleum. It was slippery, though whether from wax or ambient grease I couldn't say.

The place reminded me of Eli and ice cream and all the things I would never get back again.

I thumped my bag into the booth and sat down across from Chandra. "So now what?"

She licked her lips and started to say something, closed her mouth, focused on her cup of coffee instead.

"Come on, you're all I have left," I said. "Don't chicken out on me now."

"I found something I needed to show you," she said. "I did a little digging while you were packing, and... well, see for yourself." She hauled out her laptop and set it in front of me. It showed me inscrutable columns of notes and dates and numbers in a too-small font.

"I don't understand, what is this?"

"Revisions."

"To what?"

"To you."

I grew dizzy. The letters on the screen smeared into unreadability, and the clattering sounds of the diner turned into a sort of dull, distant roar. "Shit."

Chandra took a deep breath. "I had to know where your head was, so I used Ray's credentials and snooped around in some ultra-locked-down parts of the system at Verity. Secret sandbox. Things of Ben's that even Marjorie can't see, and the other way around."

"So what exactly did they do to me?" The waitress came over and delivered my cup of coffee and a bowl full of half-and-half cups. I waved her away without ordering anything else.

Chandra leaned across the table and turned her computer so she could see the screen, too. "See here? That's you, and it looks like you were nudged to have an argument with Marjorie leveraging Blue Ocean to persuade her you should be employed at Verity— I guess Ben didn't want to do his own dirty work. But that's not all."

She tapped a few keys and the columns changed. "Once I was looking I figured in for an inch, in for a mile, so I kept poking around. And guess what?"

"What?"

"Our boy Ben was nudged to break up with you in the first place," she said. "Somebody at Verity wanted that boy to be single real bad."

I thought about that company photo. "Marjorie is in love with him."

Chandra sat up straighter, an incredulous look on her face. "*That's* what you think?"

I shook my head. "She always seemed jealous of him. Was I right, then?"

She chortled. "Sort of, but not... really. Really not. It's complicated. The point is, they've been making changes to affect each other — even changes to each other — and hiding their tracks. You're just a ping-pong ball in their game."

"It felt like it was me."

"That's the whole problem," she said. "We can't let them continue fucking with people like this, interfering with minds and lives that don't belong to them. We have to put a stop to this once and for all. It's the right thing to do."

"Easy-peasy." I poured too much cream into my coffee. "Tell me about you and Benji."

For a second she looked startled.

"I mean it." I took a sip of coffee. It was so nasty that I put a pinch of salt in it to make it vaguely palatable.

"Me and Benjamin Adler," she said. Her voice held a contemplative note I hadn't heard before: It was amused and bitter rolled together.

"You were together, weren't you? Even though you said you weren't."

"No," she said softly. "That's not what happened."

She set the spoon down and folded her hands neatly. "I need to be straight with you," she said. "But this isn't going to make me look very good."

"Nobody's perfect," I said, but I'd already started to tense up.

She nodded, but her mind's eye had gone somewhere else already, and I felt like she hadn't even heard me.

"It wasn't Ben," she said. "It was Marjorie. She was so perfect. Sharp as a razor, funny, ambitious, hot. I was crazy about her, but she... wasn't so crazy about me. To begin with."

Ah-hah. I scoured everything I'd ever said to Chandra to see if I'd ever said anything egregiously stupid that I'd have to apologize for now. "So you and Marjorie wound up... together?"

"Not at first," she said. "We were just friendly. In the

same group of friends, I mean. So she let me share space for my research. I've already told you. We spent a lot of time in that server closet together. I hadn't told anyone about my nudges, because I knew I'd sound a little psycho, but the knowing was just clawing at my brain, trying to get out. So picture it, all of this time alone together."

She fell silent when the waitress came back. We ordered omelets and toast all around. "So what happened?" I persisted.

She added sugar to her newly refilled coffee, stirred it in. "Call it the law of unintended consequences," she said. "We were alone together at the office one night and ordered in pizza. Marjorie asked me how my mad-scientist experiment was going, so I told her some really general, high-level things to blow her off."

"But not the details?"

"I got carried away and lost my judgment, from being tired and from— from being there with her. I wanted to impress her, you know? And I really needed to spill this secret and have somebody not think I was some mental case. So I started to tell her what I was finding, just in little bits, all about the data I was seeing and how crazy it was. And everything kind of fell out."

"Of course it did," I said.

"She kept pushing me for what kinds of changes I was talking about. Could I make Elvis alive, and elected president? Could I make Canada a state? So I told her about the starbursts, the need for a receptive state— that vulnerable moment."

I nodded. "All of that early work."

Chandra took a deep breath. "By that time she was flirting like mad, and so was I, so... well. She asked about changing people, and I thought she was just being goofy, too. I laughed and told her I didn't think it could be done — how could you know when somebody was in a receptive state? I changed her bio to say we were a couple, as an example of how it couldn't work. Next thing I knew she was kissing me, and then we were in bed and our clothes weren't."

"And you fell in love?" The vinyl upholstery of the diner's seats squeaked as I shifted my feet.

Her lips puckered, like she'd tasted a lemon. "Well, we hooked up, anyway," she said. "Love, I don't know about that." She touched two fingers to her cheek, watching that ghost of a night play out again at the bottom of her cup. "It was fun while it lasted."

The wheels in my head were clicking. "So that's when you figured out you can change a person's mind and make them do something."

She nodded. "We talked about it after. She thought maybe she was in a receptive mental state and the change was that nudge at the right time. Or at least she'd never thought of me that way before. I wasn't so sure, and who wants to think she got laid because of hypnotic suggestion or something?— Sorry, no offense," she added when I frowned. "It wasn't something I wanted to pursue, though. You could conduct an ethical study — people choosing between apples and oranges, that kind of thing — but I was worried about unethical applications."

"You mean like forming a secret cabal to rule the world?"

"Yeah," she said. "Just like that."

Our food arrived then, and we ate in silence for a few minutes. I avoided Chandra's eyes and flipped through the mini-jukebox. I punched in a Bing Crosby tune that was unaccountably present on it. Then I toyed with my toast, peeling the crust off and eating it in nibbles. "Listen, I know this has been hard for you, but... look, it's been hard for me, too."

Her hand reached across the table toward mine. Her skin was hot. "I know," she said, quieter. "I don't really deserve friends like you."

Then she lifted the salt shaker and turned it around in her hands, though she was looking out the window at the street all the while. A little boy pressed his nose to the glass and stared goggle-eyed at us before his mother grabbed him by the forearm and hauled him away into the crowd. "But look, I have a plan for ending this. One last thing we can do with Ray's access."

"What is it?" I asked.

She tossed her head, her long braid bouncing and then settling back into place.

"We're going to burn Verity to the ground."

chapter TWENTY-THREE

A triumphant smile played on Chandra's face. "I looked over those notes Ray gave you, and he included how to get into Verity's hosting facility. We can walk in and take out their whole server farm. Nuke the hard disks, destroy all the hardware, hopefully take down all the backups, too. Verity will be cooked."

"No way."

"We're still in the game. We can knock them out."

I rubbed at the spot between my eyes, where my exhaustion headache was growing up to be big and strong. I wasn't up to arson and vandalism just at the moment. "Can I get some sleep first?"

"Of course. We can't afford to make any mistakes, and if we're this exhausted... mistakes will be made. Let's find somewhere to rest and regroup." She flagged our waitress for the check.

"Can you drive? I don't think I'm safe on the road by now." I passed her my keys.

"Yeah, you had a long night, didn't you?"

"You don't even know." I filled her in on the highlights of my early-morning encounter with Benji while we settled up and walked to the car.

"That's cold," she said. She started the engine and eased

into traffic. "I told you from the start that he wasn't the guy you thought he was."

"I know, I know. But when it was good, it was so good."

"At least you know where you stand." She gunned the engine to pass a box truck with ads for a halal butcher on the sides.

"Yeah, I stand with crosshairs on my forehead. Ignorance was bliss."

Eventually we stopped at a motel off the highway. Chandra paid for us in advance, in cash from her lottery winnings. We both crashed hard and slept uneventfully until close to sundown. When we woke, it was time to nail down our plan.

Verity's dedicated hosting facility, the place where all of their servers were, was only an hour or so upstate. "We'll hit some gas stations along the way and get a bunch of gas," Chandra said. "Then we get in with a little help from Ray, and burn that motherfucker down."

"Right," I said. "Let's get to work."

We made our way down the highway in fits and starts, smiling our way through a few performances of an embarrassing tale of running out of gas — just a little further down the highway. No, don't worry, we have it under control.

The sharp, heady smell of gasoline filled the car and made us giddy. Close to our destination, we drove by a state police car at the side of the road and held our breaths, hoping he didn't see anything suspicious about us. "Good thing you're behind the wheel this time," Chandra murmured. "He'd pull me over in a hot second."

We kept rolling, but it was a while again before we relaxed. "We might go to prison for this," I said at last. "I mean we might get caught."

"We might." Chandra rolled down her window to let the wind blow out some fumes. "But if we get the job done it'll be worth it."

Our ultimate destination was a windowless behemoth of steel and concrete. We sat in the parking lot in the dark, developing our final battle plan. The place was empty.

A forest of bristling antennae and satellite dishes on grew from the top of the building. "We need to knock out that one," Chandra said, pointing upward. "That's a device based on my—the Prometheus prototype."

I squinted but couldn't make out which one in the darkness. "How do we get inside?"

She played with the end of her braid for a moment. "It's a neat trick," she said. "Ray gave us a toolset that can knock out the offsite security systems for a while. But somebody is bound to notice and put it back online eventually. We've got about half an hour, if we're lucky."

"So we have to get in and out that fast?"

"Yeah. Faster, if we can. Got everything?"

I patted the pliers and screwdriver she'd given me, fresh bought from a mom and pop hardware store next to one of our gas stations.

"OK. Let's get moving." She turned to her computer, already connected to Verity's own wifi and primed to run the code that would cripple their security for the next twenty minutes. I popped the trunk and hauled out two big gas cans, each full to the brim. Chandra grabbed two of her own.

I half-expected a guard to stop us on our way in, but the building was deserted. Chandra nodded at a camera in the corner, already disabled. "They've got a central monitoring station, but they don't keep anyone staffed here," she murmured. "Makes it less vulnerable to the 'I forgot my badge please let me in or I'll get fired' approach."

She punched a long string of numbers into a keypad, and we entered Verity's server room.

The racks of servers spread away in neat rows before us. The hum echoed in my head, like a civilization of bees had set up an empire in there. The chill crept swiftly though my sweat-damp clothes and made me shiver. The floor was covered in panels that echoed under our steps, as though they were hollow, and the lights were dim. A multitude of quiet LEDs shone, some steady and some flickering madly, like the eyes of a thousand digital gods marking our presence.

"This is the right place?" I asked.

Chandra nodded and led the way forward. "Remember what I told you," she said. Her voice was low, almost inaudible over the white noise sung by all of those machines thinking in parallel. I nodded and took one last deep breath. It was almost over. My hands shook a little.

She caught my eye and put her hand on my shoulder; the weight of it was comforting. "We can do this," she said. "It's going to work. Now get ready."

She pulled a keyboard out of one of the racks and tap-tapped away at lightning speed. I went behind the row and eyed the cables, working out which went where. The priests who attended to this temple of electronic intelligence were diligent, and the cabling was all neatly tied together in rainbow-hued bundles with plastic zipcords. I uncapped my gas cans and waited.

Chandra went into Verity through Ray's secret back door, and then began a series of actions she could only take at a hard-wired admin station. She locked out every other admin account to prevent interference. Then she gave us our lives back: first she locked our entries against future changes, then she removed even Ray's double-secret backdoor ultra-mega-supreme access to them.

Next she plugged in her little thumb drive and waited, fingers drumming madly, as it began its dirty work. It deleted all the rest of the user accounts, admin or not. Then it worked its way backwards through the special secret sandbox, removing triggers, killing processes, disabling permissions, shifting pointers and deleting files until the entire data store was completely scrambled.

The process would also seek out what backups it could get to, and write them over with garbage. The random strings of ones and zeroes would look to the naked eye like they had before, but the life would be sucked out of them, all meaning lost, like a body once the soul had fled.

After that, even the codebase of Verity itself would be destroyed. Chandra's little present would follow every path and destroy every script, every service, every configuration file, until there was nothing left.

Chandra had said there would be no helping the offsite backups, not without putting innocent lives in danger. We destroyed what we had here and sent feelers probing to delete what else we could find, and hoped that would be enough. She tapped her fingers against her thumbs as she waited for the destruction to hit its tipping point. I shivered again, this time from an intolerable mix of fear, hope, anticipation.

"It's running." She nodded once, then stepped back from the keyboard. "This is going to take a while. Let's leave the gas here and go up to the roof to kill the special hardware in the meantime."

I followed her up two echoing flights of stairs toward the roof access. That's where we hit our first big obstacle — the door was locked, and the old-fashioned way, with a chain and padlock.

I panicked. "What do we do? Do we have to leave it in place?"

Chandra kicked the door in frustration, then looked at it a little harder. "Wait," she said. "We can take out the hinges." It ate at our time; we were only too aware of every second that passed by as we pried the hinge pins out of their housings. They were half-rusted in place and badly in need of oil. Once they were out, Chandra pulled the door open on the hinged side. It hung askew from the chain. "Come on."

She led me over to something that looked like a satellite dish. "This is it," she said. "Help bust it up." She brandished her screwdriver and set to work prying open its access panel. I used my pliers to cut every cable I could find, and then punched holes in its delicate aluminum face for good measure. Chandra completely removed a circuit board from its innards, then dropped it on the ground. When she stomped on it, it made a delicious crunching sound.

I checked my watch. "We've been here for twenty minutes already. Damn."

"Let's hurry." We raced back to server room to perform its baptism of fire.

When we got there, Chandra checked on the progress of her pet tornado of destruction. "It's done," she said. "It's killed. Now let's make sure it doesn't come back."

I took one gas can and handed her another. We sloshed their contents all around. The fumes made me dizzy, and at least one server popped and smoked as the gas trickled into its innards. When Verity's servers were sufficiently fueled up, I handed Chandra the match.

"This was your war," I told her. "And it's your victory."

She took the match from me and bowed her head for a moment. In prayer or contemplation, I couldn't say. The match lit on the second try.

It fell.

The gasoline caught.

Flames licked up more rapidly than I would have thought, and as quick as anything, the fire alarms went on. At this point the dry fire suppressants should've switched on, but Chandra's gremlins had knocked them offline. "Come on," I said, plucking at Chandra's sleeve, "we have to get out of here." She stood there another second, hypnotized by the fire, and then a sprinkler head went off and broke the spell.

More of the servers emitted sharp pops as we hurried out; we hadn't expected the fire to take, but if it had done any damage, then great. If it hadn't, well, the water would surely finish the job.

It was done. We won. Now it was time to escape.

We hurried out of the building as quickly as we had come in, trailing smoke and steam behind us like a comet's tail. We burst out into the parking lot already laughing aloud with surprise at how simple it had been. "We should get out of here fast," Chandra said. "Before the fire department gets here."

I peeled out of the parking lot and off into the night. We gave ourselves high-fives and settled back into the seats of our car, giddy with victory.

"Thank god for Raymond," I said.

Chandra pulled her laptop from the back seat and flashed a smile at me. "I can't believe it's all over."

"What are you going to do next?" I asked.

"Before I get too involved making plans, I want to see the 404 not found where Verity should be," she said. She tethered to her phone and then refreshed, waiting for the browser to bring up its nail on the coffin.

Except that it didn't. The Verity landing page came up, with its swooshy sleek logo and ascetic design. I swerved a little as I leaned to get a closer look. Her eyebrows plummeted together. "It's still up. Why is it still up?"

I glanced in the rear-view mirror at the burning server facility behind us. "Um," I said. "Is it possible that they had another one already set up? In the cloud or something?"

"Not the cloud— they'd never trust their data to someone else, too big a security risk."

"Maybe the new place doesn't have the right hardware, at least," I said, hopeful. "Maybe it's just data now... just a regular news site like they always pretended."

"Fat chance." She banged her head against the headrest, eyes shut tight. "I don't understand. They were planning to move, but everything said they didn't have the money without Blue Ocean. And you took care of that, right? So what happened?"

A terrible feeling settled into my gut. I slowed and stopped at the side of the road.

"What are you doing?"

I pulled out my phone and dialed a little-used number. "Hang on, I have to check something."

It rang once, twice, it picked up. "Hello?"

"Daddy. Hi, it's me," I said. "Listen, I had a quick question for you about Verity— about the Blue Ocean thing."

"Oh hi, honey!" My father's voice was a little hoarse; we were well past the scotching hour. "Don't worry, me and Ben sorted everything out. The wire went through the same day you called me, I saw to it personally. But — he didn't tell you, did he? He said he wanted it to be a surprise at the engagement party!"

Engagement party? Wait. The terrible feeling in my

gut spread through my limbs. "But daddy. I told you the due diligence should— "

"I know, sweetheart, and it speaks very well of you that you wanted to be so above-board, but we'd already nailed that down before little Michael... well, before the delays started. Our lawyers do good work. So in the end we all talked about it and decided to go full steam ahead. Consider it our engagement gift to you!"

A shrill laugh escaped me. "Engagement. Gift. Daddy, you really shouldn't have. Really."

"Oh, nonsense, I'm just looking out for my girl. You know that."

"Yeah, I do know that." I glanced over at Chandra, pale and hollow-eyed beside me. "Thanks, daddy. That's all I wanted. Love you, talk soon." I clicked my phone off.

Chandra shook her head slowly, then sank forward to rest her head on the dashboard. "We're screwed, aren't we?"

chapter TWENTY-FOUR

Chandra doesn't lose easy. She only wallowed in defeat for about ninety seconds before she took a deep breath. "We need to find out where that other facility is, and then maybe we can do a repeat performance. It'll be rough, but it's the only shot we have." She cracked her knuckles. "Mira, do you still have that thumb drive with all of Benji's email on it? There might be something in there that says where they were moving. And you can't be so worried about betraying his trust at this point."

I nodded numbly. I'd lost my computer at the Buzz, my phone, my purse. But that stupid thumb drive had been hidden at the bottom of my gym bag, so Benji wouldn't find it. "Yeah," I said. "Go ahead, look in my bag. Everything I have is in the thumb drive with the butterfly on it."

"Butterfly? Seriously?"

"Shut up."

She snagged the bag from the back seat and rummaged though it, then settled in to review emails while I drove aimlessly away from the scene of the crime. I had to physically bite my tongue to keep from asking her for a running description of what she was finding, and instead fiddled with the radio. The Talking Heads came on, singing Psycho Killer. I changed it.

It took an hour driving in aimless circles, maybe two, but

eventually my patience wore out. "So?" I asked. "Did I miss anything?"

"You missed a whole lot of things," Chandra said. "Damn, but I wish you could have given me all of this six weeks ago. Would've saved us both a whole lot of trouble."

"Shut up," I said again, sounding defensive even to myself. "I was doing the best I could with what I knew at the time."

"Yeah," she sighed, "I know. Anyway, you can't change the past, can you?" She pursed her lips at the screen. "Let's just hope it's not too late, now that we've finally got it all together. And at least now I know exactly what they're doing."

"OK, so where is the new facility?" I asked.

"I still don't know *that*. Keep your boots on and keep driving," she snapped. "I'm not a miracle worker."

I drove in silence as the night passed by us, looking over at Chandra periodically to try to read her expression. There was nothing to see there but the same fear I felt. The road noise rumbling under the tires sounded just as uneasy.

"There's not enough cell service here, we must be in a dead spot," she said after a while. "We need to find good internet again. —Turn into the next suburb."

We prowled slowly down some street named Rosewood or something equally arboreal as she trolled for an insecure wireless access point. We found one at a modest neo-colonial with white gingerbread and ceramic turtles sunning themselves in the garden.

The network was charmingly named "EffTehFeds."

"Bet they leave it open on purpose," she murmured. We rolled to a stop in front of their house, nestled against the curb. I reclined the driver's seat and shielded my eyes from the early morning sun while I waited for Chandra to figure out where we were going.

"Well," she said at last, "I have good news and bad news."

"Hit me."

"The good news is the other facility isn't crazy far away," she said. "It's in Pennsylvania. We could get there in a few hours if you drive fast enough."

"A few hours isn't far?"

"They could've moved to Bangalore."

"Oh. Right. So what's the bad news?"

She pointed to a few lines on her screen. "See this? They're trying to lock us out of the new system."

"Will it work?"

"No, not without rewriting the system from scratch," she said. "Ray's access is hard-coded in. Sneaky bastard. But... that's not all."

A little face peered out at us from the colonial, smudged with chocolate. A little fist smeared blobs of chocolate on the glass, too. The child waved, cautiously, and I waved back. The world was waking up around us.

Chandra skipped to another window. "It's your page. There are a lot of pending changes queued up."

"What kind of changes?" I asked slowly, though I knew the answer already.

She scrolled through lines of code.

"I can take it, Chandra."

"I'll spare you the details, but... they want you dead."

"I'm safe, though, right? Because you locked it? And because they don't know where I am."

She frowned at the screen and chewed on her thumbnail. "I'm not sure," she said. "None of it has gone through yet, but that doesn't mean it never will. It looks like some of the stuff we did last night affected this copy, too, but not all of it? And some of what they're doing... I don't really understand it all."

The earth rocked under us. The car's springs screeched. It subsided, came again, stopped. The little face in the window disappeared.

Chandra and I looked at each other, both subdued and ashen. "Was that... them?" I asked. Death by earthquake. At least I'd go out big.

"I don't see how it could be."

"Is that a chance you want to take?"

"... Not really. We'd better hurry," she said.

I started up the car and turned around in the driveway of Mr. And Mrs. EffTehFeds. "Where in Pennsylvania do I need to be, exactly?"

"I'm grabbing directions," she said. "Head south and west, okay?"

Everything was quiet, except for the sound of Chandra tapping away at the keyboard now and again, scouring the information I'd stolen from Benji's computer looking for a magic bullet that would make it all better.

We got onto the highway and blew by an assortment of semis and tanker trucks. The road shimmered like desert oases or pools of burning oil, but always receded into the distance. Like Benji, I thought wildly, always looking like he was right there in front of me, when he was really so far away he might as well have never been there at all.

Biology being what it is, we eventually hit a rest stop. The facilities were utilitarian and inexplicably wet; there was no flooding nor leaking faucet, but the entire floor and the full expanse of the counters were completely covered with water.

I looked a wreck. Dark circles for miles, hair wild and a little greasy from needing a shower, and I might've changed my underwear but even the clean stuff had been spending time in that gym bag. Hell, I probably smelled just as bad.

How many hours had it been since I'd said goodbye to Benji for the last time? Was it last night I'd set fire to the Joes' pride and joy, and melted away instead of helping grease their insurance claim? Or was it the night before that?

Chandra grabbed a little carb-and-fat-heavy sustenance for us, in the form of cinnamon rolls the size of our heads plus vats of iced vanilla latte. The lattes were subpar; too much syrup and a poor hand with the espresso. But I wasn't in a position to complain on a professional level about the standards and scruples of a coffee place in a truck stop in New Jersey.

Not that I was a professional anymore, come to think of it.

The cinnamon roll, at least, was warm and gooey, if so sweet it hurt my teeth. I tore off chunks and popped them into my mouth with one hand while I steered with the other.

It didn't take long before all that sugar induced a little nausea. Or maybe it was the nerves and stress getting to me. We'd pulled off a perfect raid already, but could we do it again? Even now that they were probably ready for us? Not that we had any choice but try.

With Chandra working as my navigator, we traveled through deep gorges blasted in the hillside. Raw ancient rock rose above us. Trees as old as our nation stood taller still. Every now and again we passed a wellspring cascading down the rock walls, moss and ferns framing each waterfall like paparazzi.

I took extra care to obey the speed limit. Indeed, I was the most cautious driver you've ever seen; I kept my distance from other vehicles, both hands on the wheel (well, except to grab chunks of cinnamon roll), kept my eyes peeled, and didn't engage in conversation.

Nobody could keep that up forever, and especially not me. "Can Ray's code get us into the new building?" I asked after a while.

"I doubt it," she said. "They'd pick new ones for the new site as a routine security measure."

"How will we get in, then?"

She mulled over that for a while. "I don't know," she said. "I'm sure we can figure something out."

We fell silent again as a carrier laden with shiny new SUVs passed me on the left. The driver tipped his Maple Leafs cap and winked. "So... this new place. Do you know anything about it at all? That might help our odds?" I asked her.

"It's tricky," Chandra said. "For one thing, it looks like they're a lot further along in deploying Prometheus than I expected." She stirred the ice in her coffee. "So OK, the software they've written for it works like this. They tie the AI to a whole array of these prototype controllers, and they teach it a little bit about what kinds of nudges result in what kinds of outcomes, right? So they teach it all the ways a person could die, or all of the accidents that could happen to destroy a file, or... " she trailed off.

"Or all of the ways a data center could be completely destroyed?"

"Yeah," she said. "We could try that, now that we know where it is." She opened a new window and started typing.

"But in the meanwhile it's looking for a way to kill us."

"Yeah, it is. We might've fucked up their chances, though, with our first hit. Still, if they're firing up Prometheus, that creates a field that destabilizes the horizon of probability. A... like a reality disrupter. A random event doesn't have to be quite so random anymore."

"... That doesn't sound so good."

"It isn't. If they're looking to kill you, then it makes it more likely you'll... I don't know, choke to death on that next bite of cinnamon roll. The specifics don't have to be so well defined."

I had been reaching for another chunk of roll when she said that, but at the thought I shuddered and put the pastry down, back in its styrofoam clamshell. "Pleasant thought, that."

"Well, would you rather not know?"

"I was much, much happier before I knew any of this. So yes."

Traffic slowed and stopped ahead of us. Ambulances and firefighters blew by on the expressway, lights whirling and sirens blaring. I craned my neck to see over the line of cars. "What's going on? Accident? Construction?"

"This is killing our time," Chandra said. "I'm worried about what can happen while we're stuck here."

We eased by the car carrier full of SUVs that had passed us. Well, the one that had been full of SUVs. Now it was angled off the side of the road with a ten-car wreck behind it, some of them apparently the same shiny vehicles that had been chained to the truck when it passed us.

The officer was interviewing the truck driver in the Maple Leafs cap. I rolled my window down and slowed as we rolled by to eavesdrop. "It was the damnedest thing," he said. "I was driving along and all of a sudden the cars started rolling off like all the tires had come unlocked... I've been driving twenty years now and never saw anything like it before."

Behind me, someone honked. "Just hurry," Chandra said. "We have to get out of here."

I sped up, both hands on the wheel. "Reality disruptor up and running?" I asked her quietly.

"Maybe a test," she said. "I'd say be careful, but there's no way of predicting a freak accident, so I don't know if it would do us any good."

Fair enough. But I moved into the slow lane and double-checked my seat belt just in case.

The facility reminded me of a military installation. A chain-link fence ten feet high ran along the road, the gaps filled in with black plastic to prevent spies and passers-by from seeing much. In one stretch, the slats had been torn away by weather, giving us a glimpse of the inside.

Ribbed beige buildings squatted in the distance surrounded by a never-ending plain of anemic grass. There were no trees, no bushes. Instead, Verity had planted rows and rows of antennae and parabolic dishes with delicate aluminum faces. "Those are more of the Prometheus things. Reality disruptors." It wasn't a question.

Chandra swore extensively. "With that many you could make anything happen. I hope they're not all working yet."

We drove along the perimeter until we found an empty gatehouse. The gate was closed with the same ten-foot chain link that surrounded the rest of the compound. A heavy-duty camera on a tall pole watched the entryway.

I nodded at the camera and kept rolling by. "I bet there are security guys watching from a nice cushy office somewhere inside."

"I bet you're right," Chandra said. "Let's get out of its line of sight."

The access road crunched under the tires as we traveled further down the perimeter. "But how will we get in?"

"Climb," she said.

"What if the fence is electrified?"

"Won't be," she said. "The magnetic field created by an electric fence would interfere with the data center, and especially the Prometheus arrays. Here, stop here."

"You sure about that?" I asked. It seemed like an awfully big risk to take.

She rolled her eyes as she climbed out of the car. “Of course I am,” she said. And then she walked forward and set one hand on the chain link.

Nothing happened.

I laughed, nervous and high-pitched like a bird call. “OK then, fence-jumping it is.”

We hauled ourselves over the fence, climbing up and then down one white-knuckled handhold after another. I dropped the last few feet on the other side, then caught Chandra’s bag while she climbed down more gingerly. Her skirt got caught in the wires at the top; she swore and then tore it free. But she, too, made it down safely.

We turned to face the job ahead of us.

chapter TWENTY-FIVE

The array of massive starburst makers filled the field all the way to the horizon, spaced evenly fifty feet apart from one another.

"Jesus, how many of these things are there?" I asked.

Chandra shook her head slowly. "This is insane. How much did this cost?" She walked forward and pulled an insulated access panel off the stem of one of the metal blossoms, revealing a core of wires and circuit boards. "It doesn't look like it's been activated yet. Or at least it's not on right now. Thank god for small blessings." She tossed her braid over her shoulder. "This makes me wonder, though... "

"Yeah?"

"Trouble in paradise," she said. "There was nothing in Ben's documents that even hinted at this scale, and there's no way this was built all in the last few weeks. I think he didn't know. I think Marjorie might be trying to cut him out. Ten little Indians, you know? First Ray, then me... "

"So you think he's in trouble?" I asked.

She gave me a level look. "Why, does that bother you?"

I thought about it. If he came to a bad end this way, it would be despite my efforts, not because of them. "No," I said. "No worries on my account. He had his big fat chance, Chandra. I asked him to run away with me and he said no."

She snorted and turned back to the access panel, shifting wires to get a better look. "Give up the path to godhood? Right. Even if he did really love you, and I'm not sure that was ever in him."

"It was worth a shot." I crossed my arms and stepped back a few feet. "Haven't you ever been in love?"

Chandra didn't look at me. "If I had never been in love," she said, "none of this would be happening."

She aimed a pen light deeper into the disrupter's innards. "If I could hijack this connection," she trailed off, staring at the bundles of wires and circuit boards. She pulled a multi-tool out of her pocket and started cutting wires.

Then my phone rang. It was Ben.

Chandra looked at me, her eyes sharp. "Answer it," she ordered.

I picked up. "Hi, sweetie," I said, as causally as I could manage. "What's up?"

"Don't try to play me," he snarled. "I know where you are and I know what you're trying to do."

"You know where I am?" I repeated, so Chandra would hear. She nodded, once: message received. She emptied her bag onto the disruptor's concrete pad and rummaged for tools.

"You're not the only one who can play spy games, M," he said. "And you're not as good at them as I am." In the background I heard a loud sound, like some sort of engine running at full tilt. It sounded familiar.

"What do you mean?" I asked. Maybe I could buy Chandra a little more time.

Chandra wrapped green electrical tape around a spliced-together wire, then plugged the thing into her laptop.

"That's going to be my little secret for now," he said. "Though I have to give you credit where it's due, you're a smart little cookie. I'm surprised you made it this far."

Chandra mouthed a message to me, her thumb to her ear: *Keep him talking.*

I ignored his bait. "Why exactly are you calling me?"

Chandra stretched out her fingers and began to type. She looked from her battle-scarred computer to Ray's ash-covered notes and back again.

"What, you don't want to hear from me?" he asked with mock outrage. "After all we've meant to each other?" Now I heard that heavy buzzing sound both in my phone and in my other ear, but I still couldn't place it.

In the background was Marjorie's voice, barking out orders, though the words were indistinct.

"You said we were enemies now," I reminded him.

"That's as may be," Ben said, "but I wanted to say one last thing, you know, before it's all over for you."

The little thumb drive containing Chandra's code, the little package that could take down Verity, blinked like a strobe light.

"All over for me?" I asked. "What the hell are you talking about?" The buzzing noise— it was getting so loud, so close. I looked up. A helicopter hung in the sky. It came right toward us, slowly at first and then so, so quickly.

"Sweet dreams, princess," he said, and hung up.

A canister arced to the ground from the chopper and fell to the grass, still rolling. It stopped a dozen feet away from us. As soon as it hit the ground it burst into wreaths of curling white fumes. I grew dizzy, and the ground around me tipped and whirled like a bad carnival ride.

"It's gas! Run," Chandra shouted from what seemed like a million miles away. But my legs were too heavy to work, and my eyes had turned to stone.

I toppled toward the ground. I had time enough to think about how much it was going to hurt when I landed, but by the time I got there, I didn't even notice.

I'm not sure if it was the shouting voices that woke me up, or the rocks on the ground jabbing into my ribs and probably leaving me black and blue. Or maybe it was just the gas wearing off, who could say?

I lay on the ground, the cold and damp seeping into my jeans. My back faced the argument in progress, but I had a lovely view of the expanse of dirt and grass leading up to the not-electric fence and through the slats, to our car on the other side. Afternoon light glinted off its windows, hurting my eyes.

"How did they even get here? They shouldn't know anything about this place. What did you tell her? Were you working with them the whole time?" screamed Marjorie.

"No! Of course not." Ben's voice was strained and tight. "How could I tell them what I didn't even know?"

I tried to move, slowly so as not to attract anyone's notice, but couldn't. My hands were bound together in front of me with endless loops of silvery duct tape. My feet were likewise immobilized. I wouldn't get very far like that.

"It's awfully suspicious, don't you think? Your girlfriend and Chandra just showing up here. How do they even know each other? How do you expect me to *believe* you, Ben?"

I rolled, one cautious inch at a time, so I could watch the dispute unfold without attracting attention to myself. The sun was ahead of me now, casting the whole scene in silhouette, though a storm front was rolling in.

"I don't know," Ben said through gritted teeth. "I didn't know anything about this. I thought Chandra was dead, same as you."

Chandra was bound just like me with duct tape around her wrists and ankles. She hadn't woken up yet, but the side of her face was swollen and bruised. Marjorie stood near her head, with Ben a few feet further away.

A dozen yards off the helicopter squatted, its rotors still spinning slowly. The helicopter pilot crouched in the doorway to his craft, his face unreadable through his helmet. He didn't seem particularly interested in the confrontation between his employers.

"Obviously," Marjorie said, "she is not dead. How is that even *possible*?"

"I don't know! Swear to god, Marjorie, I don't know."

Closer to me was a tangle of electronics. Chandra's work in progress — her laptop, wired to Verity to drop its deadly payload. Had it run? Did it work? I blinked and squinted to try to get my bleary eyes to focus.

The laptop had been destroyed. Holes pierced through the screen and into the body of the computer, like it had been stabbed with a spear or, or something. Fragments of green silicon and tiny curls of bright metal lay scattered all around it, like confetti after the parade is over.

Marjorie steamed onward. "Well, it does explain rather a lot that's been happening lately, doesn't it? You had to be in on this. I don't believe for a second that you didn't know— "

Chandra stirred. Her eyes opened, slowly, glazed with pain or gas or maybe utter defeat.

"Look, let's not worry about it right now, OK? Bigger fish to fry. We have a lot to do today already." He stepped closer to Marjorie and held out a placating hand.

"Wait," croaked Chandra. "Don't spin it up. Just don't. It's not safe." She struggled to sit up on one elbow.

Marjorie stepped forward and kicked Chandra's elbow

from under her with one steel-toed combat boot. Chandra's head hit the ground with a sickening thud. "That's for lying to us," Marjorie said.

"Benjamin," Chandra pleaded. She rolled so she could see him, hands clasped together as if in prayer. "Remember Ray. The same thing would happen to you."

Ben darkened. "Stop bluffing. We put in filters, it'll be fine."

"You don't understand. That's not what happened — he was fine until I... it was Prometheus. You can't turn it on. It's too dangerous."

Marjorie frowned, and for a moment I thought she was going to kick Chandra again. "So dangerous you had to keep it all for yourself, right?"

"No, I didn't keep anything. There's a *reason* I destroyed it. Thought I'd destroyed all the plans, too."

"Shut up," said Marjorie, her voice sharp. "You're just bluffing to try to scare us."

Ben shrugged. "You left behind enough that Kelly and Hal were able to reconstruct your device from your notes," he said. "It took them almost a year, but in the end they worked it out."

"It was a real team effort," Marjorie said. "You'll be glad to know it takes a lot to fill your shoes."

"Surprised you'd be willing to share with so many people," Chandra said.

"Oh, I'm not," Marjorie said. "Kelly and Hal are going to find themselves locked out of the system and on the wrong end of a tragic carbon monoxide leak as soon as everything is up and running."

I studied Ben's face, hoping for some sign that this was news to him, some human surprise or shock or at least some freaking distaste, but there was nothing.

"Benjamin," Chandra pleaded again. "Come on, you were never a bad guy. Stop this, right now."

Ben looked over at Marjorie, and studied her sharp, angry face for a while. "No," he told Chandra. "I know exactly what I'm doing."

This time Marjorie did kick Chandra in the head, with a horrible wet thud. She went limp and quiet.

Marjorie pulled her phone out of her jacket pocket. "Matteo? Yeah, that disturbance was nothing. It's been taken care of. Testing is over. Go ahead and bring it all live."

From my vantage point, I could see inside the access panel that Chandra had opened. Its innards gleamed to life with a dozen status lights and LEDs flashing in coordination. A quiet hum rose from the field of Prometheus dishes. The wind kicked up, and the storm clouds drew closer. The air crackled along the small hairs of my arms.

"What are we going to do about them?" Ben asked, nodding toward me and Chandra.

Marjorie shrugged. "Subtle has a bad track record so far. Just shoot them."

Ben pulled a gun from a holster behind his back. It was a dull, sleek thing, just like his car.

Ah, that explained what had happened to Chandra's laptop.

He knelt by my side and planted a kiss on my brow. "I'm really sorry, M," he said. "Nothing personal, you know?"

He raised the gun to my temple. I felt the cold circle press into my skin. It shook, like his hand was shaking. I guess it's a lot harder to kill someone when you're close enough for the blood to get on your fingers.

Small things crowded my head, fighting to be my last sensation. Ben's balsam scent, the damp denim of my jeans along my thighs, the bright colors of the wires trailing from Chandra's laptop. The wires. The wires—

The wires won't matter. Make a wish.

I could think of only one thing: lightning falling from the sky, putting a stop to all of this. I squeezed my eyes shut, tears leaking out, and prayed, wished, imagined.

Lightning came.

It arced from one Prometheus device to another, leaving towering cascades of sparks in its wake. Ben looked up, and I rolled away from him and that gun. He swore and half-rose as the whole field lit up in a beautiful conflagration of destruction.

The world filled with light, piercing me like ten thousand spears. My muscles convulsed in a grotesque dance of their own making. My heart stopped. Everything went dark.

When I woke again, the world was completely silent. I was cold, so cold, and shivering. I expected to be in pain, but I wasn't. Shock, I thought; this must be shock. A hysterical laugh shook me. I could feel it, but my ears didn't work.

Billows of smoke climbed up to join the clouds. The sun was dying, but enough light remained that I could see four lumps lying prone in the long shadow of the now-ruined helicopter.

I inched over to Chandra's side, slowly, painfully. She was breathing, almost undetectably.

I spotted Marjorie's cell phone on the ground near Chandra. I wormed my way toward it, agonizingly aware of each sharp stone that I crossed, every pebble. Finally I held the phone in my hands and tried to dial 911 for help.

The thing was fried, half-melted into complete uselessness.

Ben had been thrown farther away. I hunched toward him, looking for his gun, to take it before he could wake up. The gun was nowhere to be found. But it didn't matter — he wasn't breathing at all, not even so faintly as Chandra. There was a wound in his skull, smoking and charred, where his implant had fried just like Marjorie's cell phone.

I thought about trying to get Chandra's multi-tool, still there on the concrete pad where she'd left it. I could somehow cut myself free of my bonds, and then climb back over that fence to get help.

But I'd run out of everything I had. I closed my eyes instead.

When I woke up again, I was in a hospital bed.

epiLOGUE

The nurses were eager to know the truth about the mysterious circumstances under which I'd been discovered. Lucky for me my eardrums had ruptured, so I couldn't hear the gossip. Though I did catch the frequent, furtive glances my way from the nurses' station.

The lightning strike and cascading chain explosion of Prometheus devices was showy enough that people from as far as eight miles off had called in to report it, thinking a terrorist attack was under way. The nurses showed me the breathless coverage, closed captioning turned on so I could follow along.

Ben was dead, of course, and Marjorie, both killed when electricity coursed through the chips in their heads. Apparently the anonymous helicopter pilot was dead, too, from a heart attack. That happens sometimes with lightning, they said.

His name was Gerald. He had three grandkids.

Chandra was OK, maybe because she'd been lying down. Maybe because I'd wanted her to be OK. She was in the same hospital as me, only a few rooms down the hall, but I found myself making excuses for not seeing her. She didn't come to see me, either.

The police were interested in those mysterious circumstances, too. There were many questions. They even brought a tablet with them so I couldn't use my lack of hearing as a reason for not talking to them. They were especially curious about "that Indian woman," Chandra. How long I'd known her. How well I trusted her. If I could verify her identity, or if I had any hint she wasn't who she said she was.

The police had found Ben's gun, even if I hadn't, and they had some probing questions about that, too. And about how exactly you wind up in the middle of a secure compound tied up with duct tape. I told them I didn't remember much of anything.

They'd also found Ben's grandmother's diamonds-and-sapphires. They assumed it had blown off my finger. "The two of you were engaged, right?"

"Yeah, we were," I said. I couldn't think of a way to keep them from turning the ring over to me without having to answer a lot more questions. I stuck it on my thumb and obsessively rubbed my index finger over its sharp edges.

So many questions.

They kept me in the hospital for two days, for observation. A pile of newspapers kept me occupied in the meanwhile. They were filled to overflowing with accounts of freak accidents and one-in-a-billion chances, all during that few minutes that Prometheus was running. Probability had become completely unmoored, a victim of imagination in a five-hundred-mile radius or more.

At least two hundred and nine otherwise healthy people had dropped dead in their tracks of previously unknown medical conditions while in the throes of a heated argument. There had been a fifty-car collision on I-94 resulting in six cars rolling over, but no injuries.

Fifteen cancer patients at a prayer circle in Virginia had all gone into simultaneous remission. A toddler in Toronto had fallen from the balcony of her seventh-story condo and landed, completely unharmed, on the soft top of a parked Jeep. A fishing rig way out in the Atlantic had harvested an oyster with a ten-pound pearl inside.

In an industrial district in New Jersey, Dr. Hal Meadows and Dr. Kelly Peterson were found dead from carbon monoxide poisoning. A tragic and needless end.

So many questions. Not enough answers.

They discharged me before long, handing me over to the solicitous care of my parents. My burns were minor, my heartbeat was steady, and my ruptured eardrums would heal in a few weeks.

I didn't know what happened to Chandra. I didn't ask.

My parents moved me into the place on Fifth, packaging up all the stuff from my old apartment and shoving it into a storage facility. I let them do it without protest. It gave my mother the feeling that I was safe, and it beat staying with them. It gave me the chance to be alone with... whatever the hell it was that happened when I was alone.

They gave me a new phone. They bought me new clothes. They scheduled appointments for me with a grief counselor.

I slept a lot, mostly, and skipped their appointments.

Eli texted me approximately 8648392821 times without getting an answer before he finally stopped by uninvited. I guess my parents had given him the key, because he let himself in. He'd brought good wine and a hand-packed gallon of pistachio-rosewater ice cream.

"I'm so sorry for your loss," Eli said. He smoothed my hair away from my face as I lay on the couch. "Ben was— I'm sure he was a great guy, if he made you happy."

I nodded, staring at nothing in particular. "Sure."

"Listen," he said, "I... I'm sorry about that argument we had. I'll always really care about you, you know that, right? No matter what."

"Thanks."

He glanced at my still-bandaged wrists, burned where the duct tape had melted into my skin. Word about how I'd been found had spread through the media like gonorrhea, but he had the grace not to ask.

"Obviously there was something going on that you didn't feel ready to talk about. Just... trust me next time, all right?" He gave me a gentle side-hug.

"Don't worry about it," I told him, with a bravado I didn't feel. "I'm OK. I'll be OK."

It took me a solid month of staring at walls before creeping boredom began to outweigh existential suffering. Everything was terrible, yes. But there were decades ahead of me, and I didn't want them to be empty.

More to the point, I didn't ever want to relive anything like the last few months, not if I could help it.

It took me a little longer to work out how exactly to make that happen. But my solution was only ever a phone call away.

"Daddy," I said, "I want to take control of Verity. What's left of it. Can you put me in charge?"

"I'm not sure," he said. He used the fake-perky aggressively cheerful diction you generally use with a cranky toddler, or maybe an unfriendly dog. "Why?"

I had my reasons, of course. So I could personally see that anything that even breathed a hint of Prometheus was completely destroyed. So that I could dismantle all of the starburst makers in the world and see them pulverized into unrecognizable scrap. So I could make the world a better, safer place for free will.

So I'd never again have to — so nobody else would have

to die.

I didn't say any of that. "In memory of Benjamin," I said. "I think he'd want me to rebuild from his foundation. And... I almost died when that lightning struck. I've done some thinking, and you're right. Mom's right. It's time I grow up and try to make the world a better place. Coffee isn't for me anymore."

"That's very... " He didn't finish the sentence, but I had my guesses. Sudden. Ambitious. Uncharacteristic. But he wasn't one to look a gift horse in the mouth; at least I was getting off the sofa. "The management of the company is up in the air right now, since... well. Since the heads of the company aren't with us anymore. I'll try to set up a meeting."

It was as good as I could have expected.

I didn't really expect her to show up. I texted an invitation to the old number, but it was impossible to know if she received it. So when she walked into the restaurant, I was surprised and relieved and resentful all together.

I wasn't sure if I should hug her or shake her hand, so I didn't do either one. "Hey, stranger. Looking good."

She did, too. Her face was rounder, her back was straighter, she had a dewy glow like someone who drinks enough water and has a trainer. She wore a silk sweater in orange, and tall suede boots. She'd cut her hair; as she moved, it swung around her shoulders like her own personal backup dancers.

"You, too." Her eyes were heavy-lidded and unreadable.

"So how have you been? I mean, what have you been up to?" Since the horrible thing. Since we almost died to keep your secrets.

"I called my parents. They've spent a year thinking I was dead, so that was... awkward. My little brother's really grown up since I saw him."

"I didn't know you had a little brother. I didn't know you had parents."

I expected her to snort at that, or at least roll her eyes, but she just said, "You never asked, did you?"

We were interrupted by the arrival of my parents, followed shortly by Uncle Wally, the Buchanans, and an assortment of financial services personnel. These were the people who would decide Verity's fate, and mine.

First things first. I waved toward Chandra. "This is Chandra Singh, one of the original founders of Verity. You know I want to steer where Verity goes next. I need her to be right there with me."

"I'd heard she was dead," Mike's father frowned.

"The rumors of my death were greatly exaggerated," Chandra told him. "It's a long story."

"We have time," Uncle Wally said.

"Nowhere near enough." She smiled as she said it, but I think they could tell how sharp that point was. Nobody asked again.

Our meeting place was a stately steak restaurant, the kind with burgundy leather, plain white tablecloths, and pepper mills as long as your arm. Our table was shrouded in darkness. Over cocktails, I slowly picked up scraps of information on what had become of Verity.

The service was down, of course. Both hosting facilities had been completely destroyed, and there had been no plan for recovery from a disaster of quite that magnitude.

I needn't have worried about family money — apparently everything had been very well-insured, so while there wasn't any ROI for the family, it wasn't a big loss, either. And now there was only the shell of a company without a product to sell. Verity has been reduced to an imaginary thing made of bank accounts, contracts, and a few very, very important filing cabinets waiting for us in New Jersey.

One more thing: the employees had all been put on furlough while the lawyers and investors figured out what to do with the pieces that remained.

"We should pay them." I interrupted my father to say it. He was so startled that he couldn't muster any indignation over my rudeness.

I went on. "That kind of uncertainty is going to be very bad for morale. And human capital is one of the few assets Verity has left. We can't afford for anyone else to jump ship and take their knowledge with them. Everyone gets paid, and retroactively."

I looked at my mother out of the corner of my eye. She was beaming like the sun, enough to light up our whole table.

Chandra gave me a quizzical look. "Mira," she said carefully. "Can I speak to you privately?"

"Excuse us for a moment," I smiled to the table. They shuffled napkins and cocktails and acted like nothing was in the least bit awkward.

Chandra trailed me into the powder room. "Why are we doing this? What's your end game, Mira?"

"We need to clean it all up," I told her. "We need to make sure history never repeats itself. I figure you're the best one for that job. And me, I guess I'll try to run an automated news service and see how that goes."

"Did you hear about Ray?" she asked. She plucked a dried rose petal from the bowl of potpourri on the counter, then crumbled it into dust.

"What?"

"When Prometheus switched on, he set down his pencil and walked straight out of the clinic. Through a wall, as far as they could tell. Now he's just... gone." She stirred the potpourri with one finger.

"Good for him," I said.

"Maybe he fixed himself while Prometheus was up and running."

"Maybe," I said. I stared at myself in the mirror, sad-eyed and serious. "Who's going to fix us?"

Chandra shook her head. "Would you even want that?"

I thought about it. "No," I said at last. "I guess not."

I stared at the tiles between my shoes, black as night with glittering stars in the depths. I had to ask. I had to know. I didn't want to know, but... "Chandra. What exactly happened with Ray? The truth."

Chandra looked away from me, away from the mirror. "There are still some holes in my memory," she said. "I cut them out of myself when it was done. I remember doing that, a little bit. Verity-induced traumatic amnesia."

"Well, what else do you remember?"

"I was working on a probability disruptor," she said. "I was stupid, I wasn't thinking about the implications. I thought I knew what I was doing."

"But what happened?"

"It turns out that the bigger the window gets, the more places you create where you could make a revision... the less it takes to do it. You don't have to be *precise.*" She turned the tap on to wash her hands.

"Wishes," she said. "Just holding a thought steady in your brain is all it takes. With the disruptor running you don't need a neural implant. You don't even need Verity to exist."

So I was right. I'd done that, I'd made the lightning strike. I'd killed Ben and Marjorie, and poor Grandpa Gerald the helicopter pilot. I felt sick.

Chandra scrubbed at her hands furiously, as if she could

wash away the memories that remained. "They were designed to work together. The disruptor to make the windows, and the implant to choose which ones to open. When we were testing out my disruptor, I wished— I wished that Ray was different. And it changed him. It made him... like you saw. And that's when I knew I'd done a terrible thing."

"So you destroyed the evidence?"

"Even in my own brain. Not well enough. The memories come back, in bits and pieces."

"At least it's over now."

"Is it?" she said, bitter. "How many other people know, or can figure it out? The genie is out of the bottle, Mira."

"We'll see about that," I murmured. "We'll see if we can stop it."

"Right. Let's see if we can." Chandra swished out of the bathroom with her swingy hair and her tall boots.

I took a little longer to fortify myself with lip gloss. I thought about giving myself a pep talk, but the only thing I could think of was "Don't screw this up." I couldn't stall for too long, though. There were an awful lot of people expecting me back at that table.

And maybe, I thought, maybe it was time to start expecting something from myself, too.

acknowledgements

Writing looks like a solitary effort, but this is only an illusion; multitudes have touched this work. I'd particularly like to thank Brian White, my editor and publisher, for believing in me and in this book; Robert S. Davis for his stunning design work; and Lillian Cohen-Moore, my copy editor, for her keen eye and enthusiasm.

My gratitude extends further to Naomi Alderman, Michael Andersen, Adrian Hon, Elizabeth Bear, Tom Bridge, Andrew Cohen, Ian Everett, Martin Hodo, Anne Gray, Sarah Lacelle, Mur Lafferty, Haley Moore, Eustacia Moreau, Phoebe Seiders, and Will Weisser for their efforts (known to them or otherwise) in helping to shape this work and indeed me personally in significant ways.

And speaking of shaping me personally, thank you to my mom and dad, my step-parents, and my in-laws for their combined efforts in parenting me (and a job well done, if I do say so). And thank you to my own small family, Matt and Sasha and Maya, for their patience and boundless love. You all made me, so this book is yours, too.

note to READERS

Thank you so much for taking the time to read Revision. We hope you enjoyed it! We'd love to hear what you thought, either in a review somewhere like Amazon or Goodreads, or you can email us at books@firesidefiction.com.

Content Note

Sexual Assault ••
Suicide ••

• One scene of mild intensity
•• One scene of moderate intensity
••• Multiple scenes of mild to moderate intensity
•••• One scene of high intensity
••••• Multiple scenes of high intensity

Fireside Fiction Company provides content notes to guide readers who may wish to seek out or avoid particular story elements. A current list of all the elements covered in our content notes can be found at **www.firesidefiction.com/contentnotes**. We welcome your suggestions for elements to include or exclude.

CPSIA information can be obtained at www.ICGtesting.com
Printed in the USA
LVOW04s1307190515

439048LV00001B/92/P